The Stone Garden

Book 1

Tina Koutras

Acknowledgements

The biggest challenge in writing this book was having the confidence to share it.

From a young age I have written all these short stories and compiled ideas to bring these amazing characters to life for my husband and me. He has inspired my imagination and helped build this fantastical world. Patiently providing feedback and helping me grow.

To Maureen, my sister, my biggest fan, who holds her breath waiting for each book. Who not only gave me the courage to publish, but who wouldn't take no for an answer, who believed in me so fiercely that I began to belief in myself.

To Laura, who was the first person to light a fire under my butt and say you need to write more, I want the next chapter...

To my Mom and Dad, my cheerleaders who have had to listen to my ever-growing excitement and my uncles and family for all the support, love and encouragement.

To all my fellow fantasy lovers, I hope you enjoy this series as much as I enjoyed bringing it to life. I hope you fall in love with everyone in the Stone Garden.

Prologue

Her eyes were dark as she sat motionless on the throne. The cold of winter had seeped into the once warm room, chilling her to the bone. In the past this room had held grand galas and events to celebrate a new world. The guests that had graced the dance floor of the great hall were now long gone, in their steed she had immortalized them, as well-honed stone statues crafted and strategically placed in the gardens below. Monuments to their former glory and a grand age.

Entering the room, I watched her remain as still as the monuments that I had passed in the gardens enroute to the castle's inner court. She was still immensely breathtaking to look upon, though in the twilight of her life, her youth and beauty peeked out behind thin wrinkles of time. The remnants of her joyful heart evident in the smile, that now, only ghosted upon her lips. Her once ebony hair, still soft, hung in ribbons of white satin around her face.

I would have stayed long moments to watch her in that stillness, to see the years peeled back under that calm and peaceful visage. To my dismay, however, the herald drew her attention to me. Her soft purple eyes fell on me, the smile that had only played upon her lips was extended to me as a greeting.

"May I ask what was it that held you so fast my lady, that you were not aware that I had entered the room?"

"I was awaiting your visit scribe. Wondering what I would tell you. My mind had drifted into the past, so many stories." she whispered.

Her eyes had a softness that I had seen only from a distance all my life. She had ruled her husband's empire, with his death the land had fallen to her son. These last few years she had returned to her role as court adviser to her grandson in her son's absence.

"I was wondering Empress, if you would be so kind as to escort me through your gardens to tell your stories of years gone by. I would try to capture your memoirs, so that others can truly know your trials. From when it began, from the wars and all your great allies and their battles."

"You seek to put a lifetime on to pages?"

"Were it possible Empress, I would like to very much do that. So, that others may remember that when they put their children to bed safe at night, they will know who it was that attained that safety for them. Whose lives were laid down for them, and how very close they came to never waking again."

Her expression had changed somewhere while I was speaking, a fire had awakened in her heart that had seemingly slumbered for years.

"Walk with me," she paused, not recalling if I had given her my name. Seeing the moment of discomfort, I bowed politely and extended my arm to aside, "Sir Edrick Rolen."

She nodded, a gentle smile replacing the confusion. "It is good to meet you Sir Edrick. If you are to write my memoirs, we had best start soon, they are a lot longer than I have left I am afraid."

She took my arm and we walked down the long corridors that wound through the castle. Her body, though slight and small, still had a great deal of strength. She held my arm as if it was of a need for comfort, not of frailty.

We came to the gardens that surrounded the castle as the sun was beginning its decent. It lit the entire garden with a fire that took our breath away. She stood silent and watched as I looked at the statues gracefully dotting the garden. Each carefully moulded with the power of magic and desperation of one not willing to let a life, so valued, pass into oblivion. These were her monuments. Truly her memoirs could be written on the pedestals at the feet of each statue. The faces told their stories with such clarity that I did not question the names of those who surrounded me. I knew them each by heart.

I knew their legends and their hopes and sadness. These were the heroes of the new world that I had brought my children into. Knowing that they would not face the horrors that these souls had bore. They were the champions of great wars, some of the greatest love stories and some of the most tragic losses stretched out before me, all within reach. For a moment I was confused I spun and searched,

"Where is your statue?" She smiled at me and looked around at all of them with a wide sweeping gaze. I am in my children, in my friends and in my beloved husband, I did not create a statue for me, I felt no need to remember myself." I felt a moment of sadness that she was not here in this garden, that there would never be a stone monument for one who had made this world the beautiful place it had become. That I would never see her beauty again once she joined her friends that she had lost to the afterlife.

"So then, if there is no visage of you, would you mind if we started there? Where your story began. How you came to be here?"

She stared at me a moment before she sat on a stone bench that faced the greatest soldier the light had ever known. I could see the years disappearing within her mind as she stared at him, trying to decide how to begin telling me the story I longed to hear.

"Well then..." she whispered and smiled as she began in the simplest way possible. "It began when I was just a girl of sixteen..."

Chapter One

The Duke of Abarris was blessed with only one child, a strong-willed girl who had a big heart and an increasingly annoying knack for not understanding politics. He sat on the window seat in her room as she scolded him for selecting a husband that was not to her liking. This one is too old; this one is too childish. He stared at the frustration on her face and saw her mother, as she was in her youth.

Savane had only been a very small girl when her mother had passed away. The Duke was painfully aware that her nature and lack of propriety were directly related to how many freedoms she had enjoyed as a child.

She excelled in reading and could run the financials for the entire estate, she made decisions that would shrink most young ladies regarding her home. She did, however, lack the understanding that when a king wanted his son to marry her, there was very little room for negotiation.

"Why do you feel you have a choice in this matter?" his tired eyes held her a moment and she froze, her argument snapping shut behind her teeth.

"Savane," he reached for her dainty hands and held them in his, noting the distinct contrast between his and hers before looking up into her ardent eyes. "I have rarely demanded anything of you. I have given you far too many choices in this life and I am afraid that this time you have none. You will marry Prince Verentine when he arrives from the Eastern Coasts and you will return with him to his father's Kingdom. Do we have an understanding in this?"

He gently patted the hands he held in his grasp before she pulled them away with a set jaw. With that he stood and left, knowing that to linger would be to suffer the tears and rage that would certainly follow, that instead would fall to Lyselle, her lady in waiting.

Savane sat numb at the end of her bed, her hands trembled, and thoughts of her future happiness were ebbing away on a tide of panic that was rushing in.

"I don't want to marry Prince Verentine" she mumbled to her Lyselle, "He is most likely a spoiled brat."

"You will at least have one thing in common," her she teased as she pulled at her hair. Lyselle was only a year older than Savane and behind closed doors she was her most trusted friend and confident. She was the daughter of one of the lesser nobles in the township and had yet to be married off herself.

Savane cast her withering look as she endured her hair being freed of the snarls, she had earned during the ride with her father earlier that morning. He had tricked her; she would never turn down a chance to go riding with her father. A fact he was well and fully aware of. His decision to tell her of her future husband had been as they crested a hill that looked out over all of her father's lands. Like every child, she wanted to spend her lifetime in her home and that was something that was not to happen. She sighed as the reverie reignited her agitation.

"I'm going to visit with Shamus, tell father I am distraught and have decided to rest, please."

She swept from the room before her lady could protest; it would have done her little good for there were never opportunities to hold the young lady back when it came to spending those few moments with Shamus.

The cells were unguarded, and it was her usual tactic of providing food for the prisoners that bought her time with her friend. Shamus was a thief in her father's cells that had been there for many years. Savane was uncertain what the man had done to earn him so long a stay in the Duke's forgotten kingdom but there was a kindness to him that had brought her to him often. After so long in his company, she had most recently turned to him in times of frustration with the obligations of nobility.

He had spoken of many things with her. Savane's favourite story was the origins of the new Gods, he had told of a lawless world mired by darkness and cruelty. The old Gods sacrificed themselves to drive the darkness from the world they knew. In their destruction, the greatest of the soldiers of light took the mantle of their Gods, those who best manifested the qualities of the deity who had fought and died for their freedom. The God Vetis had been destroyed, to never again walk among the living.

"Do you really believe that to be true?" she watched intently as he ate the last of the bread she had managed to smuggle beneath the folds of her gown.

"I believe that the realm was affected by Vetis'

passing. That the world as we know it does not remember the darkness as our ancestors did. But there will come a day, M'lady, when the small candle that once burned as a blazing inferno to hold the darkness at bay will be snuffed out. A cold will wash over this land and shatter the veil that we have chosen to hide behind. When that comes to pass there will be a cry heard from every mountain and every valley that the shadow walks among us."

"I think you are trying to frighten me." She was breathless when she spoke, the air barely able to carry the sound of her voice.

"You will know him in your lifetime, with his cold heart and his icy hands."

"I think that you have just described my future husband, not the shadow that you spoke of."

He gave her a sad smile. Savane could see the tolerance in his eyes, as though he were speaking to a small child with no understanding of loss.

"Shamus, what did you do that my father keeps you here?"

"Better here, he believes, than to have me where my voice can be heard."

"You are telling me you have never committed a crime?"

"Every man behind bars will confess that they are innocent M'lady, they will say what is expected to gain favour or promise of salvation." He winked.

"Can I show you something?" his hands fell from view as she nodded stretching to see where they had gone. He whispered foreign words and when they rose again into view they shone with a simple light as though he were holding a flame within his closed fist.

"How are you doing that? What are you doing?" A call came from the hall, "Lady Savane?" It shattered their closeness and with it, the flame that had danced within his grasp was snuffed out and they fell again into darkness. His touch though, when he reached through the bars had warmth far beyond his prison cell.

Startled she searched his eyes for an explanation but found only the softness that was always there when he gazed upon her.

"You have a gift beloved, and you must find a way to give into it, for so long as it sleeps within you, the darkness will find a way to awaken."

Chapter Two

Savane started from sleep and sat up in her bed, her afternoon with Shamus had left her uncomfortable and restless. She stared at the open window and watched the clouds moving over the moon and trees; everything was dark beyond the walls of the estate. The sounds of night filled her ears as she tried to settle with whatever Shamus had meant. She stared at her hands and tried to recall the words he had spoken, but they had meant nothing and therefore remained idle in her memory.

A cool breeze drifted in from the window and set the heavy drapes dragging along the floor. Savane watched them settle then lifted her gaze back to the horizon. Her breath caught in her throat as small red orbs seemed to watch her from the darkness of the forest, like eyes peering from the abyss. She felt her spine tighten and cold wash over her as she began to sweat as though gripped by a sudden fever. Her cry sounded more like a wounded animal then a young woman. The guard posted outside her door bound into the room, drawing his sword and searching for the source of her terror.

"Do you see it? There in the dark?" His eyes fell to the spot on the horizon where her gaze lingered but there was nothing to speak of beyond the hills and trees. He drew the covers back over her and then drew the drapes closed.

"There you are my lady; whatever it was it is gone. I will have someone search the grounds for whatever it was that has alarmed you so. What did you see?" his brow furrowed as she shivered in the warmth of the summer heat.

She looked up for the first time to see who was in the room with her and took comfort in his company.

Dayin Drake was the youngest of her father's men and was sought after by many of the young women within the manor. He was well known for his kind heart and handsome face. Yet somehow, he was the only person inside the manor walls that was unaware of his beauty. His long dark hair and soft eyes that had an instant calming effect on Savane.

Savane watched as he lit a candle beside her bed and did one final search of her chambers.

"If that is sufficient my lady I hope you can sleep well." he made for the door and paused at the moment that he met her gaze, her eyes betrayed her and made her feel as though she were a coward, her fear was so close to the surface that he could see it as plain as the tears.

"What did you see lady that left you feeling so unsafe?"

"Can you keep a secret?" with a nod of his head he sat in the chair beside her bed, "I saw the Scorched God of Legends, he was watching me."

She eyed him closely to see if his eyes would laugh where he was trained too well to do so outright. There was not even a hint of mockery. Her fear of ridicule ebbed.

"There was a figure in the forest beyond the castle walls, on a horse, he had red eyes." Her voice trembled, drawing him into her fear.

"I will investigate my lady, if for no other reason than to bring you a restful sleep." He patted the side of her covers and made to rise and leave the room, she grasped his hand instinctively. "I would not have you go alone." His smile was endearing and gentle. If only it was someone like he that her father demanded, she marry. He placed the blankets around her shoulders once again and quietly slipped from the dimness of the room. The candle by her bedside flickered with his departure and stilled once again when she was alone. Her mind played over and over the visage of the ghastly specter on the horse, she shuddered in memory of him. The silence and warmth and the gentle reminder of Dayin's candle brought Savane gently into dreams that would not stay gentle for long.

Chapter Three

Dawn arrived too quickly and Savane struggled to start her day. She moved through her morning half asleep and listless. Her mind was still lingering on the night before. Her father took her lack of energy as compliance to the new betrothal and perhaps there was a matter of acceptance within her. After all, he was right when he had reminded her that he never asked anything of her, perhaps it was time she wore the burden of a dutiful daughter.

"My guard informs me there was a disturbance outside your window last night, I trust you were appropriately cared for."

She nodded as she brought a small grape to her lips. She played with it as though applying colour to her lips before remembering Dayin and his promise to search the grounds. "Did Dayin Drake return last night unharmed? It was he that came to check in on me, I am certain he must think me mad. It must have been a dream seeking to take hold into my waking moments."

"He did return and inquired about you, if you

were well, prior to the end of his rounds."

She smiled and placed the fruit in her mouth, "He is a very good soldier father,"

"His father served in his younger years but has since passed on. He asked to serve so that his mother may stop working. He and his brother have taken up the mantle their father once bore to take care of her."

Savane watched as guards passed in the hall but none were him. "I think I would like to go to the river this afternoon Father. The days are warm and Lyselle and I would enjoy some solitude at the river."

He nodded his approval with a mouthful of food before saying, "Take a small detachment of guards, then would you?"

"Of course, Father, I will."

It took very little time for Savane to track down Dayin to the courtyard where the guards conducted their morning training. He was focused on his drills when she fell into the front rank to speak to their commander. She carried herself with an air of self-importance that only nobility could afford.

"Commander I would like to go to the river today and my Lord Father demands I take a small escort for safety."

His eyes squinted in the morning sun as he regarded her, then a polite nod, "Yes my lady."

"Send Dayin Drake and his men to attend me and my Lady in Waiting."

If she had learned anything about manipulations it was that if you do not give a person an opportunity to debate, often they do not. When she returned to the courtyard with Lyselle, the two young ladies stood in silence as the men, including Dayin Drake formed up on horseback around their horses.

The stable hand set a stool beside their mounts and the ladies mounted their horses with grace. The ride to the river was not a far distance though it was somewhat rocky and forced a slower pace to protect the horses. Savane kept pace with Lyselle. The sun was bright overhead and the heat had already set in for the day. "What do you suppose the Prince will look like?" Savane looked to Lyselle before returning her gaze to her horse's leather reins.

"The servants say that he is young and has green

eyes that miss nothing."

"Young? How young?" Lyselle smiled at the new panic she detected in her lady's voice.

"He's of an age to marry and father children M'lady."

"Father children?" Savane's heart skipped a beat as the realization struck her.

Lyselle's eyebrow raised. "That is why you were selected to marry you know."

With a sigh Savane conceded and looked again at the road. "His father is a very strong king that has conquered lands and held them since he was sixteen years old. He too, was an arranged marriage and has the two children, the prince and his younger sister. Though they are inseparable there doesn't seem to be any talk of her, except perhaps that she is..." Lyselle looked to the water as they approached the river, "She's unusual for nobility."

The river fed into heavy rapids that wound their way to the coastal waters and out to sea. That forced them to ride further inland to ensure their safety, though both girls were not intending to swim it made the guards feel better to have them out of harm's way.

"We are far enough; it really is unnecessary to ride any further." Dayin cast his Lady a challenging glance but there was an obvious outcome to going against her will. He raised his hand and the guards halted, dismounted their horses and took up positions around the camp after setting up a leaning shelter to protect them from the sun.

They sat in the summer sun all afternoon the two young ladies and their competent protectors. Savane was embroidering the finest purple and gold flower upon a soft cloth. While Lyselle was content to watch the river and talk about the future that had been set for her Lady. With each passing moment Lyselle had made Savane's future less bleak and painted it in such glorious colours that for a moment Savane had accepted her fate and perhaps even the possibility of happiness.

First, however she had to contend with the other fate she found herself twisted into; the one Shamus had predicted. "Drake" she called hoping that it would not sound too childish, or too familiar.

"M'lady?"

"Did you find anything of concern on your

rounds last night?" He watched her for a moment as she continued to embroider the fine cloth in her hands. His blue eyes so focused on her as though he were trying to decide what he was going to say.

The calm and softness of his face made Lyselle look away with flushed cheeks. His pause was long and made Savane lift her eyes to him from the embroidering.

"I suppose, a man with concern for how his lady might appear would tell her that he saw something, some creature. But I fear that I would be only perpetuating your concern for whatever you saw or think you saw last night, so no my lady I saw nothing last night. We searched for some time before returning to the barracks. Forgive me if you would have rather had the lie but I am not an advocate of lies."

"Do you believe me?" her eyes had taken on a look as passive as she could manage in an effort to establish if this man could be trusted, if he were what she would need if the future that Shamus saw were to truly come to pass.

"I believe that whatever you saw was something of great concern to you my lady, but I do not, as of yet have any idea of what to make of what it may have been."

She stared at him a moment in silence, overwhelmed by his words. If Shamus spoke true, the world she knew was falling into darkness. She knew in that moment that he would tell her truth and be what she would need if ever she needed a champion. Lyselle rose and dusted off her dress, "I am going to wash my hands in the river before we leave."

"That is unwise," Dayin offered

"Nonsense, I'm not wading into the water, merely my hands." She made her way to the water's edge and knelt down, the water was warm, and she soaked her handkerchief to wash her forehead then made to stand. Dayin stood uncomfortable with Lyselle's proximity to the water. Just as she rose, the rocks beneath her feet shifted and she fumbled forward. Savane gasped as her friend disappeared from sight instantly carried forward on fast moving water.

Dayin cursed beneath his breath, and raced after her along the bank, shedding his armour as fast as he was able, he had to try and get ahead of her. He could see her struggling to keep her head above the water as rapids pulled at her dress and her hair covered her face blinding her to the rocks in her path. Dayin jumped into the water and was instantly rushed forward and could feel

27

the pressure as the water tried to pull him under. The rocks beneath slammed into his legs and he could feel the numbness in one leg where the rock had hit his thigh.

A bend in the river slowed Lyselle down, but she hit some rocks with such force that she lost consciousness. She had become hung up on the rocks and branches around her.

Dayin too had found a nook that was free of the power of the rushing water and he stayed motionless for a moment gathering strength. The water pressing him hard against the bank on the opposite side of the river from the rest of the men and any hope for aid.

Dayin's horse was still with the other men seeking a way across the water. Savane watched as the beast struggled against its survival instincts and the need to rescue his rider. The man holding him back was forced to release his reins or be driven into the water as the crazed animal lunged into the water just beyond his master. Dayin released the rocks and was thrust into where Lyselle had been lodged. Once he had her, he lifted her head above the water and grasped her around the torso before letting go of the rocks. Letting the rapids take him to his horse who was in a deep pool. He managed to grasp the pommel of the saddle and hoist Lyselle onto the back of the horse, clinging for dear life to the beast.

Savane was terrified until the horse managed to find purchase and hoist himself and his water-logged passengers to safety.

Savane raced to the ground where her friend lay motionless and pale, certain that the rocks that she had hit had delivered the death blow. She sought only to touch her, to see her and kiss her goodbye.

Dayin was not so willing to part with her and accept too early a defeat. He could feel all the damage the rocks had done to his body and knew that Lyselle likely had not fared any better. His hands shook as he examined the wound on the soft skin to the side of her left brow, but his eyes carried an intensity that gave Savane hope.

"You will not die this day!" he whispered to Lyselle. He held a symbol of his God, the Shield emblem inlaid with the Sword of Justice closed within a fist. He held onto it as though the wearing of it alone would give him power over death. Savane watched as Lyselle's eyes fluttered. "Wake up" he whispered and as ordered, Lyselle opened her eyes.

Lyselle coughed and spewed water from her

mouth. A collective sigh rose up between the men that were charged with her and Savane's protection. Lyselle's eyes were unfocused at first but when she saw Dayin leaning over her, his hair flattened against his head and blood from small cuts along his forehead, she pulled him to her and held him in an embrace. He froze for a moment; his eyes rose up to see Savane smiling at him with genuine joy. He returned her smile and freed himself from Lyselle's arms wrapped around his neck.

"You're safe my lady."

After Lyselle was tended to, Dayin went to his horse, he inspected his legs and joints. Savane walked over and waited for him to stand. When he did, she offered him the handkerchief she had been working on. "You're bleeding."

"I can't use this to wipe it away my lady, I'll be fine." He tried to offer it back only to have Savane push it back into his chest. "You saved my friends life Dayin, please, it is only a handkerchief." When he resisted, she held it against the spot on his forehead that was still bleeding.

"Thank you," he whispered.

"You are a hero today, Dayin Drake."

"It's my horse that saved us, without him I'm not sure I would have made it across the deepest part of that river. I had very little left in me."

Savane looked at Dayin's horse for a moment, a smile playing on her lips, "What is his name?"

"Seraphic." her eyebrows rose, she leaned forward and pet the velvet of Seraphic's nose.

"Thank you brave Seraphic. He's beautiful Dayin, make sure he gets apples to commend his bravery. But it was not Seraphic that commanded my friend to live, how did you do that?"

"I don't get to take credit for that either M lady, I simply prayed, and he answered, no special gift, no power over life and death. Lyselle was just not meant to die today and Lynstrom's will was done."

Savane watched him a moment longer, his hands lazily stroking his horse's mane. His passive content smile instantly endeared him to her.

The ride back to the estate was silent. They kept the pace slow so as not to jar Lyselle to badly. Her head was throbbing, but she was incredibly stoic.

The stories and rumors of what had transpired at the river's edge had been spread seemingly before they had returned to the estate. Every person was whispering of Dayin Drake's grand rescue and Lyselle's recovery with his command. Savane sat in the window looking out over the training grounds as the men received him and commended him for saving her life. He seemed uncomfortable and out of sorts and sought to escape their praise. His eyes desperately seeking a place to settle found hers in the window. When he found her, his smile returned and lingered for a moment before he slipped away and disappeared into the barracks.

"I hear your selection of guard was rather successful in saving your lady." Savane drew in a shaky breath as her father sat in the window seat across from her. Her hair was still dishevelled as was her mind and the thought of retelling the story was leaving her wishing she had barracks herself to retreat to.

"I am sorry father, but I truly have no desire to relive this afternoon right now." He placed a hand upon her lap and smiled at her with a reassurance and pride.

"I am only happy that the lady was rescued and that nothing permanent marred the afternoon.

Lyselle will be fine, and you will be fine too. Would you have objections if I were to reward your brave soldier with a knighthood? Given his complete fearlessness today?"

"May I tell him?

"I thought to have an event for such an occasion,"

"Father, you would honour him far more were you to whispered it in his ear, then to place him on a pedestal for all to see and cheer for. Have you not seen how he climbs inside himself with the mention of good deeds? He tried to give Lyselle's rescue to his horse. He is humble father and you would be making him very uncomfortable." Her father watched a moment as she sat across from him, looking very much like her mother. Somewhere between the horse ride that had created the rift between them and the near death of her friend, his daughter had come back to herself.

"You tell him beloved daughter and inform him that I would like to make it official at some games to celebrate the arrival of the Prince. He can fight as your champion if you would like."

He waited for her expression to darken at the mention of her future husband, but she had seemingly come to terms with his arrival and instead became excited over the idea of having a champion. As if on fire she swept from the chair and took to the stairs, in the direction of the barracks.

Chapter Four

Savane stood outside the barrack hall while another soldier sought Dayin for her. She started as the doors opened and closed, soldiers coming and going while she waited, surprised by her presence would straighten to acknowledge her. The wait however was brief; the guard must have raced the halls to find him for he was utterly breathless when he returned to inform the Duchess that Dayin would be only a moment longer.

When he opened the door he was dressed down, out of his armour and colours that the infantry customarily wore and instead wore a simple tunic over dark trousers. Over his hip was strapped his simple blade and the only indication that he was anything but a stable boy. His long hair usually bound at the base of his head was loose and blew in the wind. It took Savane a few moments to focus her thoughts away from how completely beautiful he was.

"Have I interrupted you in preparation for something?" He shook his head as he walked beside her,

"No, I only intended to visit my mother this afternoon, was there something that you needed of me. I thought myself off duty.

"You are? Of course, you are, after what happened I imagine that you were deserving of a few days."

She had not noticed that she had stopped walking and was standing still before him. Her throat felt thick and words seemed to all dance in her head as though they didn't know what direction to fall.

"My lady?"

"Forgive me, I was unsettled by the events of the day and first and foremost in the time it took to return home I don't think I said a proper thank you. I wanted to make sure that you knew how grateful I was that you risked so much to ensure the safe return of my friend."

She watched as soldiers passed them by and turned her attention to a stray lock of her hair that would not take its place before she looked back into the intent gaze that he met her with.

"I could not claim to be your protector if I did not protect those things that you value as well my lady."

"You earned the gratitude of more than just me and Lyselle, my father has requested that you accept a knighthood for your bravery and that you participate in an event to celebrate it. He would like to host games and knight you before the last event, in which he would like you to fight as my champion," the pause lingered in the air for what seemed forever before she took a breath and added, "The games to host the Prince that is to be my future husband."

Dayin breathed out slowly and looked away into the setting sun, his eyes narrowed against the bright horizon as he considered what was being said.

"You are asking me to fight for you my lady?"

"I would ask it of you" she said watching his eyes drift to the ground before her. "I have never had a champion before but were I to envision what a knight or a champion would look like and be, I cannot imagine a more deserving and noble person than you have demonstrated yourself to be."

"I cannot accept." her brow furrowed into a deep crease that made him look again to the ground to stop from trying to take it back.

"Sir, I have seen men climb over themselves to take the honour that is being laid before you. Far less deserving men that do not even comprehend what it is to be knightly, while you are those things before you even realize that you have done anything at all. Someone has told me that the world we know may change and that a darkness is coming and that I may be in the center of that darkness. If that happens I would very much like it if you were there to guide me back to the light. If you were there to ensure that I wake to face the new day instead of one of those knights that do not understand you and what you represent."

"I fear that I will fail at protecting you if that is why you seek to have me as your champion."

"Better then, that someone less noble keep me?"

"I am afraid I would accept for the wrong reasons."

Savane lifted her head up and narrowed her eyes at him, "You risked your life to save Lyselle without even a moment of hesitation. I saw you Dayin, she was not even in the water yet and you were running to her rescue."

"I accept" he said with his eyes meeting hers.

"Let it not be a battle of wills then between us my lady."

She smiled a soft and genuine smile. "So, then you will be my champion and compete in my father's games, receive whatever credit you are due and from this day forward be the commander of my personal guard?"

Savane watched him flinch and knew that his humility would have him responsible for a list of other things rather than what she had just announced to him. But the decision had been made and then she left him standing in the street suddenly trembling with anticipation.

The talk of the world plunging into darkness had reminded Savane that there was a pressing need for her to return to Shamus and ask him about the fire, about the rider that lingered just beyond the estate. About the things he had told her and shown her.

She had always heard of the mages and knew that there were some nobles who had magic in their blood. that they could study in a secret college in the capital to the south, but she had never witnessed their power. She had never felt it as she did the night that Shamus had drawn the fire into his skin. If that was to be her destiny, she was going to make sure that she knew every detail that Shamus could provide.

She moved quickly through the halls and stopped just outside his cell, the torches that burned along the walls were not lit and the silence here caused Savane to slow her steps and look over her shoulder for guards.

"What are you doing here?" the voice nearly made Savane scream like the child. She turned and faced the cell where Shamus stood looking far worse than ever before. He looked as though he had aged ten years in the time since they last spoke., His hair had whitened, and his eyes stuck out behind dark circles and creases. The sight of him forced an unwilling breath of surprise from Savane as she tried to come to terms with the man, she knew only a few days ago with the haggard visage before her.

"Shamus what has happened to you?"

"You should not be here my lady," His urgency rattled in his voice and the darkness within the halls was truly unsettling. She had to fight the impulse to run from him, to run from the cells. There was something unnatural clinging to him, making her feel terror as she did the night the rider had watched her from the window.

"Listen to me beloved Lady, there is a tower to this castle, that is old and in ill repair, do you know it?" she nodded, and he continued with his directions,

"Take the guard that you trust and venture to the top of the tower and find your mothers journal. I know it is there hidden among her things. You must find it, as I believe it will answer the questions I cannot. It will help you find the fire to keep the darkness at bay, now go."

His sense of urgency filled her with a panic that made her run from the hall without a thought about his safety. He had somehow made her forget that it even mattered, but as she cleared the steps to the dank prison, she felt a cold chase her and drive her from the hall. She raced through the halls to her rooms and bolted the door, but the fear did not ebb it sat in her chest and weighted her breath so much that it was uncomfortable to draw.

"Lady are you well?" a guard passing through the halls must have seen her panic.

"Send for Sir Drake, please, immediately."

"He has gone my lady. On leave." she closed her eyes remembering his departure earlier in the day. She felt her heart race, uncertain of how to get him back, she felt as though she would cry as all her emotions tied in knots and left her choked.

"I'll see if he has gone far my lady, I'll inform him of the urgency." Savane thought the guard was deserving of her gratitude, but her words would not come until long after he had left. He must have sensed her desperation, but then wondered what that would look like to the castle of a Lady about to marry a prince. She decided in the moment and under the circumstances that it did not matter and that she could not let it.

The sound at the door brought her from where she sat on her bed, pillow in hand and stood with her fist drawn up to hide her face.

"My Lady?"

She raced for the door at the sound of Dayin's voice and pulled the bolt free. He was still dressed in his common clothes but had his sword by his side as he had in the courtyard. At the sight of her he drew in a breath and she watched as he almost raised a hand to brush the tears that had left a trail down her cheeks. "I came as quickly as I could my lady, what is it?"

"I'm sorry, you must think I'm a horrible inconvenience, but I need you to stay with me. I need to go to my mother's tower, and I need you to take me there." She paused as her mind wandered to the prison below the estate., How had Shamus known about Dayin?

Take the guard that you trust. How did he know there was a guard that she trusted?

"My lady? You are worried."

Her eyes regained focus and stared at him, she tried to swallow and decided that rather than behave as a child she would have to find the source of this fear and extinguish it. If it was in that tower, then she would not wait a moment longer to find it and bring this shadow into the light.

"Forgive me Dayin, I had a bit of an event today and I feel I must explain so that you do not think me selfish for drawing you back so quickly after you did so much for me."

"My lady you have no need to apologize, I took an oath to serve your family and if that means I defer rest and all else, so be it. I had already returned from my mother's if it sets your mind at ease."

He smiled when she looked up at him to ensure

that she understood that all was well and there were no feelings of resentment in their new arrangement.

"Do you think I can trust you with my deepest thoughts Dayin?"

"I would hope that you would be able to." He fell into stride beside her as she made her way toward the wing of the estate that led to the tower that Shamus had spoken of.

"Then I will be truthful with you in all things and you must reserve judgment. Fair?"

He smiled again; a reserved smile that told her he was uncertain of the deal he was making.

"The night I saw something in my window, and you went to investigate did you know what you were looking for?"

He shook his head and watched the hall in front of them.

"I spoke to a prisoner in the cells and he spoke of Vetis, the one the old gods fought to destroy, do you know the story?"

"I know it well; I was raised in a family that prays to Lynstrom."

"Can you tell me?"

He seemed to wonder a moment at the direction she was going with the explanation of his presence here, but instead focused his attention to the story she asked to hear.

"In ages past, in the time of the old gods there was Adua, he was the father of the gods. Vetis, one of the lesser gods was jealous of his power and rose up creating armies of the different tribes some human and some not. He tricked the elves into serving him by convincing them that the humans were evil and needed to be defeated. While the ancient races of the goblins, orcs, and ogres served ruthlessly killing mankind wherever it was encountered."

"The gods, bound by loyalty to the laws that decreed that they could not intervene in matters of mankind, were helpless to watch but in an act of desperation to save their children, they united to stage one last battle. They met on what we call the bone fields now and gathered their forces among them. The forces of Vetis ranged as far as the eye could see and when the battle began the gods themselves fought alongside their children. Vetis' forces, through trickery were winning, when the gods made the fateful decision that would change all mankind.

They knew there was only one way to save their children. They sacrificed themselves." he paused to look at her then continued down the hall suddenly very aware of which hall they were in.

"When the Gods fell on the Bone-fields, the cataclysm that tore through the land forever changed it, magic was reborn and driven deep into the ground. The blood of the gods ran in radiant crimson veins along the ground and washed among the humans that had fought by their god's sides."

"The greatest soldiers who embodied their deities were those humans who were reborn that day, to rise as the gods of a new era. As the veins bled thin, some only possessed a whisper of the godly power but even the smallest influence would shape our hierarchy."

"But Vetis too was a God and his blood also ran in veins along the ground burning acrid rivers and char, washing over those helpless souls within his path." "Peiashchic and Valiechic were the two humans that were tainted by Vetis' godly essence; they were driven into the North lands to be swallowed by the snow and ice. The rest of the dark forces that were not destroyed were referred to as Tainted Legion. Horrible and deformed they are the children of the Dark God and their blood is as putrid as their souls, no good can come of them. The more they embrace their essence the greater hold the darkness takes until it consumes all of what once was man and leaves only a monster behind."

"In time, the people would come to see the power within the blood. The majority of our nobles possess the ancient bloodlines and have their gifts, which is why we still seek marriages that strengthen our lines as your father has done for you." Her eyes sought the ground, she had known of the bloodlines but not of the lore behind it. She knew of the gods sacrifice and the birth of the new gods. She knew that Vetis himself was cast into the deadlands, a parallel world, mirroring their own, but cast in decay where all things are in a state of death.

"Why all the questions?"

"What would you say if I told you he was trying to come back?"

"Who?" he watched her eyes as she stared at the staircase that led to the tower, "You mean Vetis? He can't come back; the gods saw to that. Do you want to go up there? It isn't safe, you could be hurt."

"I chose you because you said I could trust you, have you changed your mind Drake?"

"Trust me to do what is best for you or to do what you tell me to do?"

"Find a balance."

Her tone silenced him as he looked up the staircase. Her eyes had taken on a determination and focus that only came with self-assurance in one's path.

Savane took the stairs easily and held her dress from the floor to keep it from getting soot and ash on it.

"What happened in this wing Lady?"

"My father doesn't speak of it. Some of the servants who were here when my mother was alive believe that she was trying to grasp magic and that she failed, starting a great fire that consumed the wing. Others have more ominous versions of it. They like to believe in folk lore and still light candles when the veil is thin between the world of the dead and here. So, how is one to know what is real and what is false."

"Do you not light a candle?" he looked at her and she smiled,

"I take it you do..." Her mind drifted back to

the night he lit a candle in her room, how that simple flickering light had meant the difference between feeling the suffocating darkness and sleep.

"My mother was studying with a companion of magic, after the fire, he was never found." Savane stopped on the stairway thinking of Shamus and his deep awareness of Savane's mother and the book in the tower. His gentle nature and his loyalty to her despite being a prisoner. "She is believed to have kept a book of some importance and for whatever reason. I am told it was not destroyed in the fire and is here in the tower,"

He smiled and put his hand out for her to step over a fallen beam that stretched across the stairs. She took it and then grabbed the hem of her dress just as it hooked on the beam. He pulled it loose and continued up the stairs,

"Am I to assume that I cannot convince you to turn back if I find the book on your behalf?" She smiled a soft knowing smile and kept ascending the stairs.

When they reached the top, the door was barely hinged, it was partially open and the room beyond was in complete darkness. Savane was grateful that Dayin had taken an oil sconce and held it aloft for her as she stepped inside the room. Even with the light flickering, the room was dark because of the scarring the fire had left behind. Savane had been too young to remember anything but the panic of the night it had happened. Her mother had been alone in the tower that night and there were no witnesses to her final moments. Savane surveyed the room, the walls covered in soot and the ceiling only partially intact, revealing the stars above. Dayin's eyes held the sky longer than Savane's as though he noticed something that she had missed. "What do you see?"

"Do you see the stars, the constellation above us right now; do you know what it is?"

She lifted her eyes to the sky once again and stared at the seven stars that made up Lynstrom's eye. She nodded then continued to search for the book as Dayin stared upward. "Who did you say sent you to find this book?"

"Shamus, he is a prisoner in my father's cells." Dayin looked down from the stars and noticed a slip of white beneath the blackness of the room. He raised the light from the oil sconce drawing Savane's attention. She followed his gaze and choked with joy, she ran to the remnants of the window where just below, the pages were buried beneath wood, soot and ash. "It's here, just like he said, it's here."

The book was not only there but completely intact. The pages, dusty but not damaged at all by the flames that had consumed the room and her mother.

"I don't understand how that is possible." The sentiment barely left his mouth when the room let out an agonized groan and released its contents into the oblivion below. The book toppled down and disappeared into the darkness. Savane grabbed the window while Dayin's footing held beneath him. There was a moment where terror replaced rational thought. When Savane held the frame of the window she thought only of how far away Dayin was and that there was no way that he could save her from the painful death that awaited her below.

Her ribs burned as though they had been gouged and breath was painful to draw.

"My lady, the floor didn't release completely, raise your leg." She felt the floor with her foot and sighed as relief washed over her, she was able to pull herself to the floor support beams. She could see blood pooling on her dress from her ribs and felt lightheaded and weak.

"Savane," she sensed the panic in his voice and wanted to stay strong so that her new champion might not have to watch helpless as his charge plunged to her death.

He held the light out as far as he dared so that she could see that the floor supports still ran in a circle around the room. She had a safe path if she could just get up. She lifted herself with the aid of the window frame and put her back to the wall. The book had fallen with the rest of the floor and the helplessness that brought was starting to set in. She placed one foot tentatively on the floor beside where she stood and then confident it could hold her weight, she balanced each step carefully.

She had seen performers come to the estate many times. Gypsies that did these things all the time, and even smiled while they did it. At this moment she couldn't help but wonder what they thought of to make them smile because with her muscles burning, all she could envision was her death at the bottom of a long drop.

It felt like an eternity passed between one moment to the next when she reached Dayin's outstretched arms and felt the safety within them. She breathed in the smell of him, the slight smell of leather mixed with oil and sweat and copper. No, the copper was her own. The blood that had stained her dress now flowed freely and transferred on to his shirt as he held her.

"By Lynstrom's tears..." He lifted her up and made for the stairs. He took them as quickly as was safe with her held in his arms. He watched her eyes fluttering as she tried desperately to cling to consciousness.

"The book, check for the book..." Her words were clear despite the state she was in. Her focus extending to the need to have that book and not have it lost in the cleanup that was sure to follow. When he got to the base of the stairs, he searched the wreckage, the remnants of the room above. Between beams of aged and charred wood, again the book was found. Dayin disbelieving what he saw stared at the book, how could such a book exist that defies flames and seems to want to be found. He returned to his lady with the book and hoisted her back into his arms. He smiled at the look of complete joy that washed over her face despite her very impending fall into unconsciousness.

He arrived at her room, just as guards came to see what the clamor had been. The guards moved down the hall as he layed her down on her bed.

"I'll fetch the physician."

Savane grabbed for his tunic as he turned to leave. "Fetch Lyselle, she'll keep our secret'

53

The secret itself did not sit well with Dayin; he wondered what type of Champion nearly gets his Lady killed on his first official duty.

He turned away and felt her grasp at his arm. "Thank you, Sir Drake, for not giving up or disbelieving me." he placed her arm back on her chest and went for the door, "I'll fetch Lady Lyselle."

Savane lay still on the bed the book lay just out of reach and the pain in her ribs did not bring any desire to exceed her grasp. Instead her mind drifted to the very few memories she had of her mother. Her laugh seemed to be the only strong memory she had of the woman that every person within the estate said she was the mirror image of. Her laugh was like music and made all those who heard it smile. People would say that she had a gentle soul. They had been devastated when she died and still lit candles for her on the anniversary of her death.

Lyselle arrived and set quickly to taking care of her dearest friend, Savane winced as she tore away the gown and revealed the opened wound beneath. When the blood and cloth had been cleaned away the anger of the wound seemed to wash clean with it. It was a jagged but shallow cut that had most likely been caused by the heavy impact of flesh surrendering to wood when the floor had given way. The bruise that hid behind the cut was far more, sinister and would prove to be the source of Savane's pain for days to follow.

Chapter Five

Those days that followed were consumed by reading her mother's journal. The pages, though unmarred by the flames were aged and faded. Each passage was a reciting of history, ages before, and the link between the noble houses and the Gods who battled on the Field of Bones. There were sketches of the families and their ancestors as far back as those who fought on the battlefield and which detachment they were in when the gods fell. The narrative cited no source and Savane lay there wondering how her mother could have learned such things. Was it just the compiling thoughts of a woman grasping at heritage and legend?

There were sections of the book that Savane could not read, though she had managed to draw some words from the elvish language to which she was familiar. It was her mother that had insisted that Savane be taught to speak the languages of both the Elvin people and the Northern Dark Tribes. Savane found from a young age that one of the most beautiful languages was Elvin, and one of the most guttural and obscure languages' known to mankind was of the Northern Dark Tribes'.

There was a very detailed record of the involvement of the elves during the battle. Vetis had
tried to force the elves involvement in the battle
by bringing forth a proposal to the High King Mesorre. He told the Elvish king that if they were to
take the side against the humans, they would be
able to claim the lands that were once theirs allowing both their magic and customs to remain
intact. Mesorre, sensing the deceit turned from
Vetis and went to his brother to explain what
the dark god had offered; Railynde was enraged
that his noble brother would not take what was
offered and the power it would grant and went
to the dark god in secrecy.

The two forged an alliance that granted the
Elvin prince power that would intensify as he
corrupted other elves, drawing them to his side.
There were some who turned almost instantly,
while others saw that the death the Dark god was
promising. Though it meant the end of their enemies, death was against all that they believed
in. Railynde's forces grew and as the Elves were
corrupted, the radiance that was in their skin
faded; their light went out. The power that Vetis
spoke of, took hold, their beauty turned from innocence to a predatory allure. Their faces once
luminous cracked, became gray, and mirrored
the darkness within. Railynde and his force of

gray elves were at the battle of the Gods and received their due as the Gods died. Railynde was one of three heavily bathed in the blood of Vetis, Peiashchic, the most dangerous among Vetis human warlords and Valiechic a female priestess and the most manipulative deviant from the North lands were Vetis' newborn gods. They were driven into the Northern wastes with what was left of their forces, though it is said that Railynde and his gray elves were to have separated from the humans after they stopped running.

Savane lifted her head and closed her eyes from the book. The pages had seemingly turned on their own as her thirst for knowledge expanded. If these were her mother's words, if this is what she poured her energies into, it left Savane feeling as though her mother's death was not as accidental as others had led her to believe. Her mind drifted to the night the rider had been watching her. She felt a chill rise up and sit against her spine. It forced a shiver from her in the warmth of day.

When the door opened it was all she could do to keep from jumping. Lyselle swept through the door with a ball gown held in her arms. A beautiful rich purple gown, the colour of the Savane's eyes, woven of the finest fabric with gold piping that ran along the bust and back. The centerpiece was a rich cream satin. Savane looked at it with a heavy heart knowing it to be her father's attempt to sell his daughter to the Prince.

Lyselle frowned at the expression on her lady's face and looked back down at the beautiful dress.

"If you won't wear it, may I?" she pouted.

"Only if you can convince my father to let me go in a burlap bag." Savane sighed and sat up slowly. There were no stitches to tear, but the bruise had deepened and was near the colour of the dress that Lyselle was holding.

"Have we heard anything on his arrival?" She said as she fingered the gold piping. "Scouts put him two days away my lady and from what I have been told he has a very extensive entourage."

Savane nodded and gestured for her to set the dress down on the bed while she prepared to try it on.

"Have you been reading your mother's book?" she said as she pulled her thick waist length hair into a knot at the base of Savane's head.

"Each moment I have I am reading, I can't set it down, I feel as though each page is opportunity to know her better."

She winced as she held up her arms for Lyselle to remove her night gown and then stepped into the dress upon the floor as her lady set to dressing her. She refrained from tightening it but instead stood back from the polished metal framed against the wall.

She could see Lyselle's smile from behind her and it made the sadness that gripped her that much more troublesome.

"I feel as though my life is about to end and you are smiling for it."

"You are about to marry a Prince and begin an adventure to the Eastern coast to see things that many never get to see and someday be Queen of that land. How can you believe that it is not worthy of a smile?"

"You truly are a remarkable friend Lyselle. I know that you are right to see the good in it, but after finding my mother's book and seeing what I have in the last week I feel as though I will be missing something or leaving when I am needed."

"Did it occur to you that the Prince is where you need to be? Perhaps he gives you the far-reaching hand that is needed to solve this mystery that you have stumbled upon."

Savane remained still as Lyselle removed the dress after making minor adjustments to the length and dressed her once again in the night gown she previously wore. Her lady made for the door leaving Savane motionless in the room to think about her last words.

Moments passed before Savane donned her dressing gown and made her way down the halls with her book in her arms. Her pace slowed as she drew near to Shamus and the halls beneath the estate, recalling the fear that had gripped her and how she had run without concern for him or his safety. She hesitated for only a moment before she started her decent and into the hallway. The silence was unbearable. Part of her wanted to run to his cell to dispel the curiosity while the stronger urge held her back for fear of finding him in the cell having met some horrible fate. In the end she stepped forward and met his gaze as he stood seemingly waiting for her. Savane started at the sight of him, his eyes, though still aged, lacked the sickly look that had claimed them before. His body no longer appearing crippled by pain. "Did you find it?" he whispered. She slowly nodded her head and began lifting the book to show him. "It is yours, to read, to learn the secrets within and to guide you. It by no means is the teacher your mother would have been, but it is a start. Did you finish it?"

"No, it is a very long compilation, and I have had to rest to recover from an injury."

"There are parts within that are written in a different language, your mother was very experienced in magic and I know it is part of you as well, don't give up, it will come to you."

"What happened the last time I was here Shamus? Did my father imprison you because he thought you were somehow involved in my mother's death?" He drew a deep breath and shook his head, "None of the answers to those questions are relevant to you right now. You are not on a path of trying to solve the mysteries of the past, you have a duty to the future."

"Now," he said sitting back into the darkness, "I have a confession to make,"

Savane stared at him fearing his next words. "I am old, beloved Lady and I am running out of time. While your father has been a remarkable host, I fear our time together is at an end and we need to part ways. Learn the difference between your allies and your enemies and never treat one as the other. Find the difference between those who are magic by blood and those who are magic by theft."

He held out his hands to her which she took fearlessly. In the moment that their hands met the bars that had held him captive for years vanished and the gentle grasp upon her hands became a vice holding her fast against him and a rusted but crudely sharpened blade was raised to her throat. Shock and an overwhelming sense of betrayal choked Savane as he ascended the stairs with her in his grasp. He meant to use her as a hostage to gleam his freedom and make his way out of the sentence her father had visited upon him. For the first time in their years together, Savane feared him.

In the courtyard above there was an explosion that rocked the walls, never before had the estate been under attack nor been forced to withstand whatever could have hit with such force that the walls themselves groaned. When they breached the halls, the guards were all so busy that Shamus slipped by unnoticed. It wasn't until he reached the courtyard that he let out a frustrated cry as Dayin turned the corner. His eyes bore an intense calm about them as he recognized the danger his Lady faced, he stepped back and let Shamus pass unharmed.

"I mean her no harm Sir Drake so stay with me and I promise I will deliver her to you as she is, test me and we will see if that power over life and death you most recently used is just a falsehood."

Dayin matched each step with Shamus, meeting the eyes of his lady in an effort to stave off her fear and gauge her pain. The moments passed as hours until they reached the steps to the wall that surrounded the estate, beyond it was freedom. Just as Dayin wondered how he would clear the distance below the wall a grapple latched to the face of it and before he could react, she was falling from near seven or eight steps. In only seconds he cast away his sword and threw himself beneath her to try to catch her or at least cushion the blow on her already wounded ribs. They both felt the air rushed from them as they remained still on the ground, Savane's heart raced with fear and pain while Shamus disappeared with a wink over the wall.

Within moments a crowd gathered, and the Duke fell upon his guard, "Find him." his face red with rage as spittle fell from his lips like a mad dog. Savane had never seen her father in such a state. He had never lost control. There was more to Shamus then he had ever revealed and somehow Savane thought the answers would be within the pages of her mother's book.

Guards raced into a flurry of activity though one

remained to help both she and Dayin up, "Mind her, she's injured." Dayin commanded in a far more assertive tone then Savane was accustom.

She winced as she stood and thanked the guard before turning to watch Dayin recover his discarded blade. His eyes bore an odd intensity that she had not seen before within them. "See the Lady to her chambers and set a guard upon her door at all times." With not even a moment of eye contact he swept away and strode to the stables.

She knew she could call him back, she could force him to stay, as she wished he would, so that the trembling would subside. If Shamus had said anything that she would keep forever, it was those words he had uttered before turning on her. Know your enemies from your allies and never treat one as the other.

She was certain that those words would echo in her thoughts forever. For now, she watched as her Champion mounted his equally brave steed and disappeared beyond the portcullis.

Chapter Six

When dawn broke there was no trace of Shamus or his accomplice. He had vanished, leaving no footsteps in mud, no broken branches, and the finest trackers had searched and fallen short of success. Savane stood in front of the cell door that had vanished before her eyes the night before.

The door had been there, seemingly Shamus chiselled away at its framing and used whatever magic he had possessed to conceal his efforts from her whenever she or the servant who brought his meals, made their rounds. She stared disbelieving at the walls, how could that be, she had felt them, sat beside them, reached through them. Perhaps it was the power of an illusion to bring the mind to believe in what the eyes saw. What had he said about the difference between magic of the blood and magic by theft? She drew in a shaking breath and for the last time she ascended the stairs, leaving the prison behind her.

Word from the scouts assured that the Prince and his entourage was on schedule and that they were to arrive by nightfall. It forced Savane to participate in preparations rather than slink away to delve further into her mother's memoirs.

She spent the day having rooms refreshed, food prepared, barracks reallocated, and stables made ready to take in the large number of exhausted horses.

She spoke quickly to the stableman to ensure that all would be prepared when her eyes fell on an empty stall, Dayin had still not returned from seeking Shamus and it was near nightfall. She could feel the panic that she had swallowed all day once again rising in the pit of her stomach. Her wound ached, her head throbbed and in hours her future husband would arrive to assess her skills as a wife and matron of a small estate. Then he would evaluate whether she could run a castle, and she was certain he would be less than impressed, and to compound all these things, her champion was nowhere to be found.

The stableman was an older man with a gentle heart and a true understanding of the unsaid word. With a nod of his head Savane turned to where he had directed her gaze to see Dayin standing in the center of the horse corral with his great black horse, passively brushing his coat, seemingly lost in thought. He didn't notice when Savane closed the distance between them and stood on the other side of Seraphic. In the end it was the beast striking the ground with his hoof absently that gave her away.

"What has you so entranced Sir Drake?"

"Forgive me Lady, I didn't see you approach."

"How could you? Wherever you were, you were far from my reach."

"I could never be out of your reach." The words left his lips before he could estimate their ambiguity.

"I mean that I would not leave Lady, that I am yours to command."

"You're exhausted Sir Drake, I am aware that you sought for Shamus much of the night and into dawn. Tonight, will definitely be the most trying task in the history of all things my father has ever asked of me. I am afraid I haven't the energy to concern myself with whether or not you will be at my side tonight. So please," she drew an exasperated breath "Please sleep Sir Drake, so that I may trust you with my life tonight as I was able last evening."

He bowed his head and took the horse's lead.

Savane thought he looked like a scolded child today where last evening he had played the great defender so flawlessly.

"Sir Drake?"

"My lady?" His eyes lifted as though she had pulled him from his bereft state.

"Are you well, were you hurt at all?"

"I am only trying to reconcile last evening my lady, it is of no concern, I will return to duty as you know me tonight. With your leave." He turned and made his way to the stables where he handed off his horse with an affectionate pat to the neck before retiring to the barracks. Savane watched in anticipation of a backward glance that never came. She lifted her skirts from the ground and was about to return to the estate when the stableman caught her attention.

The subtle lift to his jaw was indicative of man who knew what was troubling her champion. "It would seem your knight has some feelings for his Lady."

Savane forced a smile and waved her hand in an attempt to dismiss the possibility that had gripped her as tightly as it seemed to have affected Dayin. "He is exhausted, nothing more."

The entourage had arrived in the latter part of the day and had requested time to prepare for the evening before making introductions. Savane watched from her window as her future husband arrived and drew in a shaky breath when he seemed to notice her from her vantage point. He was dark haired and average height though slight of frame with what appeared to be a strong physique. His eyes were light in colour and paled in the coming twilight. He did not smile or provide any indication that he was pleased to have arrived, but she chose to assume it was the journey.

Savane sat motionless as Lyselle brushed and pulled at her long raven hair, piece by piece was braided and piled upon her head in a complex pattern until only tendrils drifted over her shoulders. Gold twine interlaced between the braids and around her forehead. When Lyselle finished she turned toward the gown and smiled, "It's time."

The dress, with all of is finery was heavy and cool against her skin. Her father had ensured that the dress was worthy of a future princess and despite how it made Savane feel to be given to a stranger, forced to leave her home, for a moment she let herself feel the romantic thrill that Lyselle had tried to help her envision.

A tapping at the door announcing the arrival of the entourage drew the excitement away as fast as it has been allowed to set in. In its place, a great gush of panic washed over her. Lyselle, her lifetime friend, her confidant and ally when all things went wrong, took one look at Savane's face and laughed.

The great hall had been decorated in such a fashion that Savane almost felt that it was for the wedding. Flowers lined every wall and the sconce had been highly polished. Tables formed a great half-moon around the head table and more flowers and decor draped off of each.

A gentle breeze touched her neck as the great doors must have been opened. She turned feeling overwhelmed and released a sigh of relief as Dayin, or more appropriately, Sir Dayin Drake strode toward her. He had been true to his promise of returning more as himself. Her father had seen to him, so that he would appear fit to serve a princess and was well suited from what Savane could see. He wore dark tunic and trousers; his cloak was the deep purple of the Lady's own dress and a strip of thin gold chains linked together across his chest marked him as her own personal guard. His sword hung at his hip, tethered in a fashion to prevent the drawing of in it in the company of royalty.

To Savane, he looked magnificent. He bowed to her and let a slight smile come to his lips, "Forgive me Lady, I have never been dressed in so formal a manner."

"There is nothing to forgive Sir Drake, truth be told, I don't believe I have either. I am happy the rest you took has brought you back to yourself Sir Drake, I feel that your presence here provides me some degree of comfort."

"There is nothing to fear Lady, it would take a fool or a man with no soul to not find you a worthy bride."

She smiled and arched her brow, "You are assessing my worth as a bride now are you Sir Drake?"

His face reddened but before he could defend his thoughts, her father swept into the room and embraced her gently to prevent and disturbance to her hair and dress. "My goodness child, I failed to recognize you dressed in such finery and looking the lady." He pulled a box from within his tunic and held it out for her.

"Thank you." she whispered as she opened the box to reveal a necklace with a purple star ruby. Savane stared at the star within and remembered the night she and Dayin had found her mother's journal. "It's beautiful," she breathed.

"Go on Sir Drake, place it around her neck will you." He awkwardly took the necklace from its lined case and placed it around Savane's neck. The purple from her gown drew out the colour and it shone against her skin. "Beautiful." her father whispered as he kissed her forehead, his eyes glassy with tears.

From behind, a herald had arrived and began introducing the noble houses that had been invited to the dinner. Each in their turn arrived and greeted the Duke and his daughter. Savane was overwhelmed by the attention and tried desperately to remain focused on the evening, rather than running for the door as every fabric in her being bade her do.

The heavy knock of the herald preparing to make another introduction drew her attention to the door.

"Introducing the Prince of House Verentine of Mazen, Heir to the throne of the Eastern Realm, Prince Theries Verentine."

The Prince was as Savane had beheld from the window of her chambers, though she could not have been prepared for his visage up close. He was perhaps three years her senior and wore his standing for all to behold. He possessed a very dangerous beauty unlike Dayin whose innocence was mirrored in his eyes. The prince had a very calculating gaze that seemed to absorb everyone in the room before they fell and stayed on the sixteen-year-old girl who trembled behind her father.

She felt Dayin behind her press against her right side a subtle display of support and strength to help steady her. In that moment she matched his breathing and stood stronger because of it. But the movement was not subtle enough, the prince's eyes seemed drawn to her side before he turned his gaze away completely.

Savane felt breathless and lowered her gaze for a moment, her downcast eyes revealed all her emotion to Dayin behind her. "Am I to assume that Lyselle's vision of my Prince is inaccurate?"

He repressed a chuckle which he managed to conceal in a clearing of his throat to avoid detection. Savane smiled in return and raised her gaze to the door as the rest of the prince's entourage entered the great hall.

Both Savane and Dayin were surprised when a woman fell into step beside the prince, she stood half a hand taller than the prince and wore the same colours as he, marking her of house Verentine. Her hair was shoulder length and fine straw coloured, but she wore armor rather than the dresses that the rest of the noble houses wore. She, unlike Dayin, wore her sword across her back and it remained unbound though the soldiers had been directed to bind their weapons. Of these features, none were as distinct as the one feature that both the dark-haired Prince and the straw haired Champion behind him shared. Their eyes, though hers were the most brilliant green Savane had ever seen. The kind of green trapped in a stone not behind eyes

"Do you see that Sir Drake?" he followed her line of sight, having still not let his gaze leave the Prince, it moved to the champion that the Lady had brought to his attention. His brow raised in definitive surprise.

"Were they not his rules?" she whispered smiling ever so slightly.

The prince made his way through the crowd and stopped before the Duke who extended his arm as he made a formal gesture of welcoming. "Prince Verentine, my daughter and I, welcome you to our home."

"Duke, I see you had a bit of a disturbance on your north east wall, I trust no one was harmed." The Dukes face went instantly crimson as the breach in his home's security was so quickly noticed, he had taken every precaution to avoid that very thing.

"My Father sends his regrets toward his absence however entrusts us to see to proper arrangements regarding our trade lines opening as we discussed."

"Yes of course," The Duke smiled and patted Theries on the shoulder in affectionate display that Savane noticed was not well received. Both the Prince and his escort flinched, he to the touch and she, to what Savane thought, was of concern for her father and not the prince.

The Duke pulled his hand away, discouraged from further contact and looked to his daughter with pride, a smile beginning to surface. "May I introduce my Daughter, Savane?"

The prince's eyes barely fluttered against her before he turned back upon her father and led him away to converse about the politics of the union rather than the union itself.

Savane stood motionless, her breath sucked from her as the tide she had held at bay for so long consumed her in one last gulp and left her devoid of feeling. She swallowed hard on lump in her throat as within moment's childhood emotions rushed in and threatened tears in her eyes. She felt Dayin shift his weight behind her in an effort to help her regain focus so that she would remember where she was and not weep in a room full of her father's lesser nobles.

The champion behind the prince paused a moment as if she had some thought to share. She had a look of someone who was well aware of the rejection Savane had just suffered, but whatever sentiment slowed her pace abandoned her and she turned on a rigid heel to follow her Prince.

Savane watched them go and felt the panic ebb away as they left the room. Her guests came more into focus. She made her way to each and forced a smile. The prince had travelled all this way to seal an arrangement for trade routes and acquired a wife out of obligation. This was not the first-time marriage occurred in such a fashion and children were foolish to dream of romance when there was a matter of blood and profit.

Playing the dutiful daughter and future bride was exhausting and Savane was ready for the night to end far before the dinner even began. Sitting next to her future husband, she expected that he too would play a role, but there was no kindness extended to her. His smile was nothing more than a charming smirk that made him appear more as villain then a prince.

"Did you encounter any complications on your travels Prince Verentine?" Savane asked in an attempt to break the silence between them.

He turned slightly in his chair to consider her a moment and to see her eyes. Savane felt heat in her face as he seemed to observe everything, from the rise and fall of her breath to the few strands of hair that stood on the back of her neck. She had never experienced such scrutiny in a gaze. His eyes lingered only a moment longer on hers taking in the purple that most people loved to make comments on. He took them in in silence and then looked away. There was nothing in his gaze that felt like possession and in that moment, she wondered what he truly wanted with her. Just as she thought he would ignore her all together his gaze fell to the space between them,

"It was a loathsome trip that I am certain will be made even more miserable by your prattle on our return."

Savane lifted her chin and clenched her fists around the cloth in her lap which didn't seem to escape his notice though there was no sign of satisfaction that his words had wounded her. He merely turned his gaze away and conversed with others at the table. It took every shred of her strength to keep from feigning some illness to excuse her from the beginning of what Savane believed to be a lifetime of torment.

By the nights end, after the guests had all made their way home with their illusions of the young duchess's happiness, Savane strode to her room and tore the finery from her hair and wrists. She struggled like a prisoner against the shackle like hold of her gown before she heard fabric let go and emotion finely won over the strength of her adolescence. She fell to her knees in pitiful desperation, sobbing like a child. By the time her emotions had been exhausted she crawled to her bed and slept.

Dawn brought new determination and as she sat having her hair rebraided. She committed to strengthen her resolve and not crumple to the ground and weep ever again. If her father was going to throw her to the wolves, the wolves were going to choke.

She read her mother's journal as Lyselle prepared her for the day ahead, the tournament and challenge of champions that would come to an end with the knighting of Dayin. The thought brought a smile to Savane that made her lower her mother's book.

Lyselle was about to lift Savane's hair and pile it on top of her head when she suddenly stood and looked at her lady like a rabbit eyeing a fox.

"What is it?"

"The Prince, do you think he will prevent Sir Drake from accompanying me, do you think he will take him from me?"

Lyselle was taken aback by the panic in her Lady's eyes and then her gaze shifted and fell behind Savane to the doorway. It was then Savane who was surprised by the expression she beheld. Savane turned around to face Prince Theries in the middle of her own personal chambers.

The shock of the moment did not give her time to keep the promise she had made to herself about making this wolf choke. She knew that he could read her face and all the emotions she held behind. She took a deep breath then flexed her fist. He stood silent in her room and watched her with the fearless expression of one who never felt he was in the wrong.

"These are my personal chambers sir and you are not permitted here"

"Well, as you are about to be mine, I do not see

how you can make such a distinction."

Savane stood rigid as he approached. He moved silently and even the drawing of his breath was so controlled that he could have been behind her and she would not have known.

"Why are you trying to frighten me so? I am not an enemy; I am your future wife."

"Why are you frightened?" his eyes held hers in the first moment of direct interaction since he had arrived. She took a deep breath to try and still the wild beating of her heart, while Lyselle trembled behind her. She let the comment go unanswered as she was truly uncertain if his tactics were a ruse to gain control over her or the way he would be forever in their lives together.

He stole a glance at the journal open on a page with the writing Savane had yet to comprehend and watched as his eyes sharpened their focus before returning her gaze. He recognized the script; she could sense a familiarity in the way he had scanned the page. She was about to comment but held back instead, deciding the mystery better solved later.

The Prince turned then having new conviction he moved to the door and stopped for only a moment and without turning uttered the one command Savane would honor gratefully. "Your Champion is to accompany you. I do not want the task of protecting you."

He swept from the room in silence. With the exception of the few words he had spoken, he never made a sound. Not the movement of his clothes, the drawing of his breath or even the closing of the door. He was a ghost walking the halls. Lyselle eyed her Lady with the look of one who would spout a volley of insults were she given leave, but in that moment Savane feared her betrothed may still be on the other side of the door and waved her lady into silence.

The relief she felt at his final words left her smiling, whether they were said with kindness or not she was relieved that she would not have to face this new life alone and he would be with her to give her strength and help her endure the trials ahead.

Chapter Seven

The games were always the Dukes greatest pleasure, while the women of the court were more inclined to socialize during the event. They were always overdressed and over decorated to broadcast their stature while their male counterparts strut about in their finest armor and deeply coloured decorations.

Savane walked with her lady to Sir Drake's tent and waited as his squire opened the flap, she ducked in and stood behind him as he nervously adjusted the fit of his new armor. It was dark metal with fine etching along the neck and shoulders. His sword was again rested on his hip where it looked natural, waiting to defend his Lady. He stopped fidgeting when he noticed her watching him.

"Forgive me M'lady I have never done anything of this magnitude, and I fear I will not represent you as you deserve."

Savane looked at him with a gentle kindness as she reached her hand back to Lyselle who offered her a silken bag.

"I have seen you for who you are and what you are capable of Sir Drake, and it makes no difference to me whether you are able to defeat my Princes champion in combat. I trust that her presence at his side means that she is a worthy adversary and deserving of caution." She reached her hand into the silk bag and produced an amulet the champion was very familiar with.

"My Mother was a very strong voice of the gods, she always attended mass. After her death, my father refused the gods and their part in our lives."

The holy symbol in her hand was intricate in its carvings but not ornate. The metal was wrought and polished. "I have seen you in prayer and know that you hold your vows to your god as sacred as my mother would have held them. I would like you to have this." She stepped forward and placed the holy symbol around the neck of her champion, his gaze followed the symbol down to his chest where it rested against the armor. Savane marveled as Dayin trembled visibly. "You do not need this victory to be what I need of you Sir Drake."

Her smile brought a small one to his lips as she turned and made for the door, "Good Luck Sir Drake and rest assured that I will be praying for you."

Savane and Lyselle made their way to where her father and the Prince were seated in the pavilion, at the head of the jousting stage. The grounds were already turned up from the horses and the many knights of varying stature coming to be recognized and compete for the prize. In an act of camaraderie that Savane questioned, the Prince had augmented to a substantially larger sum then what her father had funded. Never before had the knights competed for so large a pot.

She climbed the stairs and stepped down into a large pavilion, catered with food and wine for the greater families and their attendants. Savane could feel the excitement emanating from Lyselle as she had never been permitted in the host pavilion. It lifted Savane to know that all this pomp was at least winning someone over.

The Duke turned and embraced her warmly as he guided her to her seat. Savane could smell the spirits on his breath and knew that the evening would be filled with his laughter as the wine flowed freely for he and his guests. The Prince however was not drinking and Savane was certain that he would not. He had a very careful nature that did not appear willing to lose control of his conduct or his senses. At least she could be certain he would not be one of those slobbering drunks that only came to her smelling of spirits and smoke.

In the light of day, the Prince was annoyingly handsome to look at, his clothes and posture were perfect and his arrogance from the night before, though not gone, had taken on a more polished confidence. His dark hair was freshly cleaned and was pulled to a tail at the base of his head. His hands, resting on the arm of his chair, were so meticulously manicured that she was curious if someone did everything for him.

She sat silent in her seat remembering the comment he had made to her at the dinner, knowing that he had no desire to make idle chatter, she turned her attention to the games. The pot had indeed changed the games in a way that Savane had not anticipated. The knights fought arduously, some even careless with their lives, desperate to remain in the games and not be cut prematurely.

It took several matches before Savane found the Princes personal guard, she was not decorated as the lady's champions were with chiffon flags flying from their armor or lances. The Princes guard was fast and relentless, as if she were an extension of his ego. She fought flawlessly and suddenly Savane was made acutely aware of why the Prince had so generously donated to the victor's pot.

Savane's father introduced Sir Drake in his first combat by retelling the tale of what had happened at the river's edge, how his bravery and selflessness had saved Lyselle's life, and for that Sir Drake had a number of admirers and favours bestowed upon him. Savane smiled as the knight endured the display red faced. He placed his helmet down over his face and turned to face his first competitor.

The combat was uneven from the beginning. Sir Drake had been a soldier fighting or training for the better part of his life, his father s training and then his brothers, served him well as he claimed his first victory, barely winced. He turned confused for a moment by his victory, before finding Savane in the Pavilion and bowing in respect. She nodded in return and allowed the smallest smile to show her pleasure with his effortless win.

The day's events fell one after the other with minor intermissions of jesters, plays and pageantry. It seemed each time Savane locked at Lyselle she was bursting with enthusiasm and excitement over what was to come. Savane tried desperately to cling to these moments as she was certain they would be the last truly happy moments for some time.

Even the urging of the crowd for the prince to kiss the Duke's daughter did not sway him to acts of affection or romance. It wasn't until his guard had returned to visit with him that she saw a smile creep on to his face.

She had dressed down to her greaves and chest plate, her great sword strapped to her back and her boyish hair tied on the top of her head. Her deep green eyes smiled in a constant state of amusement as she spoke with the prince. The ladies and noble men in the pavilion seemed truly distraught by her presence, a detail that seemed only to amuse her more. She had a distinct warm laugh that somehow the Prince drew out of her without having any signs of humor himself. Watching them, was as watching two participants of two completely different conversations.

When the prince left her, Savane watched as she sat against the table. Her arms folded across her chest in casual confidence. Then her green eyes fell on Savane, her smile did not fade, her eyes did not waiver or have the look of someone forbade to express her thoughts so Savane decided it was time to become familiar with this Champion of her Prince's.

As the combat began again on the grounds below

the Duchess approached her and took a glass from the table behind her.

"It is very rare to see a woman faring so well in combat against men. You must have spent your life in study."

"It is one of my favourite things, this. Beating all the boys at their games. It is a pleasure to finally be afforded the opportunity to meet you Lady, I am Balae Verentine. Your future sister."

The laugh that came out of her when Savane nearly choked on her wine was very uncharacteristic of high-born nobles. That this woman was a princess in the east was unfathomable to Savane. She gawked unabashed for a moment before she regained her composure and took the napkin Balae offered for her to wipe the wine from her chin.

"Your father insists that you are a notable rider, perhaps we can get to know each other better on the trip home. For now, I have to go pummel your new knight."

Savane stared after her in silence, watching as she took the stairs like a child skipping every other step and swinging from the last with an easy playful grace. It left Savane completely uncertain of how she felt about the prince's sister.

Was she going to be a light in the dark, or just a different view upon it? The woman had the characteristics of a man you would find in a lowborn tavern, not the sort you would find in a castle.

She returned to her seat and sat numbly beside the Prince who watched the crowd but wore an amused grin. "She's your sister?"

He dropped his chin and addressed the space between them in what Savane was coming to recognize as the way he would always address her. His smile seemed genuine and true as he watched his sister face off against another lesser noble lord's knight.

"Yes, she's my sister." he lifted his chin as she pulled the sword from the scabbard on her back and advanced against the man. It took three incredible blows before he raised his hand and yielded. She placed her sword tip to the ground and made a mock curtsy that brought howls of laughter from the crowd, before turning on her heel and strutting from the ring.

For the first time his eyes fell on her "She's a bit brutish but very effective." Then he was clapping and watching for the next bout.

Dayin Drake was everything that Savane had expected him to be, he met every challenge with grace and charisma, taking the time to help up his fallen challengers. The ladies adored him, and the crowd was quick to cheer for him when he entered the battle ring. He excelled in sword combat and mounted combat, putting him far in the lead but tied with the prince's sister and a few other competitors. The victor would not be determined until the next day of combat.

The dinner that followed the day's events was filled with more merriment and grandeur. Though many of the competitors had been eliminated this part of the festivities was free for all to attend and if they were not going to win the pot at least they could still eat well. Many of them were grateful to Sir Drake, as he had not opted to take their armor and weapons as payment for their loss against him as was the custom. Instead he insisted that they keep them and asked them to raise a glass with him. He was not only Savane's Champion, but many were already calling him the people's champion.

He stood on the balcony overlooking the grounds that had hosted the day's events when Savane found him, his eyes were tired, and his posture worn from the day of exertion. He was still however decorated in the finery for the occasion and looking very much like a noble.

"You look as though you would sleep for days

were I to give you leave to."

"My lady," he smiled as he faced her, his eyes instantly regaining focus and clarity. "You were a great motivation for me today, I thank you."

"I have never enjoyed these games, my father has always loved them and insisted they be a part of every season, but I have always found them tedious and long." She placed her hands on the rail of the balcony and watched as the game grounds were scoured by young children hoping to find the odd misplaced coin or something else of value. She smiled as one seemed to find something and made off with it before being chased by the others less fortunate.

"I used to dream of this day Sir Drake, when the games would be held in my honor and my betrothed and I would sit and watch the competitors battle. He would sit beside me with his smile matching mine. Today the only match between the prince and I was our clothes. Surely, he conceded to that only out of respect for his father, who would not benefit from trade relations if his son were perceived as an ass." Dayin's brow raised in response to the lady's use of profanity, which evoked a smile from her.

"I have been unfair Sir Drake and I need to ask you something that I only assumed to be true before this day."

He remained still and silent, his hands resting on the rail beside hers as she prepared to speak. "Two days from now I am to be taken away to Prince Theries eastern lands and I will be married to him. I had convinced myself that you would be with me and that if I had that I could endure whatever sadness would come of it. But today, as all those people called your name, I realized that this is your home, and I would be taking you from it and everything you love."

His breath expelled and silenced Savane, "No, I will come with you. My mother will have my brother and my place is with you. Whatever happens I will be by your side, to endure with you and for you if I am able."

Savane stared at the moon in the sky, so low to the horizon it seemed to dominate everything. Tears fell silently down her cheeks as she mourned the life she dreamed of but found herself waking from daily since the arrival of the prince. "Please don't weep, Lady, it compels me to bring you comfort and I cannot do that and honor you still."

She turned her gaze to the ground and trembled when he lifted her chin. He placed both hands tenderly upon her shoulders and a kiss on her forehead before turning to walk away but froze as he went face to face with the Prince and the Duke in the doorway.

"Is this the bride you offer me?"

The tears seemed to dry almost instantly as Savane's face ignited in fury. The Duke's anger matched her own as he motioned for guards to surround them both.

"Take this ingrate to the cells and lock my daughter up, I'll deal with this when I'm sober."

Such a lingering threat he had uttered, that he would deal with it at all left Savane feeling sickened. She sat numb in her room as the grounds silenced below and the festivities were driven to a halt by an innocent kiss. She wondered if by morning those who had called Sir Drake the people's champion would be demanding his head for kissing a high-born noble. Surely, her father would not have him executed for so small an offense. It was not malicious, if anything he had shown better character then herself as she knew very well that she would have returned whatever kiss he had granted her.

She watched the moon crossing the window and held her mother's book on her lap but lacked the focus required to read it. Instead she wept once again feeling the confidence draining, knowing that the champion who had sworn to bear her suffering with her would no longer be accompanying her to the east. At this point it was possible that even she would not be going, in which case she was certain she would meet Sir Drake's fate.

"Why so sad?" The voice came out of the darkness and terrified her beyond measure. Theries sat in the chair across from her with his legs crossed and his hands placed neatly on his lap. Savane had not heard him admitted, nor had she heard him come in. The man was truly a ghost.

"Well, you've made a right mess of things haven't you Lady?" He held what appeared to be a needle or pick in his hands that balanced on an end against the wood table.

"It was an innocent kiss on the forehead, intended to bring comfort."

He raised his hand to silence her, "There is no such thing as an innocent kiss." His green eyes almost glowed in the moonlight.

"It just so happens I have absolutely no desire to marry you Savane, so I am willing to get you and your knight out of this situation."

Savane sat forward in her chair suddenly feeling something other than loathing for this man. His smile in that moment seemed to radiate knowing.

"Well my childish little girl, pack your things hastily, no large dresses, and feel free to bring whatever jewels you possess as we won't be going to my home either."

Savane's eyes widened in shock as she moved quickly to gather her things and her mother's book. He offered no explanation just took her small bag and made for the door. "Step silent now." They stepped into the halls where a guard had been posted earlier but had no sign of one now, she looked both ways down the halls and followed in step behind her mysterious prince. He turned down the corridor to meet with his sister and passed off Savane's bag before grabbing her roughly at the elbow and leading her toward the prison below. She was about to protest when he turned on her and snarled, placing a finger to her lips. "I have freed you and now if we are discovered, it is I who will pay for it, so silence yourself and move swiftly."

They got to the prisons and as before they were locked but unguarded. He spent only a moment in the dark at the lock before it clicked open and the two raced down the stairs.

Savane stopped at the cell that housed Dayin as Theries calmly removed the keys from the wall and turned to the cells. Dayin sat up and stared, blind in the darkness, "Lady Savane?"

"Please come with me Sir Drake, I will explain on the way."

"I can't, I have dishonored your father I can't run"

"Oh, by the Dark Mistress," Theries cursed and raised a knife to Savane's throat. "Well Sir Knight, you can do me the courtesy of caring for your Lady or you can leave it to me, either way, we're off." Savane's eyes widen in shock and Dayin raced to the bars. Satisfied that he would do as he was told; the Prince released his hold on Savane and turned to leave. The knight advanced on Theries, only to have that weapon turned on him with such speed that Dayin was pressed against the wall to prevent his throat from being nicked. "Knights and soldiers are good at obeying commands, when one isn't, they are rendered useless and put to the front lines to die. Since we are not in a combat Sir Drake, I would hate to have to put you down. But as I detest prison and I am currently breaking some laws; I am certain the Duke would place me in one for your half-witted duchess. I think you can see my dilemma. You will come with me silently and protect her or I will kill you both and pretend this night never happened."

His eyes never wavered in the dark, there was no sign that he was uncertain or nervous. He held the weapon pressed against the knight's throat until he felt the shift in his body, like a dog succumbing to a masters will. He released him and once again made for the door.

Savane and Dayin followed obediently, through halls and into the courtyard. Savane was certain her father's guard were more vigilant then this and when she spotted the Prince's sister, she began to question the safety of the sleeping estate.

As if he read her mind the prince pulled himself up onto his horse and motioned for her to do the same, Dayin hoisted her up as Theries looked at them both.

"A night of celebration however briefly cut short is the best opportunity for revolt Lady. Soldiers, loyal as they are, can be bought with coin or spirits, either way the gate is open, and freedom lay beyond it."

"The riders stole into the dark and were long gone before the Duke would awaken to deal with the night before. His prison empty, his daughter gone, along with the majority of his guard incredibly hungover due to the Princes generous donation of spirits left over from the festivities."

The Empress made a small sound, startling me out of the story she was telling, turning my gaze to her until she shifted. The light had long faded in the gardens and servants had come and gone, lighting torches and braziers to keep the dark and cold at bay. His statue before her seemed to almost breathe with the life she had infused into him. The determined set in his jaw and the warmth in his eyes that was tempered by a sadness.

"He was my first true love and this statue does not do him justice. Forgive me I have spoken for so long; I did not notice the castle go to sleep." Her smile was filled with melancholy as she stood and reached for my arm. Which I offered gladly before we began walking toward the castle.

The archways were decorated with winter vines strong enough to withstand the coastal winters and would even bloom on occasion. As we stepped inside the castle the warmth surrounded us and we smiled at each other, having had no real recollection of when we had become so cold. She walked down a hall and stopped at a door, "I would like you to stay Sir Edrick, as I am enjoying our conversations. the story is only beginning, and I would like you to know it all, but I need my sleep as you can imagine."

"Let me escort you to your room Empress,"

"That won't be necessary, my son is home." There was not even a breath that passed before a middle-aged knight strode down the hall. His hair short and well-groomed, his armor well used but well cared for. The Emperor was still a very commanding figure and I forgot myself as he advanced to greet his mother.

It had been years since he had been home and to see him now, he bore very little resemblance to her. Where her hair was raven in her youth, his was brown. His strong robust figure contradicted her slight frame. Their eyes, however, were the mirror of each other, that beautiful enigmatic purple I had been lost in as she had woven her story earlier.

"Forgive me, my son, this is Sir Edrick Rolen," she released her son to bring me to his attention "He is writing my memoirs" she added, before her attention was drawn to the woman who was advancing down the hall.

"Sir Edrick, I hope you have a great deal of ink." The Emperor smiled. The woman the Empress greeted was a strong looking woman with a great sense of purpose about her. She had blonde hair and warm eyes that in some way were familiar to me though I had never met the Emperor's wife. She, like he, was dressed head to toe in armor and looked so completely at ease in it, though I was certain she would be as beautiful in the burlap bag the empress had jested about when the Prince and she had met.

She left me then to join her son and daughter in law down the hall. I felt as though I would never sleep, as I sat at the grand desk in the room, she had provided for me. Morning seemed so long away, and I was desperate to know more. I settled for writing what she had shared this day, sleep would come later.

Dawn was marked by a beautiful sunrise that streamed through my window and roused me. The sounds of sea birds searching for their morning catch and the bustle of the city below all rose up and filled me with a sense of what it was to live here.

My bones ached from the chair I had fallen asleep in, the wax of my candles had long extinguished the flames I had been using to write long into the night.

My belongings were piled neatly on the bed and plate of foods I had never seen the likes of before, were waiting on the personal dining table in the room. A small note with the finest script was folded neatly on the table at the head of the plate, it read simply, "Shall we continue?" Signed S.

I ate the food quickly and attempted to make my way back to the gardens, several times becoming turned about by the many halls and corridors that encircled the Empires largest and longest standing castle. It wasn't until a servant noted my frustration and with the most polite manner, led me to where the empress waited for me in the gardens.

This time she was dressed in furs and had a blanket on the stone bench, a brazier was lit beside her and two of her grandchildren were with her. They were perhaps the age she had been when all of this had begun. The girl was perhaps fifteen and the boy a year or so her elder. They were a match to each other and the image of their mother. When they saw me, they each in turn kissed their grandmother on her cheek and returned my respects as they passed, having never spoken a word.

"You could not have slept well with your face in your writing all night" she teased.

"It is an unfortunate reality that a writer will write when inspired. It sometimes leaves us unable to sleep until the body makes demands that the mind can no longer stave off."

She smiled at me with the look of one who knew of what I was speaking of. Her eyes fell on the next monument in the garden. It was one of the few that at first glance I did not recognize and as I stared at her, reviewing the people in my mind I still could not place this woman.

Her features were strong, and she bore the look of a northerner. Her hair was long and wild, her eyes focused like a hunter. Her body was covered by stone furs that fitted her from head to toe, in her hands was a flail frozen in mid swing. She looked fierce and determined and her anonymity was driving me to irritation.

"Who is she?" I asked confessing my ignorance.

"Well" the empress said as she motioned for me to sit, "In order for you to understand what happened to me, you must know what happened to all of us. This is Danica."

Her name rang true in my mind as I found her in the songs that had been sung of the heroes. Hers was not so bright a story as Sir Dayin's, and I found myself suddenly very excited to learn the truth about her.

The empress seemed to stare for a moment as though trying to find a place to begin and finally started by saying,

"Danica was the greatest unknown for all of us, she had endured more loss in silence then any of us and when we found her, she had an entire culture to war against before she could ever truthfully belong."

Chapter Eight

Danica was born in the North Lands to a tribal Chief. It was a land of chaos where the strength of the sword and the ability to manipulate were the only two factors which governed right from wrong. The frozen wastelands that had been the home of the banished Legions were endless and harsh, and it bore harsh, strong people.

Peiashchic, the newly imbued god of War, was a dark soulless man who in his human life sought power and was merciless in battle. His followers were granted strength and stamina in battle. His female counterpart and his lover in life, was the manipulative witch of the north, who used her guile to gain position and power. Valiechic was beautiful and deadly to behold, very few could resist her will.

Danica's mother was a high priestess of Valiechic, who assumed her position through her commitment to her goddess. She gained favour in the tribe and was offered to the chief as a prize when her husband was killed in battle against him. As a show of loyalty, she killed the dead chiefs' children to rid herself of his hold. She bore Danica after having two sons to the new chief and one daughter that followed her.

They were a hard, merciless people, who never knew if they would live beyond one winter into the next. The ground never thawed, and the wars never ended. But war was war and there was no mercy for cowards.

Danica was a furrier trained from a very young age by an elder in the tribe. She and her sister both were expected to skin and tan the hunters catch and had little time for anything else. Her brothers were both training to be hunters and warriors. Mishka, the older of the two was a good-hearted jester while Urrie had no time for his brother's games. Where Mishka would be the one to talk to Danica with tenderness, Urrie would be the one that would beat the boys who tried to get too close to her. In their own way they both were affectionate to her.

It was when she was ten years of age that the rules that governed them began to pull them apart. As the young men were allowed to train and fight, Danica was forced to let her brothers come to her rescue. It was a source of constant aggravation. Her mother was one of the most powerful women she had ever known, but the rest of the women in the tribe were faceless child bearers.

Danica wanted more.

Karra, another girl in the tribe felt the same horrible need to be more. Danica and Karra became fast friends that would dream of battle. Karra's father was a weapons smith, his son's and he were well respected.

The two girls would slip away in the dead of night to train. They had drawn a circle with the blood from deep cuts upon their hands, praying to Peiashchic, the god men prayed to, to bring them the strength they deserved. They were certain that their prayers would be heard for theirs were the only voices crying out in battle born of women.

Years of training would strengthen their bodies and they were always careful to obey as daughters ought to, in an effort to avoid suspicion. It changed them both. Making them more determined to be hunters. Danica knew that for her to defy her father and chief she would have to be very formidable to ever be accepted. She had the blind hope that she could change laws which had been obeyed since the battle on the bone fields half a millennium before.

It was the night of the full moon when Danica was in her thirteenth year that her brothers were due for their rites. When a boy came of age, he could challenge another, the victor would be set to a challenge by the chief. Mishka and Urrie were less than a year apart and were able to compete together. They had both defeated their challengers and as the children of the chief, their tasks would be more arduous, and the rewards would be less.

Urrie sat on Danica's bed furs as Danica painted his face. His eyes followed her as she focused on his eyes making him appear fierce. "What have you been doing to your hands?" Her eyes went from the paint to his, "I am a furrier Urrie, they get cut,"

"You are a furrier not a liar. Tell me true sister or I'll throw you at father's feet and call you one."

"I cut it to pray to Peiashchic."

"Do you pray for me?"

"You have your own blood," she smiled "pray yourself." He smiled and it cracked the fresh paint along his cheeks making him look older than he was.

"What will you hunt?" her eyes fell to the flail that he kept at his hip, it was a spiked ball that was bound at the handle by leather strapping. "I haven't been told"

"Will you go with Mishka?" Urrie made a sound in his throat that parents used to reprimand children, "Mishka has his own fight, you know better."

"Your paint is done," he went to touch it and she slapped his hand away., He returned the strike and the two exchanged blows in good humor until he struck her ribs where Karra had injured her the night before. Her intake of breath drew out the protective nature in her brother, he forced her to the ground and raised her furs to expose the massive purple welt along her ribs.

"Who did this?" Enraged, Urrie got to his feet, dragging Danica up with him, "tell me."

Danica tried to hush him, but it served only to push his anger to the point where it drew Mishka's attention. Danica left the longhouse and stormed away to try and regain control of her brother.

"Danny, tell me, let me take care of this." She stopped in the snow and turned on her brother. "You cannot take care of this Urrie, it is mine."

Confused he eyed her from beneath the blue mask she had painted on him, she could see his emotions at war within him.

"Tell me." This time barely a whisper, she closed her eyes against his plea, "I cannot." He hissed his disapproval at her, the sound ripping her apart inside. Of all things she needed, Urrie's approval was one of the most desired.

"You will be distracted from your task Urrie and I cannot have that. I want you to be the greatest victor today and make father proud to call you his son."

"This injury," he motioned toward her ribs, "Please tell me that it was not more than this."

She breathed out, suddenly aware of what Urrie suspected the injury was and smiled at him. Holding his face cradled in her hands she pressed his forehead to hers and whispered, "I told you I have been praying to Peiashchic brother, there is nothing more."

Satisfied he took a handful of snow and washed the paint from her skin.

"No battle paint for you little sister." Danica's jaw clenched tight as he washed the remnants of the paint away, mocking her, that she may never wear it. He turned and made his way to where Mishka waited in the doorway to the longhouse.

The two ducked under and disappeared. Danica stood in the wind; her face raw from the snow he had used to wash it. The pain of having never told him carved a hollow in her. She wanted to, but she had bled over the pact that she and Karra had made that neither would speak of it.

She looked around to see her friend on the other side of the camp watching her, her eyes soft and empathetic to her plight. She mouthed the words "are you alright?" to which Danica nodded curtly and closed her fists.

That evening the tribe was in a frenzy over the challenges. Each boy would leave and in turn a man would return before dawn. Mishka and Urrie left one after the other, the other four boys on their heels. It would be hours before they would return, so Danica and Karra did what they did every night. They trained. "Your brother thinks you were violated."

Danica smiled, "you should take better care not to violate me." They laughed from within the circle they had drawn this night. They could hear the festivities from the longhouse and knew that most of the tribe's warriors were drinking, celebrating, sending prayers to Peiash-chic for a good hunt.

They trained for hours until the first horn blew

signifying the return of the first of them. Danica raced out of the circle and toward the long house and watched as one of the new men returned. His catch in hand, he held it high before her father and declared himself. A wolf had been his challenge and its fur was red with blood. Danica looked at it, knowing that there was little left for her to make any kind of trophy were he to ask for one.

The next to return was Mishka with his stag, the great beast had run for hours, its fur was slick with sweat that frosted on it in death.

Each in their turn made their way back and each held their victory for all to see. All but Urrie. Danica sat at the foot of her father's chair; her furs pulled tightly about her as she waited. The tribe had drunk more in that night then they could make in a week, but the spirits were high as they made games as they waited for Urrie.

It was just before dawn when Danica felt him shake her awake, his painted face hung over hers as he smiled down. "You slept through it, little wolf" he chided. She hit him with a sleepy blow that forced the air out of him, made him lose balance and sit on the ground before her.

"Is it a victory if no one is awake to account for it?" He asked as he scanned the longhouse and all the sleeping members of the tribe.

She smiled a devious grin and moved toward the horn in the hands of a tribesman. She pulled it from his hands and let loose with a mighty blast that brought them all to a confused panicked wakefulness. "Great chief" she said, "your last brave has returned."

Her father eyed her, gaining focus as the tribe waited for him to react to his daughter's display. Then a great cheer rose up among them as Urrie was welcomed as a huntsman in the tribe.

The wolf that Urrie carried was twice the size of the other hunters. There was no denying that Urrie had taken his time, the animal had no damage to the fur at all. It had been killed by Urrie's hands; he had managed to break the beast's neck.

Danica worked tirelessly in an effort to use every part of that fur for Urrie, she made everything for him. Including a helm out of the skull with its face frozen in a snarl. When she presented it to him, Urrie smiled and pulled her to him, confessing that she would make a good wife for someone lucky enough to best him in combat for the right to her. To any other it would have been a compliment but once again she felt the anger boil up inside, thinking that it should be her that would be bested if it was she that would ever be taken.

The weeks grew mild and the days longer which only served to steal training time from the two girls who had to train in secrecy. They had to travel further out to prevent the sounds of their battle from making it to the tribe.

It was late in the thaw when the snow was thin that they had trained all night and were near exhaustion, eating at the edge of their circle that they saw it.

The great bear was Peiashchic's totem and all the tribes of the North respected the beast. It brought great honor to defeat one. This night it stood on the other side of the circle from the girls as they ate their dried. They had barely heard it approach and now it stood a stone's throw from them.

They were frozen facing the beast, fear knotted their stomachs and numbed their limbs. A band of hunters with spears would serve well against this monster but not two slight girls with nothing more than discarded weapons and courage.

The bear raised its nose in the air, sending clouds of frozen breath upward as he snorted. Danica stared at it for long moments, defying all knowledge that she should keep her eyes averted. There was a deep intelligence gazing back that captivated her, his eyes stayed focused on her until it rushed forward so suddenly and stood upright before them. Danica sucked air through her nose in a desperate attempt to remain still while Karra outright fell to the ground from surprise. The heat from its body washed over them as he stood tall before them, snorting and salivating.

Then in a moment he dropped to his four legs and sauntered out of the circle and into the dark. The girls collapsed to the ground and drew long breaths and as they lay still.

"Did you see the way he stared at you?' Karra marvelled, "Did you see Danny?"

"I nearly wet myself, how could I not? We should go." It was a moment she was certain would stay with her forever. That beast, so deadly, so close, and yet somehow it chose to let her live. Danica spared a glance over her shoulder to see him still in the darkness, his hulking figure looming over an outcropping of ice and snow.

Karra looked back and motioned for her to hurry. The two returned to camp without speaking of it and crept back into their bed furs. Adrenaline pumping through her, Danica stared at the smoke rising out of the hole in the roof of the longhouse. The bear's eyes burned in her mind and made their way into her dreams as she drifted into exhausted sleep.

The rest of the house was silent, when Danica finally awoke, they had all taken to their tasks and she was certain she would get a thrashing for sleeping so late. She got up and put her furs over her already tender body before shoving her feet into her boots and running for the furriers. She passed Karra who was already helping her father in the smith, widening her eyes at her as she raced passed. By the sun in the sky she knew she had slept well into the latest part of morning and didn't attempt to make excuses when she ducked under the flap of the furrier's tent.

The haggard old woman stared at her, perhaps shocked that she arrived at all, and reached for a new kill that lay on the ground beside her sister. "Keia, you are done for the day."

The old woman said, "your sister will finish your tasks, and her own."

Danica took a deep breath and started to work. She would not finish until long after the day was done.

When Danica finally returned to her longhouse

Karra was waiting for her, sitting with Mishka and Eiessa, a young woman that Danica was assuming would soon be his wife. He was permitted now to take a woman. She was a plain looking girl with dirt coloured hair, but she smiled when he spoke to her and that seemed to be important to him.

Danica made her way to her bedroll without a word to anyone and sat upon it with great relief. She pulled a bowl of cold stew from beside it and set to eating for the first time since she saw the bear.

Karra's brow raised in surprise and amusement. "Was the crone hard on you today?" She teased.

"Shut up." Danica snapped back.

"Am I to assume we are staying in tonight?" Karra played with a fur mitt that Danica had been working on.

"We can't go back there, Karra." She pulled the mitt from Karra's hands and stared at her friend.

"That bear, he lives there in those rocks, he warned us this morning and we would be foolish to go back"

"What bear?"

Urrie was suddenly there, rolled onto the bed-roll propping his head on his elbows.

Karra growled loud enough that he raised his eyebrows and made that sound that Danica hated to hear. That condescending chiding. She smiled as it seemed to irritate Karra just the same. "Karra and I found a bear in the woods."

"What were you doing in the woods little sister?" The tone in Urrie's voice made Karra jump to her feet and abandon Danica to the conversation.

She smiled as she waved to them both before slipping out of the house. Danica turned to Urrie and told him about the bear in the woods but stopped before she got to the why.

"I don't want to be helpless my whole life Urrie, Karra and I were fighting in the woods." His eyes widened at her confession.

"Are you out of your mind you silly little girl, any man in this tribe would take you and you want to ruin that? No one will support this Danny. Father will strap you to a post and flay the skin off your back, then throw you to the meanest man he can find to husband you and teach you a lesson." Danica sat sullen and silent,

"I didn't ask you to agree, I just wouldn't lie to you about how I found the bear."

His eyes softened, "Danny you need to stop this madness, tell me you will stop."

"No Urrie, I will not."

"Show me the bear." He sighed. She stood weary from her training and her day with the furrier, put her furs back on and started for the door. She walked beside Urrie, having little need to look up as she knew the path in the dark.

When they came to the circle, the snow crushed and icy by weeks of combat, the odd splash of red in an otherwise ocean of white, Danica looked at him. "Do you see the outcropping there? It lies within it."

"Danny, you must stop this,"

"You stop Urrie. If you had failed at your hunt you would have been less than a man and you would have had to take up what? Furs, smith work, you would have had to work with us women. You would have been miserable, so do not bid me to suffer in silence what you could not endure at all." She turned and trudged away in the snow. Urrie watched her go, suddenly aware that even her walk was not that of the girl she had been but that of one of the tribe's warriors. Her shoulders had broadened, and her gait had a certain confidence that came from battle.

Chapter Nine

Danica was sleeping when the horn blew. The blast had half woke her, but the tribe rising and making cries of battle was what had truly brought her to her senses.

She got to her feet and dressed as quickly as she could before running from the longhouse with her sister on her heels. The tribe had gathered at the center fire pits, she could make out the figures of several people forced to their knees at the feet of her father. The tribe's huntsman were surrounding them hooting and calling for blood.

The eight or so prisoners would be traded as slaves for furs or livestock to the other Northern tribes, they would live bleak dreary lives, and to be ignored would be a blessing.

Danica watched as her people reveled in their capture, her brothers among them. Mishka with his weapon held high and Urrie leaning against a stump with his arms folded over his chest. It was when Danica drew closer that she saw the faces of the men on the ground. They were not of the northern tribes. They were southern born, with their light hair and red wind burnt faces. Their blue terrified eyes. What could have driven them into the North? Danica's eyes settled on a woman in the center of their circle. They had tried to conceal her with furs and hoods, but her hair had spilled free in the combat and now she struggled to remain unnoticed. One of the tribesmen caught sight of her and strode over pulling her from the rest. The men all rose to defend her but were beaten down in seconds.

Danica's father stepped forward and all fell silent. The tribe waited for direction as the men who had rose to defend the woman shivered in pain and cold. The woman at the feet of the tribesmen sat silent in the snow, her eyes cast off to some distant place free of whatever fate was about to befall her.

"Kill the leader, trade the rest," he looked to his wife who stood at his side. "Priestess, do you claim the woman?"

Danica watched as the woman's only hope at salvation passed before her in the form of her mother's slave. She would be abused; she would be harassed but she would live.

Her mother stood and walked over to the woman, standing over her. The dark strong features of the Northerners embodied in her mother, contrasting the softness of the southern people in her prisoner. This southern woman did not break at the priestess gaze, though her eyes were glassy from fear she sat silent. Her eyes trained on the woman who held her fate in her hands.

They say that a wild thing should never be stared down, Danica thought, that it provokes attack. Her mother was no different, she backhanded the woman, sending her flying across the snow. Blood was dripping from her torn lip, still fearful but having learned, her eyes stayed locked on the snow at the priestess' feet.

The old woman moved quickly and took the girl by the arm and dragged her away to the longhouse, provoking angry cries from the remaining seven. Once again, they tried to rise up against their captors, it was in that moment that Danica's brother carried out her father's first order and killed the leader. The violence that followed made Danica look toward her mother but caught a glimpse of Urrie watching her with blood on his weapon. A look that said, you see, you can't be what I am. Danica snarled at him in response before turning and following her mother and sister to the house.

The fire inside was warm and already seemed to have defrosted the woman who sat shaking and terrified, like a rabbit in a snare, wounded and waiting for death. Keia set about heating water while her mother was preparing something else. When Danica noticed what she was doing she knelt down beside the woman and stared in her eyes. The blue there was like the sky and Danica had never seen it in the eyes of a person before.

She looked up at her mother to ensure she was not watching and looked back at the woman. She took a knife from the sheath at her boot and motioned it over the furs of her ankle lightly to show her what was coming. The woman's eyes widened in fear as she suddenly understood what Danica was trying to tell her. Danica lifted her hand to the woman's face and ran her hand over her tears, shaking her head.

"Don't cry out" she said knowing the woman would not understand her words. She took a branch from the firewood and then turned to help her mother prepare. It took them a short time before they were ready, it was customary to nick the slaves as a warning and cut them if they ran.

The Priestess turned to Danica and motioned for her to hold the girl down. She gave the girl the stick to put between her teeth when her mother wasn't watching and staring down at her with a final warning. The girl panted in fear as the knife was heated in the fire, her eyes widening as the woman raised it and exposed the skin at her ankle. Danica stared at her and shook her head in one quick movement before it was dragged hot and searing across the thin skin of the ankle. Not deep enough to be anything more than painful, she would heal. Danica had known it was a test to gauge the strength of the woman to bare pain, she had whimpered but did not scream. Danica pulled the stick from between her teeth, concealing it under the furs as her mother dressed the wound. She stood and nodded to Danica.

"Dress her in something more appropriate and make sure she understands the rules. Since you feel a need to protect her little wolf, if she runs Danica, I will punish you."

Danica watched her mother set back to work then turned on her new charge. The woman, perhaps only a few years older than Danica, lay horrified on the furs. Danica got up and took her to the back of the long house and sat her down, binding her good leg to the post intended for that purpose. It would take some work, explaining the rules to her. With her mother's words, she sensed the girl had best learn fast or Danica herself would be the one to kill her.

The days were long for Danica teaching her slave

how to understand the rules, working in the furrier and still training at night with Karra. She lived in a sort of haze between sleep and awake. Her slave learned quickly and never took the kindness Danica had shown her for granted, in turn she was afforded a certain amount of protection.

Danica learned the slaves name was Majolyn as well as many words in the southern tongue. She listened whenever the girl was alone with her as she spoke of her home. She had been part of a farming village in the Barrens, so named because it was the border lands between the North and South. It still experienced the change of seasons but was vast, in an effort to deter raiding parties from the Northern tribes encroaching on Southern land, most villages were walled in and safe. The winter had been brutal and drove the Northerners south. They slaughtered her village and took everything, food and livestock both. The tried to flee but windstorms had turned her party about, and they had become lost.

"What do the people in the south value?" Danica said in slow broken southern as she stopped and sat on a fallen tree. Majolyn looked at the tree and glanced down the path in search of others before sitting next to Danica.

"I think they value the same things as your

people do, they value family, land, and the right to it. They fight wars over land and bloodlines." She sighed and looked at the gray sky above them.

"What do you mean by bloodlines?" Danica pulled her arm from her sleeve and stared at the veins under her skin provoking a smile from Majolyn. She placed a hand on Danica's arm, "Not those lines Danica, the family lines that date back to the bone fields where the gods died and gave mortals their essence."

"Your people believe in this story as well?"

"It isn't a story Danica, it is truth. Some people have small gifts and only possess a flicker of the old god's power while others control great mastery of it. Some can wield the essence in words to turn things to their advantage, while others can see and feel things from generations past, yet others can heal." She dragged her forearm against the tree they sat on and turned the angry red flesh for Danica to see. She closed her eyes and moments later the red was gone and the skin soft and white once again.

"It was why I was so carefully protected the night your tribe took me; I was their healer. I can only heal small wounds, but it has been helpful combined with my medicines."

127

Tina K Koutras

Danica's eyes were wide with disbelief, "it is magic?"

"No, it is bloodlines, and it can be stolen." Majolyn took a deep breath and pushed her hair out of her face. "If I am killed by someone who possesses a stronger bloodline than my own than mine will pass to them." Danica eyed her a moment, "and if it is a weaker line that kills you? Or none at all?"

"Then I just die and my line disappears." The words hung in the air as Danica absorbed them in thought. Majolyn watched her a moment before looking again to the sky.

"What are you thinking of?" Danica asked her quietly lifting her head to see what Majolyn was watching. "I was praying."

"For what?"

"That no one tries to establish if my line is stronger or weaker than theirs."

Danica smiled and patted her back, "Your secret is safe with me, and no one else here knows how to talk to you anyway." A small smile softened the edges of Majolyn's lips. "We need to get back."

Majolyn fell into step behind Danica and walked the remainder of the way in silence. Danica glanced to the skies a final time and then to the trail ahead of them. The sun was setting and the village was still a distance off.

Majolyn had struggled with the distances they walked daily once but now she moved over the snow and ice like one of the tribe. In her year with them she had endured beatings by the priestess and learned the values of the tribe, what she had to do to survive. The beatings had all but stopped and she was no longer chained to the post at night. She came and went among the tribe.

When they returned to the camp there was a number of hunters and tribesman gathered around the priestess tent. There was shouting and someone was screaming. Danica broke into a run, leaving Majolyn to carry the water back, a sick feeling was knotting in her stomach as she recognized the screams of pain. She forced her way through the crowd at the flap of the tent and ducked under to see her mother working over Urrie, his body arced in spasms of pain, involuntary convulsions raced through him as she tried to reset broken bones. Danica collapsed beside her brother as her mother worked to heal him, she gripped his hands in an effort to steady him and scanned the tent floor wildly for wood to brace between his teeth. Majolyn entered the tent and crouched down beside her and offered her one, wide eyed by the sight of Urrie's legs. Danica spared her a glance as she desperately tried to think of a way to save him. His eyes focused on Danica's as she knelt back over him propping the stick between his teeth. She smoothed his hair and kept her eyes dry and intent on his. She left her emotions far in her stomach so he could draw on her strength as she held him down. "It was the bear Danny..." he panted "I thought I could kill the bear." he gasped through the stick between his teeth.

Danica's eyes widened, "We'll kill the bear Urrie," his eyes rolled back and his body went limp. Danica stared at her mother who continued to work quickly to support the bones of his legs. They squished into place as she tied strong planks of wood as supports, before working on Urrie's ribs.

Once her brother fell unconscious, Danica sat back on her heels. she watched her mother work through glassy eyes that blurred her vision. Her mother spared her a moment's glance and then banished her from the tent.

Danica rose without protest, leaving the tent and her dying brother behind. When she came back into the waning light of the day, she looked at the tribesman gathered there.

"The bear still lives?" she growled, and it set them almost instantly into plans for a hunt.

It was hours before the priestess came from the tent, her face an emotionless mask as she washed the blood from her hands. Danica watched her from a wood stump she and Majolyn had been sitting on with Karra, the three didn't move until Danica's mother motioned her toward the tent.

"He will likely die," she said off handed and cold, then left.

Danica growled inwardly and ducked under the flap with Majolyn following close behind. Urrie was still asleep when she entered. "Can you help him?"

"I can stop him from dyeing, but I am not sure that it would help him Danica. You heard the sounds his bones made when your mother tried to set them, he'll mend but he will mend wrong."

"Please Majolyn, I can't lose him, not like this."

Majolyn knelt beside Urrie and put her hands on his chest under the furs, his skin was slick with sweat and blood. A calm settled across Urrie's sleeping face, Majolyn looked to Danica with a nod, "It is done. I should try again tomorrow."

The hunting party returned the following morning with the bear being dragged behind their mounts. Danica and Majolyn set to work immediately on the fur. If Urrie was going into the afterlife this fur would be wrapped around him and if he was going to survive, he would be wearing this fur. She worked tirelessly to prepare it, long after the tribe was asleep and into the following morning until her eyes blurred with fatigue and she could lay out the salted skin. She fell asleep next to Urrie in the tent and when she woke, she watched him. His brow knit in pain, even in his sleep it dogged him. She tied her fingers into his and felt the strength as he closed his fist holding her fingers within.

When she raised her eyes, his were trained on her, the pain driven out by conscious effort. They said nothing between them but sat until fatigue washed over him and pulled him back under.

The circle had been ignored for days, when Karra and Danica returned, it was with the knowledge that things had changed for Danica. The anger inside would push her to an intensity they had never felt in the battles before.

She was more intense than ever, and it pushed them both to a new level. When they finally stopped, they realized what they had been lacking was finally filled. Urrie was near death and that sense of desperation would be fuel within Danica whenever she called upon it.

The days that followed drifted into weeks that brought heavy snow. The tribe hunted constantly to prepare for when the food would be sparse. The fur that had once warmed the bear that had spared Danica over a year before, now wrapped her brother as he slept.

Danica stayed with him in his waking hours though as each day passed, he became more irritable and viscous, trapped in a broken body. He healed and watched as his brother married and had their first child, celebrated great hurts that Urrie could no longer be part of.

Urrie would hobble around on a crutch made for him. Danica knew he would never choose to live in this world as he was and did whatever she could do to keep him with her. She taught him how to skin the furs, repair the damages caused by the hunter's weapons, but all these things were reminders of his fate and only made him insufferable for even Danica to bare.

She took the rage she felt into the circle each night and forced Karra to endure it. The two became stronger and faster, and soon their tribe would know what they were.

Karra finished dressing a small cut she got from Danica's blade when she looked to see Urrie watching her. His eyes dark with resentment.

"Go back to camp." He snarled. Danica looked up and eyed him a moment before she nodded to Karra to do as he had commanded her. Though he no longer had the strength to enforce any commands, Karra respectfully chose not to remind him. He saw it in her eyes though and lashed out at her. She nimbly dodged away from him, upsetting his tentative hold on balance, sending him sprawling awkward to the ground.

"Go." he shouted

Karra turned gracefully and walked away leaving him prone on the ground. Danica walked over and stood above her brother. Her eyes, no longer a visual indication of her feelings, were unreadable. She waited as he tried to right himself, but the fresh snow was soft, and he was deeper than he was strong. He stopped struggling and rolled to his back where Danica stared down at him. His eyes trapped in torment were glassy as his emotions came forward in a way only Danica would understand. She knelt down after she knew Karra was out of sight and placed his arms around her shoulders and heaved him out of the snow. He stood awkward before her as she knelt to retrieve his crutch.

They made their way over to the tree stumps that Karra and she often sat at and talked about their circle and their training.

He had watched them all evening. "You really are good Danny. You're fast and nimble, you adjust constantly so you're unpredictable." She looked at the ground at his feet as he sat a moment longer with silence between them. He sighed, "if you want this to work Danny you are going to have to make father favour you before he even knows who you are."

They devised a plan to hunt night and day to accumulate furs and food to give to him in an effort to appease him and let him see her worth.

The next day Danica and Karra set to work. They were able to easily hunt small animals with snares, but fox and deer were harder, they required patience and strength to return the carcasses to the camp. They accumulated several by the weeks end, each night they left them outside the longhouse.

The girls were both exhausted when they heard the horn blow. The tribe made their way to the center fires and gathered to listen to the Chief. At his feet were the pelts of the kills that Danica and Karra had made, skinned and separated.

He raised his hands for all to listen and a silence fell over the tribe. "These past few nights a hunter has gifted me with the furs of several kills, who among you claims these kills."

The silence that followed brought all the tribe looking at each other with curiosity. Danica and Karra watched each other and finally nodded and stepped forward, fear gripping their stomachs as the tribesmen noticed their claim.

"It was I father and Karra who lay the animals at the longhouse for you, it was we who made those kills, who tracked the deer and brought it back."

An outraged cry rose up among the men that Danica's father silenced with his hand. Urrie sat back from the congregation and nodded to his sister, puffing up his chest to remind her to look fearless. She stepped forward again and called out, "I seek the right to challenge." Karra too, repeated the words. The tribe stood silent. If no one answered the challenge, they would not be awarded the right, and all would be for nothing.

Urrie stood up and called from the back of the tribe "I accept Danica's challenge." Again, an uprising as shouts of anger washed over the tribe. Danica's father looked to Urrie his eyes alight with warning, "If no one takes Danica's challenge then Urrie will"

The implications hung in the air, even Urrie flinched at his father's unsaid words.

"I accept." One of the boys Danica's age made his way to the front of the tribe. Karra watched her friend choose a weapon and face off against the taller boy. The rest of the tribe cheering his name. Urrie made his way to his little sister and stood facing her before she entered the circle the tribesman had formed.

"Listen to me girl," he said, "Don't let him anger you, and don't let him become brave, make him think twice before he swings. If he's always doubting, he won't attack."

She felt an easy calm wrap around her as his hand clamped around her shoulder. "I need you to win this" he whispered. He cut his hand and painted her face with the blood. The way she had painted his on the night of his challenge. Then he pulled away leaving only the boy in the ring in front of her.

Danica drew even breaths, her heart in her chest pounding to break free, with the fall of her father's hand she lunged at the boy. He would have trained as often as she perhaps, each day and with far better teachers than just her and Karra, but he like everyone, she would face, did the one thing that Urrie had told her would be her advantage.

The boy forgot about the kills that had lay at the longhouse, he forgot about the training that she had done. He lay on the ground, sucking air, his chest heaving from pain and surprise. Danica had won because he had not believed she could. The circle of braves were silent. The boy humiliated on the ground, Danica's body shaking with adrenaline over her victory, blood spilled from her nose and one wound over her shoulder, a superficial nick that would heal in a few days.

Danica's father stood silent eyeing her and the rest of the tribe, while her mother stood at the entrance to their longhouse, her eyes dark and unwelcoming at her daughter's deception. Danica's chest heaved with breath as she tried to recompose herself. "Have I earned the right to a challenge?"

Her father nodded his head, but Danica could see

in his eyes that he had no intention of giving her a challenge that she would survive.

She looked to Karra who watched the dark look in her chief's eyes and called out. "I would have a challenger."

The circle still silent, watched the chief, who took one step forward and called for all to hear, "If these girls are to be hunters, that provide food for the tribe they must pass my challenge. Danica has defeated hers, who will stand against Karra before I give them their challenge?"

Urrie looked to his father and then to Danica and the realization of what Danica had already guessed washed over his face. He stared at his sister whose eyes closed as she drew an uneven breath.

Another boy rose to challenge Karra. He was younger than any before. He knew he would have another chance the following year if he was to fail, unlike the young man that Danica had driven into the snow.

The tribe had put their trust in the chief's ability to devise a challenge that would rid the tribe of two unsuitable girls rather than weaken the hunting party.

Karra stood against him in the new circle and waited for the hand to fall, she unlike Danica, waited for the boy to attack. Karra had been stronger in the circle than Danica, stronger in anticipating movements and predicting her opponent's weakness. She worked with her father near the training grounds and was able to watch the boys train all day. She had the added advantage of her choice of weaponry, to play with when no one was watching. It was the reason they had agreed that Danica would take up the challenge first, to prevent the tribe from offering a more dangerous opponent to the weaker of the two.

The boy that fought against Karra was impulsive and wild with the way he moved. When he attacked, Karra countered with an accuracy that had been her strength in the circle against Danica. Where Danica had been able to rely on strength, Karra was unable to end the fight quickly and had to trade several blows before she was able to put him down. She too, stood victorious, her weapon and face bloody, small insignificant wounds on her forearm and legs. She looked at the chief as Danica had. He watched a moment, his brow knit in the concentration of his next move, whether to break from tradition and let two girls join the hunters or to break them in their challenge.

Danica sat outside the longhouse, the wind had picked up and threatened to carry fresh snow. She watched as clouds rolled over the sky like the snow over open plains and then closed her eyes. She felt Urrie sit beside her, his clumsy awkward presence, and the warmth of another body next to her.

"When you first told me that you were praying to Peiashchic I thought you were praying for me. When you told me about the bear, I thought you were telling me so that I could gain honor by taking it's fur, but when I saw you in the circle with Karra, Danny, it made me hurt inside to know the struggle you had been facing all this time, we are so alike, you and I. You with the battle you face in a camp where women are not hunters and me a cripple."

She opened her eyes and stared at him. "You have wounds brother, but you know things that keep you from being a cripple, you just choose to ignore them. In the south and in the elf tribes there are bowmen who can kill from great distances. If you had a weapon like that, you would not be a cripple."

He watched her in silence, she knew he wanted to dismiss her, but something had changed in how he viewed his little sister and now her words held wisdom.

"You are so different from us Danny, you see things, believe in things that we are too stuck in our ways to ever understand. You will drag the North out of this curse we have lived since Peiashchic was banished and unite us all."

"The tribes war against each other too much to ever unite much less unite under a woman."

He sucked in a breath and rolled his head back against the longhouse staring up at the rolling clouds. "Tell me again how the bear spared you," he whispered. Danica stared at him, his words weighing in her mind, "What does it mean when a god spares a girl fighting in secrecy in a forest, forbidden by her chief and then breaks her stupid brother on the rocks but lets him live to have this conversation?"

"Urrie it was just a bear,"

"Then Danica, you are just a girl. The day you are ready to accept that you aren't more and abandon your will to fight and become one of the hunters, then, I will believe that it was just a bear."

The door to the longhouse opened and her mother stared at her under dark cruel eyes.

"It is time for you to learn of your challenge." she turned back inside, and Danica rose to follow.

"It will be hard Danny, it will be made to break you so that you never make it back or never want to fight again when you return. He will not want to have people challenge his leadership ever again so understand that whatever you do, if you survive and if you return, you will be dooming our father."

"If I survive, if I return and others feel a need to challenge father, then it is up to him to survive."

Urrie smiled as she ducked under the door. The heat inside the longhouse warmed her almost instantly, she could feel the eyes of the tribe's council burning into her adding to the heat she felt inside. Karra was first to receive her challenge and walked past her with dark eyes that Danica read to mean that Urrie had been right. They would have wished each other luck and a good hunt as was custom between the challengers but this was not a customary challenge and she could feel the men of the tribe scowling at her.

"Daughter step forward," Her eyes snapped toward her father, then she advanced and stood before her chief and father.

"You have dishonored the tribe with your actions, but I have seen fit to recognize your right to a challenge rather than string you up for crows and wolves. This day you have tested my leadership and challenged me. Your mother however feels that Peiashchic is guiding you. That war is in your soul for a reason." Danica eyed her mother who stood motionless beside him, her eyes a mask as always. She had support where she least expected to find it.

"Succeed in this task and I, and the tribe will honor your claim as a hunter and warrior of this tribe. Because you have dishonored your father and your chief, the test will be twofold.

"There is a gorge to the east, within lies plants that grow in the snow, they are needed for your mothers medicines, the gorge is an unfriendly drop and hard to navigate and it is more than a day away so you are permitted to return in three days. If the challenge is not met, then you and Karra will be executed. You both must succeed for you both to survive. Do you understand your challenge? "

Danica nodded, and turned from the war council and her mother. She left the tent nearly choking on her fear. Three days alone in the wild was more than every hunter had ever been given, she gathered up meats and furs, snare wire and her weapons before meeting Karra at her tent.

"I'm going east, three days to return."

Karra nodded, "I am bound north for two."

"Please come back," Karra whispered.

Danica stared at her then ducked back under the flap and left.

She stopped to say goodbye to Urrie and offered him a quick embrace before she turned and looked toward the east.

"I will wait for you." He said.

"Just do it where it is warm," he smiled and kissed her forehead.

When Danica set into motion, she could feel the heat in her legs, pulsing through her and igniting a fire that fear had tried to extinguish. Running was easy for her, covered in furs head to toe she had always run between snares as a child and still to the day it was how she dealt with frustration and uncertainty.

She fell into an easy rhythm and only stopped to eat and rest before she started again. With the clouds high in the sky obscuring her view of the stars she had to take her directions from points she set from the camp, The mountains at her back were the only way of knowing she was going the right way, but if a storm came she would be lost.

Dawn brought the snow that the night before had threatened, but it was only light drifting snow that shifted on the wind. The sun high in the sky was hazed in clouds but she was able to make out its general direction. It wasn't until she saw the wolf that Danica realized her task was going to be a challenge after all.

He was not a skinny wolf which to Danica meant he was part of a pack. His yellow eyes watched her from a distance as he stayed back from her slinking along the tree lines and dogging her the better part of the afternoon. When she came upon the gorge, Danica felt the relief of knowing the wolf would not follow, but she also knew there was a good chance the pack would be waiting when she came back.

Danica slid down the first drop into the gorge, but as she hit her first plateau, she realized getting down would be difficult but getting out would be near impossible. She walked along the thin plateau searching for a viable path into the gorge, she could see breaks in the shear drop but they were few and not spaced well enough for her to make a safe decent.

The wall was ice making her weapons useless as climbing tools, she had little more than two days to make it down and back up before her time would be up and her life forfeit.

Danica sat at the edge of the drop, with the distance masked in the whiteness of the snow and ice, depth was difficult to gauge, in the end it was not the descent she would have to solve, it was the climb, so she started from one plateau to the next, each time sliding as she landed. She was grateful for her think layer of furs that took sharpness out of the ice and left only a dull ache from muscle use and heavy impacts into unyielding terrain.

When she reached the bottom, she let her eyes float upward, she had only lost a few hours of daylight climbing down and from where she was, she could see no way of climbing back up.

Danica stopped for a time to eat and check to make sure she wasn't too badly wounded in her climb down and to steal a little rest. The sky over head was finally clear and with it brought the cold. The night would be the kind she loved to train in when the stars and moon would light up the snow and make her feel alive, but with fatigue setting in and the time dwindling away she was certain that she would not have the same appreciation for the stars and the moon.

The snow in the gorge was deep but was a mix of ice and powder that made her trek through it perilous. More than once she had to race as the ice platform, she thought herself safe on, threatened to dump her into the icy grave that waited below. The cold numbed her senses and made her mind wander to other things about Urrie and Mishka, his little boy and the shame he would feel when he thought of her if she never returned.

It was getting dark when she found the cave that her father spoke of. She stared at it in fatigue and desperation, with just over two days to find the plant and make it back up the gorge she had to make it home.

The entrance was a narrow climb but once inside, the cave opened to reveal icicles alight with the dying sunlight. The cave was made up of ice walls and high above a spiked ceiling. It was more beautiful than anything Danica had ever seen and yet looked so deadly. Every sound she made echoed and there was a ghostly moan emitted as the wind raced through the cave. She made her way inside a ducked under an over-hang of ice that once again opened to reveal the plants. There was a mix of berry bushes and flowers that sprouted up out of the snow in a way Danica had never seen before. As she drew closer a knot tangled in her stomach, she looked up to see a pair of glassy eyes staring at her from behind a mask of furs.

The darkened gray skin of Railynde's elves were only spoken of in legend, this one was young and alone. Her silent posture against the ice wall told Danica that there were no more within calling distance or she would have attacked for certain. They were not known for their diplomacy with the human tribes and were even more dangerous when they had Vetis' taint. Danica pulled her weapon only to have the elf look to the high ice spiked ceiling at the threat of the noise that came with a battle. Danica was suddenly aware that the girl had no intention of fighting here as she slipped backward along the ice and disappeared from sight.

So, this had been her mother's plan, to pit her against the legendary elves to be killed mercilessly. A hatred opened up inside her for the first time toward her mother's heartlessness. She growled inwardly as she gathered up the plants. The elf would not just let her leave, if she made her way back to her tribe before Danica was out of these caves, wolves would be the least of Danica's concerns.

She doubled back the way she had come and pulled herself through the narrow opening into the sunset that had turned the gorge into a brilliant red. She raced to the gorge wall and began a relentless struggle to the top.

Several attempts were in vain as she slid back down at times further then she had scaled upward. The moon opening up above her lit the gorge wall, the crisp air frosting her breath. She felt numb as fear stole her will to climb. The wolves she knew, the cold she knew, but these elves, these dark children of Vetis that had been exiled with her tribes hundreds of years ago, that worshipped different things and were in the war on the Bone Fields because of their hatred for humans. She knew very little of them.

Danica steadied herself against the wall drawing deep strong breaths then turned and once again started her climb.

There were moments that passed in the dark that Danica sat in the snow, drifting into near unconscious sleep until a yip of a wolf or some other stray sound would rattle her awake. By dawn however she pulled herself to the top and lay in the snow wheezing and breathless.

She tied the sacks with the plants against her

legs so they wouldn't move as she ran, took time to eat and then set a vigorous pace to get some time to spare. The day spanned out before her as vast as the snow-covered plains. She had only this one day to make it back. Karra would already be back if she had succeeded, waiting in the chief's tent for Danica to return. Danica would not know if Karra had made it until she got inside the tent and when she arrived it would be too late to run if she hadn't.

The wolves found Danica when the sun was sitting on the mountain top, they could smell her perspiration and fatigue. They knew better then she how exhausted she was and gave chase as a pack. Everything in Danica told her to run, everything but her legs which cried for rest. Her stomach was nauseated with exhaustion and her head ached from dehydration, but if these wolves wanted a meal, they were going to have to fight for it. The fire light from the village began poking up as the sun fell below the mountain and Danica's will to run rose up within her.

The first wolf that ran past her nipped at her furs at her ankles, sending a wash of memory over Danica of the slave with the blue eyes. How like wild animals they must have appeared to her that night that she was taken in.

They danced about Danica, nipping and trying

to weaken her before she drew her weapon to make a stand. Like the tribe the night the southerner came, the pack, would allow no time for her to mount a defense and snapped at her weapon hand, opening a gaping hole in her furs and tearing flesh with it.

Danica fell forward on the ground the pack yipping and singing to their achievement. She could see the weapon just out of reach as claws and teeth tried to tear through fur and flesh, the soft skin at her neck and the sinew of her thighs. The bite that tore into her leg drew a howl of pain from her as she lunged for the weapon and gripped it with slick hands, rolled on her back and thrust it through the first wolf. The wolves lurched backward as one of the pack fell.

Danica hobbled to her feet and turned to face the yellow eyes of the alpha. His face twisted and bloody, snarling his warning. Like Urrie's helm, a calm rose inside her as she thought of the night she left, how he needed her to survive. She met the wolf's eyes and snarled back at him, holding her weapon in weak trembling hands, she was uncertain what would happen if he met her challenge.

He didn't. He changed his posture and with it went the pack. Receding into the darkness of the forests to howl and mourn their dead. Danica stared at the lights of the village. It seemed so far away and the blood on her back was cold and sticky. Her legs had lost feeling and all she wanted was sleep.

She dragged one foot forward, her mind keeping with her promise she had made to Urrie and Karra. Step after agonizing step the lights drew closer. Until she numbly reached the chief's longhouse. The house she had been born in and lived all her life. Inside there was no celebrating, the men did not drink to the challengers, they did not revel in the new hunters. She opened the door and fell inside and then she slept.

When Danica woke, she was in the warmth of the longhouse on her stomach. Urrie sat with his back propped on furs as he worked at a piece of leather. His eyes caught Danica's and he lowered it to his lap.

"I was wondering if you were ever going to wake. Your fever broke a day ago and still you slept." he put his hand on her shoulder as she tried to pull herself up, but an explosion of pain ran through her, forcing her into stillness. "You still have great wounds on your back and legs, lie still so you don't open them."

"Karra?" he nodded, "She made it back after only a day, I think father believed you wouldn't return in time and was happy to tie her fate to yours."

Danica lay still and watched his eyes. "There were elves Urrie, I saw one."

"Only two days away?"

He nodded and motioned for her to rest, "that is for another day little wolf, you need to get well so you can claim your victory. Karra's life is still tied to yours."

Danica drifted back to sleep. Feeling the pain ebbing away.

Dreams of wolves chasing her were driven off by a great bear standing on its hind legs and embracing her before she was swallowed inside it and she and the bear became one.

It took days for Danica to be able to stand but as soon as she was able, she was brought before the war council and her chief. She could see the look in her father's eyes was not of relief that she had survived, instead there was a distant cold gaze.

"I have succeeded in my challenge."

"No Danica you have not, not yet, I told you when you left that your challenge was twofold, and you have yet to full-fill the second part of your challenge." Danica let her eyes fall to Karra who seemed to be holding her breath in anticipation of what they both believed to be the end.

"Then what is my second task?" Danica stood as tall as her sore and torn body would allow until the Majolyn was brought in. She was bound at the hands and staggered as they pushed her to Danica's feet. "Kill her." The chief commanded.

Danica felt the air rush out of her as his words fell on her. She had become her friend, she had saved Urrie and now he would snuff out her life. She had endured so much only to have her life cast aside with such indifference that it sickened Danica that this man before her, her father could command such a thing. She let her face reveal nothing of her emotions as a war raged inside her. The girl's blue eyes staring up at her glassy with tears of understanding.

"Danica," she spoke in her southern tongue that no one but Danica had taken the time to learn.

"I forgive you, take me from this life, but live yours and never forget." Danica let her eyes say what her voice could not. She drew her weapon and cut the ties that bound the girl, Danica ran her hand over her eyes to close them and pushed her sword through the soft flesh of her shoulder, into her lungs and into a still and quiet death.

Her eyes never leaving her father. Danica pulled the blade free as the blood pooled around her, a gasp from Karra forced Danica's gaze to shift, and the blood shimmered and ran like veins over the ground toward her. She shifted her stance uncertain of what was happening, the entire council stood from their furs and watched as the magic in her blood blackened and seared the ground before running over Danica's feet and finding the openings of the fabric. When it touched Danica's skin it was like a cold fire washing over her, painful and yet exhilarating, it was unlike anything she had ever felt before. Her pulse quickened and the room seemed to grow bright before her eyes. The girls' life seemed to pass through Danica's mind, with moments in the south and love of a man, then the darkness that her life had become. Danica picked up the body of Majolyn, holding her lifeless frame protectively in her arms despite the rush of pain that doing so incurred she looked to her father who stood breathless as he watched.

"I claim my right as a hunter of this tribe."

The war council had unanimously voted in favour of Danica's bid as a hunter. Though it had been many generations since the blood of Vetis had transferred into a member of the tribe. To have all the elders witness it at once ensured her place in the hunt and would likely one day win her a seat in the council.

Danica had taken the body of Majolyn with her. She would see her buried as the clans buried their dead. She would sing for her as was the tradition to welcome the brave into the after-life.

She was at the edge of the camp when Karra and Urrie found her, she had already wrapped the girl in cloth and was painting her face when they stood behind her.

"What happened to you?" Urrie asked. Danica spared a glance over her shoulder at Karra who had to have revealed everything to Urrie. Then she looked at Urrie before she turned her attention back to the paint on her friend's face.

"Why such tradition for a slave?"

"She was brave." She whispered "and that deserves to be honored, she could have cried and begged, she could have been bitter and twisted by the rage inside her but instead she was brave. Her last words to try and make me feel like what I was doing was for her, not to her." Urrie stared at her in silence, his jaw slack with disbelief.

"The southerners think we are mindless killers; today is the first time I have ever agreed with them."

Karra made a disgusted sound in her throat which turned Danica on her. "It was one or the other Karra, I buried her, or I would have been burying you. Her life bought you yours."

"She was a slave; she was already dead." Karra snapped and turned away.

Danica stared after her, feeling anger rush through her. She could see her with such clarity that even the rise and fall of Karra's chest was visible to her. She was more than just irritated, Karra was angry. Danica looked to Urrie and sighed.

"Is this what mother spoke of when she told us of the blood of Vetis on the Bone Fields, is that what happened to me Urrie? Is my blood tainted?"

"It's a gift Danica, if you have the blood of Vetis you will have gifts that go with it,"

"Gifts that will someday cost me my humanity, turn me into something? Right?"

"It is only those who lose control that become disfigured Danny. Look at you woman, you are burying a slave in traditional tribal ceremony, you have a long way to fall sister."

"A slave I killed to save my self...Not so far as you might think."

"This is a great victory for you Danica, mourn your slave if you must, but do not waste what she has given her life for, feeling sorry for her. She didn't"

Chapter Ten

With the passing of the trials the requirement to train in secrecy vanished, Karra and Danica drifted from their routine in the circle and instead hunted with the rest of the tribe's hunters. The bond that had held them together all of their lives had suffered with Karra's resentment of Majolyn. Both Danica and Karra had become the hunters and warriors they had dreamed of becoming.

There were a few who opposed but kept silent or faced the chief in combat.

Life had begun to take on a sense of peace for Danica, though no one would have her for a wife she enjoyed the children Mishka and his wife had. She lived in Urrie's company, both Danica and Urrie, were both crippled in their own way.

The tribe was preparing for a long hunt, Karra had told the chief that she had seen a herd of animals heading south and the tribe meant to take as many as they could. The warriors stayed behind while the hunters left to see if they could pick up the herds tracks.

The moon was high in the sky when they reached where Karra had said they were, but there were no tracks. It wasn't until they heard the horn blast cut through the night air that the hunters realized something was very wrong.

They raced back over the snow to find the tribe under attack, Danica's first thought was of the elves but her newly sharpened vision picked up Karra with men Danica didn't recognize. She was enraged and moved toward the long house calling for the men to "find her."

Her, could only mean Danica. She broke into a run and killed anyone that rose to block the way between she and Karra.

Mishka's tent was a blaze and the whole village was filling with smoke.

Karra came out of the long house cleaning her weapon still searching the grounds, when Danica heard someone approaching from behind and ducked just in time as a sharp pain ripped across her back. She turned and faced a strong, tall warrior whose face was tattooed, a stranger to Danica. She returned every blow he dealt but every time he hit her, she thought she would pass out from the pain. She could feel the blood slick in the grip of her weapon and blurring her vision. In a last attempt she fell to her knees and when he rose to deliver the death blow, she drove her sword up through his ribs. She fell forward in the snow as he fell back. She was unsure how long she had lay there but she blinked repeatedly when she felt something on her side and opened her eyes to see Urrie poking her ribs, "Up, get up,"

He was wounded and bleeding but still had his senses about him, "Come on Danica, all my will cannot help me carry you, get up,"

She pulled herself to her feet and steadied herself against her weapon in the snow. She had barely focused when he ripped her from where she stood dragging her to a heavy treeline and started to force her upward. "Climb damn you," He struggled against her weight and his own poor balance as she flopped listless against the tree.

"Listen to me Danica, you have to climb this tree, please." She could hear the pain in his voice, she could feel the years he had suffered as a cripple and his need for vindication.

"Please climb," he whispered desperately. She pulled one hand over the other pulling branches and limbs, until she found a place strong enough to hold her and free from sight. It wasn't until she was there that she realized she was alone. Urrie hurriedly brushing away her tracks and ensuring that they would find him far from her. Her eyesight, so keen now saw as Karra advanced toward him, "Where is your sister cripple?" Karra's face was painted for war, she had known this was coming. She had prepared, divided the tribe in search of the caribou and taken out the first half before the others could even make it back. Urrie stood on his knees before Karra, his weapon in hand he tried to force himself to his feet, but she beat him down with a heavy-handed blow to the head.

"I'm going to kill him Danny." She screamed to the air.

"Are you hiding little wolf, is that the kind of warrior you are?"

"She's dead," Urrie choked out. "Your tribesman killed her." he motioned to the one that Danica had killed, "before I got him." He spat blood at Karra. "You can't call her a coward Karra, she fought bravely, it was you who betrayed your tribe."

"Strength and manipulation Urrie, I was theirs long ago, they accepted me, as a woman. Years I trained to become what you were born into.

163

Years of blood and sweat, for what, to have the chief, your father say that if she failed my life meant nothing? He was the first to die, and like the rest of you he never believed that this simple little girl had it in her, didn't respect anything I have lived and fought for." She knelt down before him and dragged her tongue along his cheek, Danica bit back rage as she watched but Karra was surrounded by her tribe now and there was no way to stop what was coming. "If I can't have her blood Urrie, I'll take yours."

She drove her sword through Urrie's chest the weapon cutting through skin and bone effortlessly, Danica choked and held her own chest where the pain was strongest. Her eyes scanned over the camp; fires were burning everywhere. As Urrie hit the ground his blood rolled over Karra's feet and seeped into the snow. Karra stared at it, in rage,

"Why isn't it working." she let out a terrible scream of frustration and turned to scan the ground for Danica's body, "Find her" she screamed. The clan separated and began searching while Danica sat in the tree and stared at her brother.

It was late into the next day before the last of them left, Danica's sight picked up even the slightest movement and it was when the wolves came out that she climbed down and made her way to Urrie. She fell beside him and lay in the snow. Her mind filled with conversations and memories. His face was cold and bluing in death and his wolf helm had been bloodied and cast aside. She picked up his flail and tied it to her hip as tears froze on her cheeks, she willed him to stand, to help her walk away and forget everything, but will alone was never enough.

She closed his eyes with her hand and dragged herself to the fast river, she pulled one of their canoes down and lay inside feeling the water rush under her, she let go and drifted down stream.

Chapter Eleven

Danica was found by a half breed who had lived all his life in the Barrens. His father had been a northerner that had raped a poor southern woman. The half breed and his mother had been ostracized, she became something of a healer, they lived apart from either world until her death.

He was a cold sort of man who made his living trading furs and medicines, he had no real love for anyone. But when he found Danica, her body broken and near death, for him it was a challenge, to see if he could bring her back. He pulled her from the river and brought her to his small home, dressed her wounds. Marvelling that one with a back so scared by claws and wounds from weapons could live at all. He fed her and dragged her back from the brink of death. She spent days bewildered, silently staring into the fires that in her mind were still in the Northern lands, she talked to Urrie until her fever broke, then the reality of what had happened washed over her.

∞∞∞

"That is where we found her." I stared at the stone rendering of Danica feeling so lonely. The Empress watched me; a sad smile lingered on her face. "It got better for her," she said, feeling sympathetic to the emotions she had evoked in me.

She placed a hand on my shoulder, "We can continue tomorrow." she said as she stood and pulled her furs around her shoulders. I fought the urge to drag her back to sit beside me and continue, which must have been apparent on my face for she laughed. A musical sounding laugh that made me smile up at her. "Perhaps more over dinner," she conceded with a smile.

We got up and walked along the garden path, she, always holding my arm with the both of hers. She was such an elegant creature that her nearness brought a calm about me that words on a page could simply not capture. We left the gardens that were quickly becoming my favourite place to be and started for the dining hall.

"Empress could you please tell me how you could possibly remember so much of this, all their details. Her eyes took on a distant look and

I feared I spoke out of turn, but she smiled at me and asked simply. "Do you remember your family?" to which I responded, "yes of course,"

"They were all my family Sir Edrick and even the darkest of them I loved. We spent every moment in each others company, shared our greatest victories and our most painful sorrows." She looked up as I seated her at the table and waited a moment.

"Now our story can truly begin.

Theries and Balae's story will come in due time, as will Gwendolyn's." She waited as servants placed food on her plate to which she thanked them with a smile before turning to me to begin again.

After their escape from the Duke, Savane, Sir Drake, the Prince and his sister travelled North in an indirect manner to avoid detection. Savane dressed down in the most conservative dress she could manage while the Prince felt there was no need for him to be common as people would leave well enough alone with two moderately skilled swordsman in their company.

The Duke had never been one for having his lands patrolled heavily, the threats thus far in Abarris had been manageable by each town magistrate. The roads were safe for them to travel without fear of detection and the inns along the way more than accommodating when offered a sum of coin for silence and privacy.

Balae rode beside Savane and watched her riding. "You manage very well for nobility you know. Three days on the road and not a complaint," she turned her gaze to the Prince, "Brother I think you owe me coin."

"Were you betting against my resilience Prince Verentine?"

"Why not at all Lady Savane, it was your ability to keep silent I questioned." Savane gawked at him for a moment with complete disregard for rank or stature. Every time she tried to carry on a polite conversation he would belittle and treat her to scathing remarks. Dayin, riding behind them all had come to recognize the nature of the prince and closed his eyes as the Prince once again dropped Savane into silence.

"He isn't always this way. He can be very loyal and has his redeeming qualities." Savane stared at the Prince, his nonchalance that echoed in-difference to the way he abused her at every turn.

"I think by the time he shows his redeeming qualities we will all be aged and gray. How is it that you differ so much if you are siblings?"

Balae, who insisted, was not to be referred to as Princess Verentine, was every inch a warrior. Her brother had proper etiquette and manner she was boorish and conducted herself with less than lady like behaviour in the inn's. Scandal-izing herself in a fashion that both Dayin and Savane blushed at. Despite that very strong dis-similarity in their character, Savane had grown very fond of the Prince's sister. She looked at Sa-vane and smiled.

"Well, my mother was a very soft-spoken woman whose single desire in life was to have a daughter. When I came into her life, she was happy and while my brother was learning to become prince, I was being spoiled with fancy dresses and having my hair brushed and made to look like the princess my mother always wanted. I, like you, was very young when my mother took ill and died of a viscous fever that claimed her mind. In the end she barely knew me. She gave me this necklace before she died."

Savane watched her. "So, my father, who never had a moment or a kind word for me sent me off to be trained in military combat. To serve as my brothers' protector." She puffed up her chest in exaggerated pride and then deflated against her horse drawing laughter from Savane and an amused grin from Dayin.

"I know that you think he is cold and indifferent, he is one of the best men I have ever known, he always speaks the truth, and he is a loyal friend. I will always risk anything to save him."

Dayin looked up at her, his eyes focused on the Prince ahead, "Do you think he would do the same for you?"

"I think that it is not knightly to speak so of royalty Sir Drake," she grinned, "But since you have, I think that it is not his place to risk his life for me is it? Sister or not, he is the heir to the Eastern realm, and it is my duty to see that he becomes King, just as it is yours to protect your Lady."

Theries looked back over his shoulders his eyes cast toward the ground, "If the lot of you are finished debating the hierarchy of our little dysfunctional flock, there is an inn ahead on the road. It will be dark soon and we have a need to

171

establish some sort of plan, I have no intention of running from the Duke for the entirety of my life."

Savane looked back at Balae who only grinned and shrugged her shoulders, "I said he was loyal, not personable."

They stabled their horses in the inns corral and made their way inside. A thick haze of smoke hung in the air casting everyone inside with blurring visage. Savane gagged on the smell bringing unwanted attention that the prince glared at her for. They made their way to a table at the back and sat, waiting for service.

Balae watched as the men eyed the duchess and tried to estimate her worth against the very real threat that she and Dayin would present.

"Seems we are going to have to dress you down even further Savane or you are going to bring Dayin and I some added work."

The girl that came to their table was perhaps Savane's age and had dirty brown hair that she wore in a tie at the top of her head. Her dress was far more revealing than both Savane and Dayin felt was appropriate for a girl of her youth and her manner as she saddled next to Theries was even more inappropriate. Savane starred as the Prince whispered to her, all the while she maintained her soft smile, then pranced away as though he had given her life new meaning.

"What did you say to her?" Savane asked as she watched the girl preparing a tray from behind the counter.

"I asked her to bring us food and drink, get us two rooms and promised her your dress and a small gem for her silence in our part of the transaction."

"You promised her my dress?"

"Balae is accurate in saying that you are a danger to all of us with your perfect posture, your picturesque beauty and your somewhat mediocre finery. So, please do us a favour and braid that ridiculously long hair, learn to slouch and go with your knight to fetch some more appropriate attire. Put a weapon on her Dayin, even if you have to secure the hilt to the scabbard so she doesn't endanger herself."

Savane's eyes widened and her face reddened, her jaw set into a stern show of retaliation as she stood up. Balae watched the fire in her eyes go from a dull fury to rage and slowly closed her own eyes breathing out an exasperated breath, "Uh-oh" Savane pulled the tie loose on her gown and it dropped to the floor leaving her standing in her under clothes as she stared at the amused Prince.

Dayin rushed to conceal her with his cloak as she strode from the room, the dress in a heap on the straw laden floor, for the girl to collect.

"Well brother I can honestly say, I have never seen you have that effect on a noble born girl before." Theries took a sip of the wine the girl offered him and smiled at his sister, "Nor have I." he mused.

Savane felt the anger burning her face as she walked through the town with Dayin close behind her, his cloak securely fastened around her to conceal her. As the anger ebbed all that remained was the horrid embarrassment at her own temper which until she had met the Prince, she was unaware she had.

She stopped at a merchant and looked at his cloth wears before she looked helplessly to Dayin for guidance.

"I really don't know what to purchase." she conceded feeling the heat in her face.

Dayin looked to the counter and took a pair of riding leathers and plain white tunic, some leather straps and pair of riding boots to replace the silk slippers that were currently on Savane's feet. He paid the man his coin and looked toward the back of the store and nodded to the merchant.

"Could she please change in the back?" The man nodded to Dayin and the knight escorted his charge to the back of the room. Behind a dressing screen. Savane was grateful the clothes were simple to fasten. She pulled the tunic over her head and fastened the ties, drawing a deep breath she came around the corner where Dayin was holding a simple unadorned dagger in his hands. The blade was longer than the ones she had seen the men use but it was thinner.

He looked up; his eyes passive though she could see the change when he saw the way the clothes fit. He nodded his head and re-fastened the cloak over her shoulders, turned her away from him and began securing her waist length hair into a manageable braid.

"Should I cut it?" she whispered miserably.

His hands stopped and then restarted, and then finished and secured it with the leather strap. He turned her around to face him and stared in her eyes.

"Why would you do that, when just the manner in which you asked, you revealed that you do not wish to? Lady you have been the head of a house for nearly ten years making decisions on how to run everything as a Lady does, this prince comes in and belittles you, mocks you and steals your confidence and your peace of mind to the point of removing your dress in a room filled with men, in defiance of him."

He placed his hands on her cheeks, below her eyes where tears threatened to fall. "Do not give him your tears too. You are so much better than he sees you, do not collapse your spine, do not change your nature," he paused and pulled her into an embrace.

"And do not...cut your hair."

Savane sunk into his warmth and felt her heart warm and her spine strengthen with resolve. He was right, she had already given Theries too much, she was after all not his wife, nor would she ever be.

"Thank you, Sir Drake."

He pulled away and kissed her hand then turned toward the door, as a number of riders came into the town. Dayin shielded Savane from view until he realized they were not the Duke's men rather several commoners perhaps from a neighboring village. He kept her at his back a moment longer as he watched the riders exchange words with the merchant before they carried on out of the town.

Dayin took her hand and walked with her, stopping at the merchant and looking toward the riders, "He seemed out of sorts, was there a problem?" Dayin asked.

The merchant was packing for the night and looked toward Dayin, then to Savane for a moment before he returned his gaze to the riders and said, "They said that the village North of here has rebelled and executed their Lord. Said they were paid to and carried it out."

Savane choked and looked up at Dayin who nodded to the man and pulled her into movement behind him and made for the inn.

"Rebelled against what? Lord Garth was a kind man who ruled with a noble heart. Who would pay for such a thing?" she gasped, her hands flying to her mouth in sudden realization, "he has a wife and children, were they executed as well?

"I don't know," he took her hand from her face and started again for the Inn, "Until we know more, please gather your senses and try to act normal, Theries may have just saved your life with that little performance regarding your dress, we need to move."

They returned to the Inn where Balae was standing on a table and singing with some of the drunks in the tavern, Theries was nowhere to be found and the tavern girl was wearing Savane's dress. Dayin growled in the back of his throat as he took Balae's arm and motioned for her to step down which she did breathless and enthusiastically. She smelled of spirits but still had the look of someone in her right mind.

Dayin whispered to her, her smile vanished, she sobered instantly. She gathered her things, making apologies that her encore would have to wait before she darted up the stairs with Dayin and Savane on her heels.

They got down the hall of rooms and stopped at one that was locked when Balae tried the knob. Voices from in the room silenced and Dayin looked to Balae who returned the gaze with a shrug, having no answer to the questioning look as to who the Prince had in the room.

When he opened the door, Balae did a quick search and frowned, "Were you talking to yourself?"

"How else am I to have an intelligent conversation?"

"We need to move, there are problems in a neighboring village."

"What sort of problems?"

Balae picked up her brothers' things and looked at him sternly, "Can we talk about this when there is no threat of a repeat offense from this little village?"

"You're overreacting Balae, it is most likely a small rebellion that has succeeded in whatever they wanted and have no reason to come here. We need sleep and a plan."

"I was reading in Savane's book that there is a trader close by that may know something."

"You read my Mother's journal?" Savane blustered.

"Oh, why Lady, I barely recognized you with your clothes on."

Dayin placed a hand on Savane's shoulder as she moved toward the prince. She steadied and lifted her jaw.

"Do not touch my mother's book again."

He turned his gaze toward her, she could feel the humor drain from him and his usual condescending and cruel demeanour took residency in his gaze.

"Perhaps the lot of you should leave my room and get some sleep, we ride North in the morning to the Barrens. I hope your Northern tongue is still fluent Savane, your mother says he's a bit of a hermit." he tossed the book at her dismissively and nodded toward the door. Savane looked to Dayin who stood appalled, staring at Theries.

"Have you no concern for what happened in the village?" His emerald eyes focused on Dayin as he ushered them from the room, "This is the sort of commotion that we can disappear in. Good Night." The door closed in Dayin's face and left the three of them in an awkward silence. Balae pulled a key from her tunic and turned in the hall to the door across from the Prince.

Savane cast Balae a withering look that seemed to condemn her previously positive remarks toward her brother before they all filed into the room and prepared for sleep.

The tavern below the inn was still in high spirits with song and revelry, while it had no negative effects on the Princes sister it left Savane unable to find rest. She tossed and turned in her bedding until she heard a sigh from Dayin. "I'm sorry, Sir Drake I can't get comfortable, and I'm angry that he read my mother's book."

"It is as I said my lady, he will do countless things to get under your skin, if you let him. You mustn't."

She lay with her eyes focused on the wooden ceiling. In the dark the grain of wood was like a river and Savane tried to focus on it, but when Dayin's breath lengthened and deepened, she pulled the book to her lap and lit a candle. It had been days since she had read from the pages and as she ran her fingers over the binding, she felt an excitement that had quieted since she had last put it down.

The pages that the prince had referenced were indicated with a leather tie folded into the center. She scanned over it propping the book on her lap as she resigned herself to read what he had stolen from within the pages.

I have had some difficulty tracking down ingredients for my most recent spells, I have been told there is a Northern half breed that trades in the city and I will try to establish contact with him to get what I need. With these ingredients I should be able to ascertain the script on this page and learn the meaning behind the prophecy that it refers to.

Savane unfurled the enclosed sheet and looked at the ancient script, beyond any language she had ever seen, beyond the elvish tongues. She stared at the page and let her mind fall back to Shamus. "Learn the difference between magic by blood and magic by theft." she turned the page over in her hand fidgeting with the leather tie as she relived the night Shamus had made his hands glow. She searched through the pages of the book until she found a note about the birth of the new powers.

When the blood of the gods flowed through mortal veins the essence gifted them with power. In the original bloodline it was magic drawn upon in time of need and of the gods choosing: some with the gift of healing while others the gift of truth, some the gift of strength and others, the greatest of the lines whose ancestors bore the brunt of the essence, they were gifted with true greatness and power. It wasn't until the northerners began raids on the southern lands that the people realized the essence could be stolen, ripped from the dying and then corrupted.

Savane looked to the window and felt a chill rush through her. Is that what he had meant? She continued to scan and finally found what she had looked for since Shamus revealed his magic to her.

She read it silently at first, letting her mind recall the way Shamus had said each word. Then quietly, she whispered, closing her hand as he had done until the air about her felt charged like in a storm. She felt it wash through her, setting her hair up on the back of her neck until her fingers had become numb with the energy. She then uttered the words out loud. No longer afraid to say them, she let the words fall from her lips in a fluent tongue born into her from the death of the first Gods.

Her hands warmed and light spilled from her fingertips as though she had dipped her hands in liquid light with a purple hue, it burned far brighter than Shamus light had and felt warm from the inside.

Dayin opened his eyes, confused by the sudden illumination that spilled into the room. He sat up suddenly from his bedroll on the floor and stared open mouthed at Savane as her magic manifested for the first time.

When she saw Balae stir however she closed her fist and the light winked out leaving only the warmth in her fingers. Balae opened her eyes and stared at the both of them for a moment before rolling to

her side in a sleepy fog and drifted back off.

Savane looked to Dayin who looked as she must have the night Shamus had shown her the spell for the first time. She brought her finger to her lips, it would be their secret, at least until she knew she could do it again.

His eyes had the concerned look she had come to recognize from him, but she smiled to put him at ease. The magic had taken its toll and her pillow looked far more appealing than it had only moments before. She set the book under her pillow and rolled to her side facing away from Balae. She felt the excitement of what her mother had been, coursing through her. Fatigue had also taken root and in the battle of excitement and magic induced fatigue, excitement lost. Savane yawned and pulled her pillow to her side and closed her eyes as a shadow passed outside her window.

Chapter Twelve

Dawn brought the sunlight streaming through the window and filling the room with warmth. Savane woke easily, having found a new source of energy. The aura of mysticism that had encircled the memory of her mother was slowly unveiling its secrets. With a new excitement she sat up and pulled her mother's book into her lap. Flipping through the ancient scrolling text that seemed over night to have new meaning, each spell that had been blocked to her seemed to reveal itself and make perfect sense. From the ingredients to cast it and the time it would take, it all unravelled, though it was clear that some of the magic was far beyond her grasp. Her mother warned in her journal that the spells power was something of a life force and that to draw too much too quickly could cost the caster their sanity or even their lives.

Savane shut the book when she heard Dayin stir on the floor nearest her side of the bed. He rolled to one side and sat up looking confused for a moment before he seemed to settle. He stood and massaged his lower back before glancing over at Savane as he re-tied his hair and strapped his sword to his waist.

"Did you sleep well?" he asked as he tied his boots and strapped the shin guards on.

"I have truly never slept better." She too rose and started packing her book into her travel bag and tied her hair in a rope that hung to the small of her back. Dayin watched a moment before picking up her things and walking to the door. In the bed Balae still snored quietly with her face buried in a far less then regal manner.

Savane nudged her, "Balae, we're off to pick up some things before we leave." The prince's sister sat up abruptly and stared at Savane with confusion.

"I'm up."

Savane smiled at Dayin whose brows were arched at the uncertainty of Balae's level of consciousness. Then a smile as he placed a hand on the small of her back and escorted her from the room.

They walked down the stairs of the inn to find it nearly empty. The straw on the floor was damp and smelled of ale and smoke hung in the air from the night before like a thin veil over one's eyes.

The streets outside however had regained life as people busily started their day. The smells of fresh bread and meat cooking drowned out the memory of the smoke and dank straw and awakened their hunger. They exchanged a smile and made their way to a vendor.

Dayin stopped Savane and looked down at her. "What did you do last night?" Savane tried to conceal her excitement as she recalled the way the magic felt as it coursed through her, the way she suddenly saw her mother for who she had been.

She told Dayin about how the pages seemed to change with the casting of the spell and how it seemed that all the magic made sense to her. He listened intently, fighting his fear that something bad would come of this simply because of the part that Shamus had played. He had taught this to her and then threatened her life in his escape. The use of magic was rare, and he had no reason to trust, not yet.

They walked through the village, Savane occasionally eyeing a heavy storm cloud that sat on the northern horizon.

"We need to keep away from that storm Dayin or I fear we will have to seek shelter. With the death of Lord Garth, there is no way of knowing what type of welcome we will receive in the north."

He nodded his agreement and the two made their way back to the inn to retrieve the Prince and Balae from where they were feasting on leftovers from the evening before.

"We need to get moving" Dayin directed "there is a storm in the North western sky, and we need to be clear of it or face whatever village may be responsible for the death of Lord Garth."

Balae stood and stretched her back before she placed her weapon across it and waited for her brother. He packed a few things and joined the others at the stables to ride north.

The road seemed unusually busy as they made their way to the Barrens. It was as though some wave were forcing them in a tide to venture with families, farmers and merchants alike. A sad sort of melancholy that followed them as they travelled. It was mid-day when Theries seemed to stare off at the storm clouds that still lingered in the north eastern sky.

"It's smoke" he declared matter of factually, "it isn't a storm, it's smoke."

Savane's head snapped up from where she had been staring at the pommel of her saddle, "What is smoke?"

"There, over the village, we thought it was a storm but it's smoke, can you smell it on the breeze?"

Savane took a deep breath and then closed her eyes with the realization of what must have happened. Garth's village must have been sacked. He and his people had to have been killed, that was why all the travellers were on the roads, they were displaced and on the move.

"That's horrible, who could have done such a thing, I have to send word to my father, and he has to do something."

"At the risk of soundly uncharacteristically selfish, we can't do that. If we give your father any idea where we are, I guarantee we will be adding to an already precarious situation."

"You have unbearable lack of concern for people, it leads me to question what type of king you would truly be, were you to take your father's throne."

"They aren't my people."

A growl quiet and threatening came from Dayin, it seemed to be almost unconscious, as his eyes never left the road ahead of him. It seemed however to only amuse the prince.

Savane sat back in her saddle feeling overwhelmed by the loss of life that must have happened to bring such a cloud of death over the village. She watched the faces of the people as they passed until they reached the fork in the road that divided the northern road east and west.

By the end of the second day of travel they came upon the home that could only belong to the half breed. There was an abundance of furs left outside to dry, wood in piles freshly chopped and a massive spiral of smoke rose from a hole in the top of the hut.

"Do you know what to say?" Dayin asked Savane as he pulled her from the horse and adjusted her cloak, "I am certain he will remember my mother unless she was killed before she was ever able to contact him. At the very least I can speak both languages so I should be able to communicate with him."

She walked to the hut with her small entourage in tow and was about to knock on the door when it opened suddenly. Savane drew a quick startled breath as the man who stood within the doorway was a giant to her. His build was strong and postured with the threat of confidence but not arrogance. His eyes were a deep brown and his hair hung to the middle of his back, a mix of black and steel like his braided beard on either side of his strong jaw. Savane had never seen a man his size in her life and she found it difficult to not say so.

Her words felt lost in her throat as she tried to speak.

"Are you the trader the Duchess of Abarris wrote about in her journal ten years past?" His brows lifted in a fashion that gave him a far more personable demeanor and set Savane at ease.

"I am. I knew her very little though, and you are her daughter perhaps?" His voice still rough and raspy from ill use had a distinct northern accent. Savane nodded.

"Could we perhaps have a moment to speak?" He opened the door and stepped aside to give them an opportunity to pass and then carried on inside himself.

The room was filled with stifling heat that originated from a large fire pit in the center of the hut. A very exotic individual with auburn hair that hung in braids around her face sat by the fire. She was as pale as the snow and had the deep brown eyes of the northern tribes but lacked the fierce look within that had always marked them as savage and barbaric. Her back bore fresh scars that seemed to mar her from rear to shoulder and was a mix animal claws and weapons. Savane stared at her horrified for a brief moment and was grateful that for whatever reason the woman did not seem to see her or acknowledge her presence.

"What happened to her?" Savane whispered in fear that she may be overheard.

"She floated down the river a few weeks back and was a challenge to bring back from the brink of death, I had never seen someone so close that didn't slip away."

He moved to sit across the fire and watched as Savane watched his first guest staring into the fire, her eyes dancing with the flames, "She doesn't speak, or at least not to me, not yet. But she understands everything, in both languages I think."

Dayin stood a few paces next to Balae with the door propped open as the heat in the room was more than both the armored guards were willing endure. Theries on the other hand seemed very intrigued by the woman at the fire and watched carefully as Savane stood a distance from the fire directed her attention to the half-breed.

"My mother referred to you in her journal, she mentioned that you may be able to help me by providing some ingredients for a scroll she had been trying to translate. She spoke of a prophecy and that you might be the one to help."

"Your mother stumbled on something that someone was willing to kill to keep silent. I would be very cautious about toting that book and sharing its contents with anyone, were I you little lady. Your father has a tenuous hold on his land on the best of days and there for beyond the walls of your estate I think you have very little understanding the type of danger you face."

Savane watched his eyes, he had the look of a man who had known betrayal and seemed as though his intent to protect her stemmed from a genuine concern for her well being.

"Do you have the ingredients that my mother was seeking then? I think I can make use of them."

He sighed a deep fatherly sigh and made his way to the other side of the hut to search for a package that had been set aside nearly a decade ago.

Savane turned her attention to the woman as she drew closer to sit across the fire from her. She marveled at the strength of purpose this woman would have to have had in order to survive such a tremendous ordeal. There was something deep within her that Savane could feel nagging at her, like the way she had felt the night she had found her mother's journal. The nagging sensation that had drawn her eyes to search for it under the debris after it had fallen with the floor. The air around her felt charged like static in a storm and Savane could feel the hair on her neck raise in answer to whatever was passing between them. The woman raised her eyes and watched intently as Savane reflexively opened and closed her hands. Whatever magic flowed through her seemed to almost charge her skin, leaving her anxious and breathless.

The half breed returned and slowed his pace as all eyes had fallen on the exchange. Savane was now only an arm's reach from the woman. Their eyes locked, whatever Savane felt, the woman seemed unaffected, but she took in the intensity of Savane's purple gaze. Dayin had moved into the room his hand rested on the pommel of his sword, a detail not missed by the northern woman. Savane motioned for Dayin to stand back as the woman went from curious to defensive and stood. Her hand near the weapon at her side.

"My name is Savane, daughter to the Duke of this land." Savane said her northern tongue weak from neglect.

"I am Danica." The woman responded her eyes intent on Savane, "How far south have I come." Savane looked over her shoulder at the half breed whose mouth was agape that Savane had broken the silence that had lingered on Danica through the last few weeks.

"You are on the southern barrens," he said regaining himself,

"The river carried you, I found you while checking my snares."

Danica stared at him with a look that was unreadable. "You saved my life?" He nodded slowly suddenly uncertain that she had wanted to be saved.

"I, and the gods, for certain had a hand, for you were only a breath from death when I found you, I've never seen worse that survived."

Danica's eyes glazed as she seemed lost in a moment in her mind, recalling earlier events that chilled her. She slowly returned to her seat by the fire, her hand falling away from her weapon. A weapon that a moment ago seemed to bring her comfort, now seemed to burn her as hot as the fire before her.

Savane felt her chest ache as the look on Danica's face registered. So much emotion, even Dayin, halfway across the room who had not understood a word of the conversation seemed to understand what ever loss had befallen this northerner.

The half breed turned to Savane, "here are the things you asked for, are you hungry, will you eat?"

Savane looked to Dayin and repeated the question in the southern dialect to which Balae responded, seemly unaffected by Danica, "yes, we will definitely eat, but I've got to get out of this armor if we're staying." She proceeded to strip down to her leathers and stretch her shoulders. Her brother on the other hand did a quick surveillance of the small hut and frowned. Danica looked up at him, her eyes taking in his look of comprehension, something akin to recognition or awareness that seemed to darken his features.

Savane looked to the half breed, "What is your

name?"

"My mother called me Kazmir, as a reminder of my bloodline, that I am tainted by Vetis."

"Tainted how?" Savane asked, his brow arched, and he looked toward Danica. "Not all who have Vetis blood are part of the tainted legion. Those of us who have the blood gifts are left to our own to decide how we are corrupted by it. My gifts for example are in the realm of creating poison and I use that gift to make salves for healing as my mother did.

The blood knows when you are using it for dark purposes and the more it is used for the darkness the greater the corruption." Danica stared intently at him.

"How does that work if there is no distinction in your gift?"

"You mean if it is not as cut and dry as poison and healing salves?"

"My mother used to tell me it is in you and you control its intent. If you are evil, so is your blood. If you are good, then you must fight every day to stay that way." Danica looked back to the fire, watching the flames weaken with the consumed wood. Urrie had believed the same and that her gifts were granted to her by the gods in the death of the southern slave. Her mind raced with the possibility that somehow, she was meant to come here and be a part of these people.

Before Majolyn died, she had never seen any of the legion, never heard anything but fireside stories. She looked down at her hands, flexed them against the heat of the fire. A scar ran through the center that had once been a source of pride for her, but now was just evidence of how Karra had fooled her. She looked up to see Savane staring at her with compassion and warmth.

"Will you return north now that you are well?" Danica shook her head. "No, I have nothing to return to in the North. They are all dead and I am not ready to return."

"You could come with us." Savane noticed Theries eyes close slowly in exasperation. She feigned ignorance on his stance and returned her gaze to Danica.

"We are gathering some things, but sooner or later I will have to return home and perhaps you could find employment with Dayin in the capitol." She looked to Dayin, who seemed to suddenly realize that his decision to run with the

Duchess and the Prince would have branded him a traitor and would drive him out of Abarris. To seek employment elsewhere, it also meant that his mother was without means. He dropped his gaze.

Kazmir began placing food on the table, stew that had been simmering since before they arrived. They gathered around the table and ate, all but Theries who turned his face away from the offered bowl and left the hut to sit outside. Balae watched him, her warm expression extinguishing with the realization that he was not well protected with her eating at the table. Kazmir seemed to notice her conflict and nodded to her, "Take it with you." She nodded her appreciation and made for the door, while the rest of the table began their meal.

Balae shuffled out of the hut with her bowl of food and her sword tucked under her arm. She struggled at the door and then sat on the large tree stump which had been Kazmir's chopping block. Theries watched her, his eyes revealing his amusement at his sister's less than graceful display. "For one who fights like a dancer, you are a clumsy thing."

"For one who is intent on taking fathers role as king, you are a callous one." she mimicked, "Since when were you keeping score on how many verbal death blows you can deliver? I have never seen you like this."

His brow furrowed at her contempt, for a moment she assumed it meant something. Then a distance grew between them in that moment and he seemed to gaze at her with the same condescending scorn he had offered Savane and the others. Balae's eyes narrowed, "Theries, where are we going from here? Are we to fall in the shadow of the Lady as she skips through Abarris on some fool errand from her mother's past or are we going home?"

"No sister we are not going home or were you not in the room when father said, 'Theries, whether you are inclined to marry the girl is of little relevance, I need those trade routes.' He was very clear, and I know that if I return home, he would just demand I return and make it right by whatever means. So, I would rather endure her company until I can figure out a plan that he will agree to, then have to endure her company until I am old and gray and praying for the peace of death."

Balae stared incredulous at him, her jaw slack with surprise, her brows raised. "Don't be so quick to judge my discontent," he chided, "I don't see you volunteering for a suitor."

A smile suddenly started on both their faces, "Could you imagine?" she snickered.

"I could imagine him running the same way I am." They burst into laughter almost instantly at the truth of it. "Fair enough, I'll stop nagging, but you know, you could do far worse than Savane, she's good Theries." His eyes darkened in a manner that made Balae wish she had left it at the laughter. "This isn't about her Balae.' was all he replied. They sat in silence as Balae ate her stew, he ate the rations he had in his saddle bags. His gaze had ventured north, and the silence seemed to suit them both. This was how Balae had spent most of their recent years.

In her youth they had played together whenever he had one of his rare moments that were not consumed by his father secreting him away. He was a master of hiding in hide and seek and she was never able to hide for long before he found her. They would sneak out together to the castles highest ramparts and watch the night sky long after they were meant to be asleep Theries had been her only friend through her youth. He had been vicious when their mother had died, and their father sent her away to become a sword master. Years had made her a deadly master of the blade while Theries seemed to have perfected a different weapon.

Their reunion had been a cold one, not the one she had dreamed of. He had become his father with his cold demeanor and his scathing criticism. It was all Balae could do to remain loyal to the memory of the boy she had loved as the man before her faltered in her eyes.

Inside the hut, Savane sat near to Dayin and relaxed into simple conversation with Kazmir. Danica seemed content to listen though there were signs of her attentiveness in her eyes. She was intrigued by Savane's stories of the south and the plans to follow the book that had once been her mother's end.

"If you are certain that your mother was killed for what she knew, why are you trying to learn more?" She asked her voice thick with the Northerner accent.

"If your people were trapped and you knew the odds were not in your favour, would you simply not try or instead change the odds?" Danica's face darkened and Savane watched as a shadow devoured her expression and silenced her.

"I am sorry Danica; I didn't mean to upset you. I didn't know,"

"You could not know," she responded softening, "My family was murdered by my childhood friend, so I have every intention of changing the odds. Your choice of words was very," she struggled with the translation, "perfect."

Dayin watched her, "When will you go back to avenge them?"

"When I know that there is no chance that she will defeat me. When I know that I can look her in the eye and see her soul flee." Dayin raised his brows at the intensity in her voice. He knew the pain his father's death had brought upon his family and could not fathom what Danica described.

"If I may come with you, into the South," Danica offered, "I could help defend you against whatever killed you mother and perhaps fill this uncertainty I feel."

Savane nodded, then looked to Dayin who seemed to hesitate before nodding in return. "I think I could use all the help I can find, Thank you."

Danica looked to Kazmir and nodded to him, "I thought I would hate you for saving my life. When I stared into that fire these last few days, I thought I would never find a way to move on. It seems I have; I owe you my life." She stood and placed her hand on his shoulder, "I am thankful."

Dayin watched the exchange, not understanding the language as they had returned to their own, but he understood their eyes. He could feel the release of tension in the room that signified that they had gained a new protector for Savane.

It seemed that both Theries and Balae were content to sleep outdoors, so when the rest of the hut drifted to sleep Savane gathered the things she believed she needed to work the magic in her mother's book. She placed the various ingredients in a half circle around the book, then she followed everything that was written and began muttering the words that had been hidden within for nearly a decade.

The magic seemed to stutter from her lips as though it protested in fatigue. With each attempt it flowed more freely more accurately until it almost sounded like music. Savane could feel her pulse quicken, could feel her blood rushing through her and the hair once again on her neck tickled her. Within this spell though there seemed to be a reluctance, like something greater waited inside. She repeated the chant until her stomach heaved and her head throbbed then in a moment there was a numbness and the words on the page changed and spoke of the prophecy that her mother had written about. The words however blurred together in a haze and the numbness that had been mild only a moment ago consumed her from top to bottom and she fell back and slept.

Savane woke to Dayin above her, his face etched with concern as he spoke her name.

"What did you do?" he whispered as she came out of the haze the spell had wrapped her in.

"I can read it," She muttered excitement starting to rise up in her, "I could read it before I fell asleep."

"You mean before you lost consciousness." he chided.

He stood taking her hand and bringing her to her feet, the hut around them was empty and outside there was a red glow that seeped from the hut door like the promise of sunrise.

"Where did they go?" She asked fixing her cloak and reaching for her book. He gently pulled her away and held the door opened and waited for her to pass through it.

When Savane saw the night sky still on the horizon she took a breath and joined the others as they stood under the star filled sky. In the middle of which was the source, the brightest star

Savane had ever beheld, as though it were trying to reach for the ground. She stood beneath and watched it shoot across the darkness in a slow arc that burned a streak through the night sky. "What is it?" Balae asked,

"Lelandra's Tear." Savane breathed with such certainty that even Theries looked at her.

"The Goddess?" Dayin stared at her. "Savane what did you do?"

"I let you see what she was trying to tell us."

"What does it mean?"

"It's in the spell, I saw the words change but I didn't have a chance to read them before I... lost consciousness." she admitted as Dayin looked at her. "It seems to be moving across the sky so perhaps it's going somewhere."

"Is it a star?" Danica asked, Savane shook her head with uncertainty and stared at it with a sense of longing, wishing that her mother had been able to succeed. That whatever the reason Lelandra had created this beacon could have been resolved long ago.

Savane returned to the hut, intent on reading what she had missed in the book after the spell was cast. The pages were hard to see in the darkness. Without thinking she raised her hand and uttered the words that Shamus had taught her and within seconds the room was a light stemming from her hands. It had been such a challenge the first time but now it flowed from her like it had been waiting to be released. The words on the page were simple. They spoke of a great love, that in overcoming a great severance, would rise again and birth the freedom from the darkness. Savane stared at the page as Dayin entered the hut. His eyes registering surprise at her hand gripped in a ball of light. His face, worn and concerned. He looked so tired as he sat next to her.

"It speaks of a love that will face challenges but will birth the freedom from the coming war of darkness."

He closed his hand over hers, Savane let the light wink out and felt the fatigue set back in as the rush of magic left her.

"You wanted it to be your secret, and now you show it to the world, be careful my lady, you face too much, too boldly."

She nodded her head and leaned against him, caught up in the romance of a love so great that it could fight the darkness. Wondering who it could be and what it was they would face. She could feel Dayin's face against her hair as they sat side by side in the darkness, his breath quiet and controlled, his lips brushed her forehead before he moved to separate them.

"Don't..." she whispered.

"I will not be what your father accused me of, no matter my heart, I am not meant for you."

Their eyes met in the dark and she could see the pain in his, how he yearned to stay with her, but the determination that drove him to his feet and placed a blanket about her shoulders. "Sleep, beloved Lady and I will wake you in the morning to seek this love you speak of."

Savane watched as he left her side for the fire that burned up the last of the wood that had been fed to it, it's dying embers casting ghosts across his face. His eyes closed as he leaned against the stool and sleep seemed to grip him quickly. She could not imagine another man making her heart hurt the way just his visage would grip her. She placed her head back against his rolled cloak and breathed in the scent of him. If he was not meant for her, then who would it be that claimed them and drove them apart? The thought hurt more then she dared think for now and she closed her eyes as the others entered the hut.

Balae stayed outside under the burning sky long after the others had slipped back off to sleep. Her mind flew with questions, Theries had explained what he had overheard of Lelandra's tear.

The Goddess was the child of two of the gods who had earned their place among the deities on the bone fields. There were only three gods born of the new ones; Bromwyn the god of wrath and battle was Lynstrom's impetuous son, Viserra the maiden of shadows, Lelandra was last, the young goddess of love. Most believed with her birth, that a new hope came with her. It was not her birth, however that would bring hope. After two and a half centuries, it seemed that she was intent on bringing to life whatever small magic could be gained to save mankind, despite being told she must remain out of the lives of mankind.

Balae watched the tear in the sky until she felt a presence close by. She looked over her shoulder thinking that Theries had returned to sit with her but found instead a figure on horseback at the fields end. His eyes blazed an eerie red orange, like the heart of a fire. There was a potent feeling that rushed over Balae.

From the very beginning of her swordplay she had shown promise and confidence. But in this rider's presence it slipped away and left her feeling as though this were the very first time she had reached for her blade. He stayed motionless, watching her through his ghost like eyes, wind carried the smell and chill of death. Balae felt her stomach knot with a sensation she was so unfamiliar with that she barely recognized it as fear. Then, before she could find her voice he slipped away, turning his horse and riding south with the silent promise of future encounters should they choose to follow.

Chapter Thirteen

Savane's dreams were restless, filled with a sense that someone was pursuing her. She could feel Dayin trying to catch up, but this presence was faster, and more dangerous. She woke startled, scanning the room for him and finding him where she had left him by the fire the night before. His eyes closed and his brow knit in what could only be the same kind of troublesome dream. She was about to wake him when she noticed Theries not in the hut. She stood to her feet, pulling Dayin's cloak around her shoulders and stepped outside into the warmth of the morning.

The sun was barely cresting the eastern horizon and the morning was still being reddened by Lelandra's tear in the Southern sky. There was a soft fog that hung low to the ground promising to dissipate with the suns first rays.

She walked around the hut and scanned the treeline, but Theries was nowhere in sight. She made her way over to where the horses had been tethered and found his with a bag of feed over his face. The back and withers were moist. She raised her eyes to the others to see if any others looked as though they had been ridden but they were all still, only his.

She looked to Dayin's horse whose head was raised and towered over her as he smelled the air. He was such an intelligent looking beast, Savane drew closer to him. She placed her hand on the velvet of his nose and felt his breath. He gave her a moment of stillness before she saw his eyes shift and his ears go back as he noticed something behind her. Savane looked over her shoulder as Theries stood behind her. Despite the horses warning she still started at the closeness he had achieved without her knowing he was there. The horse seemed to sense her fear and protested with an aggressive snort. Theries paid him little mind as he looked over Savane with a scrutinizing gaze.

"What has you awake so early Lady?" His voice had an edge that Savane had come to recognize as his usual condescending tone.

"Dreams. Nightmares really." she put her hand protectively against the velvet of Dayin's horse again and looked back up at Theries. Her eyes caught the hint of blood on his tunic, just beneath his ribs. All her disdain for him was abandoned in a moment to the concern that he may be wounded.

"Theries are you wounded?" she reached for his tunic only to have her hand slapped forcefully away drawing a surprised cry from her. Before either had a moment to gather thoughts they were separated as Danica appeared from within the hut and rose to defend Savane. Her weapon drawn and her face drawn in a fearless display resonating conviction and calm. The tension between them even gave Savane a moment to pause before she placed a calming hand on Danica. "It is alright Danica, he's with us."

"A man who disappears in the night and returns with blood on him is either a hunter or is hiding something. He doesn't look like a hunter." Her voice sounded cold in her thick accent and Savane watched Theries to see if there was any fear in his expression but there was nothing. His eyes flashed with life as though he wanted her to move closer, to cover the space between them and engage. Savane stared at him in confusion then gently turned Danica away from him. They left Theries with his exhausted horse and his wound.

"You should not trust him." Danica's eyes were still lit with a protective ember. She flexed her grip around her weapon and watched as Theries sat and ate food from his own rations beside where the firewood was piled.

213

"It isn't about trust Danica. It's about a debt. Dayin would possibly have faced an execution had Theries not rescued us and for whatever reason he has stayed with us. I am not willing to do wrong to him when I owe him so much." Danica watched Savane as she spoke and then her gaze slipped to the weapon in her hand.

"Why did you choose to join us Danica? Why not stay here where you would be safe?"

Danica looked north and placed her hand over her brow to shield it from the coming dawn. "I had a..." her words stuttered as she thought of her slave, "friend, who needed me to be brave and I failed her. She was a southerner like you, brave and wise. In the time of her death she showed more courage than some men and I feel that if I help you, perhaps I can balance my blood."

"You feel it then? The bloodlines? You can feel Vetis?" Danica swore at the mention of his name. Her eyes closed to a not so distant memory. "My brother told me of the legends., He told me what it was to be tainted, but he swore it was a gift, he thought that I was destined to help my people." a coldness had settled into her gaze and Savane felt as though somehow this burden that Danica was carrying had been leveled on her shoulders for her to share and maybe help Danica carry.

"I will try to help you Danica, I don't know what you feel inside, but I do know what it is to feel overpowered by your fate." She looked back at Theries and then to the weapon in Danica's hand. She cradled it in a fashion that she had never seen Dayin do. Her fingers gripping lightly over the red leather grip that ran the length of the handle, moving as though caressing the weapon. Danica saw her line of sight and became suddenly conscious of what Savane could see.

"It was my brother's" she whispered, "he died saving me. He made me climb the tree, I thought he was behind me and when I looked, he was already engaging the others. He was already near death and I couldn't let his dyeing sight be of me running to rescue him and meeting the same fate. I had to watch him die, then in order to honor his last wishes I had to hide in that tree. That was the last time I will ever hide."

Savane watched her new friend with such pain inside and swallowed hard. She placed her hand on Danica's shoulder and held tight for a moment. She thought to offer promises of the future and to help keep her blood balanced as she had referred to it, but Danica seemed very much the sort that actions spoke louder than words. Savane would have to earn her place at Danica's side. She thought the irony of that was that most nobles would not seek an ally in a northern woman. Yet something in Danica had reached Savane and she would keep the unspoken promises that she chose not to share.

The journey back down to the south was quiet, though watching Danica try to ride a horse for the first time required all of them to refrain from laughter. Theries even seemed to have a controlled smile at her distrust of the animal. Danica was fortunate that the only horse she had to choose from was Kazmir's old and very docile mare. Had she been on a more spirited beast, it may have been truly comical. Despite obvious discomfort however Danica rode in silence, enduring the beast and lost in thought.

Her goodbye to Kazmir had been brief. In the moment they said goodbye, Savane could see their culture. The understanding that passed between them that she knew she lived because he had saved her, and that every breath she drew from that moment was a gift from he and the Gods.

Balae had not said a word of her encounter, instead it sat inside her as the southern road led them back to where the rider had vanished in the dark. She glanced back to Dayin and slowed her horse to where he rode solemn at the back of the procession.

"What are you thinking on?" Dayin looked up at the abrupt break in his silence. He shook his head not offering to share and noticed the look on her face. From their first introductions she had been high spirited and fearless, but something had eaten that away and left her noticeably shaken, lessened somehow.

It was a jarring that Dayin needed, to see her like that made him forget about him and brought him back to life.

"What is it? What happened?

She looked to the others and then back to him. "The night the tear appeared in the sky, you all went back inside, I stood watch outside. I was unable to sleep any way because of this thing blasting into our lives," she motioned to the tear in the sky, still visible in the day light hours but lessened in its beauty and intensity.

"I felt as though someone had come to join me outside but when I looked it was not one of you." Her throat felt dry just recalling the figure, the unnatural fear he had leveled within her. "He was a rider concealed in a black garb head to toe and he said nothing. Dayin, I have never felt even intimidated by others in combat. My father used to say it was my blessing to be stupid in battle. This rider, he totally disarmed me without even closing the distance between us. Even the thought of him makes me tremble." She closed her fist as if it could steady her, but he could see it, the sweat on her brow and the look in her eyes. Like an animal in a snare.

"The Lady Savane saw him from a distance one night I was on watch. She spoke of the cold he made her feel even though he was so far from her."

"Dayin, he went South." he looked at the rode ahead of him and then back to her.

"I think that the Lady Savane really doesn't know what she has awakened."

"If her mother was killed to keep her silent, perhaps it never slept."

Balae felt a knot rise in her stomach, "I have never met anyone I can't fight. This thing Dayin, I couldn't even draw my weapon."

She watched Theries and Savane riding in awkward silence, "Keep this between us, please, I don't want to cause alarm when we aren't even certain what it was, perhaps it was a dream."

Dayin let her ride to catch her brother with the knowledge that they both knew it wasn't a dream, whoever it was, or whatever, both Balae and Savane had seen it.

"The third day was when everything changed, and we believed that something far bigger than we had ever imagined had tangled us in its web. Going south again seemed the only way to go. We had to make amends with my father or face being fugitives in my own lands. Theries was less then pleased about returning but I think Balae convinced him because she wanted the entourage back under her command."

"That leads us to our final introduction." The empress opened the doors to the garden once again, having exhausted the candles in the dining hall she felt the need to personally introduce me to the woman that most still remembered as the "Angry Maiden"

Her statue was however not angry. Hers was carved out of something different than the other statues, that left a red hue to the carving. She and her son were kneeling cradled together with their noses near touching and laughter frozen forever on their faces. Standing guard was her smiling husband with his arms embracing them both.

The empress watched my smile as I stared at the emotion she had captured within them and smiled herself.

"I would love to tell you that she chose the name of her ship as a ruse to keep other pirates away. But in her youth, she was as angry as the sea itself. To understand Gwendolyn Bannier, one only need remember that a wounded animal has sharp teeth. She grew up in a small coastal village that was oppressed by their noble Lord Resnick who was like a pariah on the land. He had been rumored to have climbed out of the gutter, making deals along the way. Those deals bought him his nobility and only came at the cost of any who got in the way.

Her father turned to piracy to be able to pay taxes, though most people believed him to be a merchant whose trade routes included the coasts of Abarris and beyond. He was very well loved by his crew, but even more so by his daughter and wife, who never knew of his piracy.

When Gwendolyn had been in her fifteenth year there was a celebration for the village, she was so excited because her father had given her a beautiful dress to wear. She had danced with the people of her village with such carefree joy. When they had returned home however another pirate named Dirk was waiting for them.

He felt slighted by Bannier's success, many believed he was in the pocket of Lord Resnick. He had Bannier skewered against the wall and was made to watch as both his daughter and wife were violated by he and his crew.

Bannier died that day, and the girl who had danced carefree on the beach at the festival died with him, only the angry maiden remained.

She was beaten and broken inside and sought only to find revenge. Her mother became a priestess of the Goddess Shoanne and removed herself from civilization. Gwen became a pirate, taking her father's ship and crew for her own and making certain that she stayed out of the path of Dirk until she knew she would be able to confront him. Her ship was faster but carried nothing to do damage were they ever challenged by Dirk's massive war ship.

We met Gwendolyn when we went south to make amends with my father. She, like many, had come ashore because of the rainy season starting and the need for provisions. Her first mate was a great hulking man that towered over everyone because like Kazmir had been, he was a half breed. Braxus was half ogre and half human. His mother had died giving birth to him and he had been cast to the sea to die.

Bannier had found him, wailing on shore and raised him. In that relation, he and Gwen were siblings., Gwen had not known, and it took sixteen years and Bannier's death to know each other.

They were inseparable. The beautiful red-haired angry maiden and the grotesque gentle giant. Gwen, a formidable pirate with quick wit at sea, and Braxus, the priest of Shoanne. Most stayed out of their way.I watched her drift back in memory and knew that in a moment she would see those memories so clearly in her mind, reliving it as though it were only yesterday. I had become familiar with her story telling and knew each time she was about to torment me with a break. She had been generous enough to stave sleep and all things were filled with her story.

"Sir Edrick are you fatigued?" My eyes must have betrayed me for she had an air of concern as she regarded me.

"It is late," she confessed. "Perhaps it would be better continued in the morning," She knew my objection was coming before it left my lips.

"Please after you explain how you met.'

"Fair enough." she smiled "After the introduction." I settled back into place and she continued, content with her devout listener.

"Let's see, Balae had been shaken by the presence of the rider and with the exception of Dayin, she had kept it to herself, though it ate at her as we rode south. She was uncharacteristically quiet and as we neared the town that was in a state of absolute chaos, that silence broke into something that twisted her stomach with fear."

Abarris most Southern town was broken into two parts, the Seaport and Townside, where the Duke lived. The guards were desperately trying to regain control of a panicked mob as people tried to crowd for the estate. From the north west of Townside there were clouds of heavy smoke that could only be fires as people raced around mindless with fear.

Savane tried to see a cause but from where she was there were too many people. Dayin grabbed the reins of her horse in a desperate attempt to keep her close while Balae was making similar attempts with Theries. He shoved her horse away and called out, "I'm fine, find out what in hell is going on."

She looked to Dayin who nodded a silent promise to watch over them both and then she veered off against the tide of people they had been caught up in.

The people were more panicked than Balae had ever seen. Mothers clutched their children in an effort to keep them from being trampled in the mass that seemed driven toward the estate. The smoke got thicker and began burning her lungs before she was able to find the source of the terror that had gripped the town.

The rider, that Balae had witnessed in the Barrens had kept his unspoken word and sat upon his black steed in the center of the burning town. His body seemed unaffected by the clouds of smoke that drifted around him while Balae was already beginning to convulse involuntarily as it sent her into fits of coughing,

This time the rider was not alone. Through the tears in her eyes, Balae could see behind him, there were three figures on foot that wore heavy blackened armour.

One was not human; he was tall and broad with teeth that jutted from his bottom lips over the top like an ogre. His hands were massive and within them was clutched a great mace that he swung and struck anyone unlucky enough to get caught in his path. The second was tall for a human but was dwarfed by the first. His appearance bore a resemblance to Danica's people with hawkish features and a terrible beauty. His raven wing hair tied at the back of his head; he was covered in the blood of the victims in his wake. The last was between the two in stature. His eyes were the colour of ice and filled with intelligence and hatred. He moved in swift decisive attacks and killed with every blow. The three were killing anything in their path and scores of townspeople were lying in the streets behind them.

Balae's horse could smell the blood in the air and terror gripped the beast turning it back into the throng of townspeople racing for their lives. Balae tried to fight the urge to let it carry her as far from this place as possible, she pulled on the reins as hard as she could muster and drew the beast back.

She turned and faced the rider assuming that he was the commanding force behind the actions of the other three.

She drew her sword from over her shoulder and kicked the heels of her feet into the horse as hard as she could. The beast whinnied and surged forward toward the rider against all impulse for survival, they advanced.

As the distance between Balae and the rider closed, Balae could feel the terror that had driven the horse away the first time beginning to rise up within her. Her eyes burned with smoke and tears were flowing down her face. Her stomach knotted and the momentum of the horse was the only reason she didn't turn and run like the others. The rider had drawn his own blade and was waiting in the open for Balae to bare down on him. When she did, she was horrified that fear had gripped so tightly around her that her muscles would not respond, only a numbness clinging to her limbs like death and left her defenseless against him.

His red eyes bore into her, the features of his face lost beneath his cowl. She all but lost her sword in the frailty of her swing but the rider did not even show effort as he raised his weapon and in one movement drove it down her shoulder. Pain snapped her out of fear as flesh and bone surrendered to steel. Her sword clamored to the ground as all strength that had held it ebbed and fog settled over her vision.

Within moments she felt her horse turn as she reeled back in the saddle and was dragged through the throng of people as far from the rider as the beast could get. The wound throbbed from her shoulder to her abdomen, it felt like ice had buried itself inside her and pulsed with each step the horse took, until unconsciousness gripped her. She looked around one last time, certain that she would never wake again.

The Rider had said something. Balae had thought it was the hiss of his blade, but he had said something. A whisper. Ghost-like and filled with envy or longing. Olavnia. Balae's eyes opened.

Pain ripped through her as it set fire to every nerve. She could hear voices, distant, though as the pain ebbed, she could see the face of the ogre before her. he was concerned, this was not the Riders ogre. His eyes were calm, the colour of water and filled with compassion and tenderness. The air still burned with smoke but there was a rocking movement that could only mean they were on a boat. She tried to sit up but cried out as the muscles flexed and she could feel tearing.

"She's panicked, get her brother" she heard the

ogre say, his voice thick with an accent that she didn't recognize. Within moments, Theries sat down on his knees before her and stared at her. His hand resting on her skin made calm settle over her and the pain ebb away. Focus returned and the terror that had nearly driven her mad vanished in the beauty of her brother's face.

"Be still. You are still very near death as you were when they found you. Your arm nearly severed, Braxus is a priest of Shoanne and he was able to mend you, but you are far from well sister. You need to be still."

"I'm cold Theries." he looked at the sky and the heat that surrounded them as he took a cloak that was offered to him.

"Think of the fire in Kazmir's cabin" he whispered as she drifted back to sleep.

Chapter Fourteen

I spent the remainder of my waking moments writing what the empress had told me and trying to capture the fear that she had expressed Balae experienced. Trying to grasp what they must have thought when they saw her. I wondered whether the prince allowed a moment of concern to pass over his egotistical face or if he had become stone under his father's instruction. The healing hands of the priest of Shoanne had been the only thing that separated Balae from this life and the afterlife.

When dawn came, I found myself dreadfully hungry and took my morning meal to the garden to sit before Balae's statute. She, unlike most of the empress' statues, was alone in her carving, she bore no resemblance to the way I had envisioned her previous to having seen this stone visage. She had short hair that met her jaw and wore armour from head to toe. There was nothing in that carving that resembled fear. She appeared unconquerable. I was lost in her image thinking of her bravery when a voice behind me startled me back.

"She would channel all of the fear she felt and would never again be as terrified as she was that day. She felt fear, as we all did, fighting what was coming for us but she was different. Fear is for the unknown and her shoulder would always be a reminder of what and who was out there. Balae knew the rider better than any of us."

I took a bite of my food and continued to stare at her visage. "I wish I could have beheld her when she looked like this, when she fought, she must have been magnificent." The empress smiled at me, a soft smile as she placed her hands together. "She was. The bloodlines were only just awakening within us because we were so young. Balae's was, as you said, her bloodline was that of Adua's and was more powerful then we knew. I get ahead of myself. I cannot jump to the middle when we are only at the beginning." she paused "But I can grant your wish."

I raised my brows in surprise, and excitement. Before I could ask, she reached her hands upward and I could feel the hair on my arms tingle. Magic, I had forgotten her magic. She was by far one of the most powerful mages in the capital.

I watched as images began to form in the mist that clung to the garden floor, the empress eyes were alight with a childish glee as she controlled the fog to take the shapes of some great battle. Balae was her focus and I could see what she had described as a fearless, confident, battle hardened woman fighting for her cause. The image flattened returning to fog as I was turning my attention away from Balae to the people who surrounded her on both sides of the battle. "You didn't think I would let you jump ahead did you Sir Rolen?" She smiled a very sly smile and then pulled her fur back around her shoulders.

"Where were we?" She settled and began again, her hands wrapped around her furs clutching them to her chest as she stared at Balae.

The terror that Balae had endured was what had occurred on Townside and Port side had been cast on it's end. Somehow, the people had managed to gain some control of the nobility and were forcing them into a corral. The sheer numbers left them powerless and Savane watched horrified as their fate hung in the hands of the people they had once ruled.

There was an anger to the people as they circled the fencing. Watching for any foolish enough to try to escape. The guard had been retracted to the estate and the people had been denied access. Savane could feel a suffocating fear as her home surrendered to chaos. Theries, too, seemed taken aback and glanced at Savane with, for the first time, what appeared to be empathy. Dayin and Danica guided them toward the docks noticing that it seemed the only place unaffected by the madness.

As the noble's lives hung in the balance, the people of the town were scouring for any that had escaped notice. Theries had disappeared from sight all together which sent Dayin into a search while trying to conceal his Lady. She desperately tried to keep her head down knowing that at any moment someone could recognize her and corral her with the rest to face an uncertain fate.

It wasn't until the Rider arrived, that the throng of people separated and made way for he and his three soldiers, the fate of the nobles was revealed. Dayin grabbed Savane drawing her behind him and reaching his hand to his weapon as did Danica. The air was suddenly suffocating Savane, she found herself clinging to Dayin and filled with an inner terror at what was coming. The entire town had been herded here and all the people sat silent, as though their will had been drained from them. The rider radiated a chill despite the humid summer air. His red eyes gleaming from beneath the cowl of his cloak. He nodded to the three men accompanying him and they went about slaughtering the nobles penned and helpless.

Savane felt the scream rise in her throat as Dayin clamped his hand around her mouth. Not a single voice rose in protest as the nobles died. The commoners seemed unaffected and indifferent to the carnage that only moments ago they had fled from.

"They are under some sort of trance." he whispered as she buried her head into his shoulder.

Danica watched the rider move through the bodies on the ground. His red eyes closed as he passed over them. Something about the way he moved and shuddered as he passed over them was familiar. Her eyes fell to his feet and she watched as the blood leaving the nobles pooled in veins along the ground in bright rivers before darkening and scorching a path to the rider. Each step he took he drew in more essence and from what little Danica could understand, more power.

"Get her out of here." She hissed in broken southern. His eyes followed her gaze to the ground and horror and realization replaced confusion. He pulled Savane into him as if her nearness would shelter her from their eyes. Danica stayed on the street. Her eyes focused on the riders three guards. She took in their visage and the last of them, with his dark hair and eyes and distinctly Northern features. She stared a moment too long, her gaze drawing his, his eyes focused on her. He was older than she by easily ten years and in the North, older meant they had survived more wars, they had survived more winters and they were almost always stronger for it. She felt the sickened feeling that had consumed her when she watched Urrie die and then it ebbed away as his eyes narrowed with purpose then drifted away from her.

She knew that her blood was tainted, imbued with the same godly essence that the rider was consuming and yet he ignored her. She backed away and kept as close to others as possible until she was able to clear the center of town. She turned when she saw Theries watching her for a moment before turning away and moving for a boat with Dayin and Savane behind him. Ahead of them, it appeared that Balae was being carried by some massive man and three strangers.

Danica ran to catch up as she watched them scurry about the ship. "First a horse and now a ship, soon they will have me in a dress." she groaned bitterly in her northern tongue.

Savane gazed off in the direction of Abarris, it had been consumed in fog and smoke from the moment they embarked and now they sailed blind along the coast. Her tears had dried on her cheeks and left her face feeling tight and cold despite the heat. The priest sat near Balae and watched for her to improve while the crew of the ship made preparations to sail into open waters.

Dayin had spent some time talking with a fire haired woman that Savane believed to be the captain of the ship, Danica had not left her side. She seemed ill suited for sailing, her posture, slumped and her head held protectively in her hands as though it could somehow shield her from the rise and fall of the tides.

Savane sat quiet in her misery until the captain made her way over and sat between her and Danica. "Your friend looks like she is through the worse of her mending. She should be able to use her arm again." She said as her eyes stayed focused on Balae.

"How was he able to save her, I saw her arm, it was barely attached?"

Gwendolyn looked toward the massive man lingering over Balae and back to Savane. "I have seen him mend far more broken then she. He has Shoanne's touch and has dedicated his life to her worship. You need only question why did they slaughter all of those nobles and let your friend lay dying. To me that is more the question." Her eyes fell to Danica who gracelessly dry heaved next to her before running for the side of the ship. Her red brows rose in amusement before she turned her attention back to Savane. "And you, Lady, why do you suppose they let you live?"

"They didn't see me."

Gwendolyn shook her head in doubt.

"You presume to tell me that these marauders came from the north having no familiarity with your people, come riding into town with vengeance. Coincidentally they manage to select only the nobles to stock pile in the pens to slaughter and you think they didn't see you?"

Dayin was suddenly there a rock for Savane to set herself against.

"I think that the lady has been through enough and that your questions are coming too soon in the wake of what has just occurred. So respectfully Captain Bannier, would you please give her time to mourn those counted among her friends that were slaughtered today."

Gwen stared at Dayin; her eyes narrowed in an unreadable mask. Then she nodded, stood and made her way over to where her first mate sat next to Balae and seemed contented to leave the line of questioning for another day.

"Thank you," Savane whispered breathless in an effort to control the emotions that threatened her tenuous hold on sanity. "I feel as though I have been dreaming and it is gradually shifting from dream to nightmare." She looked up at him and caught his eyes shift from the book she held to her eyes.

"You think that my mother's book has something to do with this?"

Dayin closed his eyes and shook his head, "No, I don't. The night you saw something outside your courtyard you had not yet found this book. At that moment none of what we face had yet revealed itself. I think he was looking for her and found you."

"Then why look to the book just now, what are you not saying Dayin?"

"That you were brave to share what you feared was coming. Most would not share that kind of thing for fear that they would be deemed mad."

She smiled in an effort to lift his spirits, "Did you think me mad Dayin." He looked up at her, his eyes saddened, and put his hand to her cheek. "I wish you had been."

Balae made a sound that drew everyone's attention, a pained mournful cry from deep within.

Braxus put his massive hand on her good shoulder to steady her as both Dayin and Theries rose to see if they could be of any use to the healer. Braxus pulled away the cloth that had been wrapped around the wound to reveal what should have been a mortal wound but instead revealed a thick rope like scar that wound from her neckline to the underside of her ribs. His head tilted as he looked at the colour. It should have been bright red, or pink, but the wound had taken on a blueish tint, like the colour of ice.

Theries eyes widened upon seeing it, "Is it infected?"

"That is not like any infection I have ever seen." Braxus muttered, uncertain how to respond to Theries sudden interest. The sounds coming from her were as though she were being torn open all over again, her eyes opened, and tears welled within. Theries watched from standing above her. His face frozen in apparent apathy.

Dayin dropped to his knees besides her allowing only a moment of an accusing gaze to fall on her brother before he pulled her in and held her up against him.

"Theries?" Her voice cracked with the effort of the words against what had been screaming moments before.

"No Balae, It's Dayin, I have you."

"He's coming Dayin, I can feel him. I'm so cold."

"We are at sea, and nothing is coming for us." Braxus interjected. Though he scanned the horizon. The crew had gathered around her and were watching as she began to claw at her shoulder. Dayin lifted her, struggling to get his balance against the weight and the tide. Braxus put a hand across his back and in one easy push helped him up. without further words Dayin carried her to the captain's bed and closed the door.

The crew stood silent and confused until Gwen shouted at them to carry on with their duties, "Move on." she cursed and then looked to Braxus and the door that was now closed in front of her. She looked to Savane, "Are they lovers?"

Savane blanched and looked to the door. "No!" Gwen's brows raised, and a slight smiled swept across her face.

"Dayin most likely didn't appreciate that someone who relies heavily upon her intimidation in battle be viewed in so miserable a state. He recognized how humiliated Balae would feel to have so many stare at her in such a shameless manner. If you will excuse me." Savane turned her attention to Danica.

Dayin sat across from Balae watching as her eyes blinked in an effort to focus. "Can you see me?" She nodded, her voice losing its panic she reached up and sought his hand. "Where's Theries?"

"I think he is unnerved by your state Balae and fears for your life." He felt her stiffen as the reality of what was unsaid was understood.

"You mean he thinks whatever is wrong with my shoulder is unnatural and it frightens him for his own life."

"It is not my place. Are you still in pain?"

"It is hot and cold at the same time, like a burning poker inside the wound with ice upon my skin." She looked to her shoulder, pulling away the bandages and staring at the blueish line that scarred her. She moved the arm in a slow circle and looked to him in surprise. I was certain it was severed."

"Balae, you would have most certainly died had the Priest of Shoanne not been the one to find you. He was able to staunch the bleeding and carefully mended you. He's been at you for days and did not leave your side."

"And my brother?"

"To his credit, Theries was very distressed by your wound and stayed as well. It wasn't until this morning when you started to scream that he seemed bothered enough to keep his distance."

"Did everyone else make it out well enough?"

"The nobles were executed in the square, all were killed. Savane was with me and blessedly no one recognized her. Your brother perhaps saved her life with his demands on her humble attire. Now, it seems there is a fog along the coast that has consumed all of Abarris."

Balae's eyes had grown wide as she listened to Dayin, her hand clenched in a fist, "And Savane's father? Was he counted among the dead?"

"No, he was locked up tight in his estate and all the guard with him."

"Did Savane notice that none of her father's men were there to help the nobles? What madness, what cowardly behavior." Dayin placed a hand on Balae to calm her, "I was there, and I did nothing," he whispered, miserable.

Balae eyed him coolly, "You were alone, had you the men Savane's father had, you would not have remained idle"

"You need to rest Balae, whatever we are in for, I am certain I cannot do it alone and that I will need both your strength in combat and your bravery. Please mend and get well."

Dayin watched a smile start on Balae's lips, not her usual playful smile but a genuine warmth. "Thank you Dayin." Her eyes drifted passed him to where Theries had made a silent entrance and stood still in the doorway. Her smile instantly returned to its guarded playfulness as she acknowledged him. "Theries," Dayin stood and turned for the door. Balae could feel the animosity in Dayin as he passed her brother without a word or even a glance. To some it would be perceived as cowardice to say nothing, but Balae could see the indifference in Theries eyes and knew it to be more of realization of wasted effort on Dayin's part.

"You are fairing far better now than this morning I see. Sitting up and talking instead of screaming. May I see?"

Balae looked down at her shoulder as Theries approached her bed side. He gently pulled away the bandage to reveal her scar.

"I have never seen a priest so adept in the healing arts before. I have heard there are some here in the West," his thought trailed off as he examined the fading evidence of his sister's near death.

His hand sat idle after she re-wrapped the wound and Balae watched the turmoil as years of training to control his emotions wrestled with his affection for their childhood.

"Where are we going?" He looked up at her, grateful for the distraction, he glanced around the cabin for the first time. "I think the captain intends to wait out this fog and try to return. She apparently has some need in Abarris and wants to ensure she makes it back before the rule is compromised."

"Why is the fog a concern?" She lifted herself to look out the window and winced as it sent a new wave of white-hot pain through her shoulder.

He eyed her a moment, his breath caught in his chest until she was comfortable. "Her brother, the Priest, says it is unnatural and she believes him, and so we wait."

Savane sat with Danica's head rested on her lap. The Northerner had not slept since they had set sail and exhaustion had finally taken hold. Savane had managed to give her herbs to settle her stomach and the two were sitting out of the way when Dayin emerged from the cabin. His eyes squinting in the light of day. He looked down at Danica then to Savane who still idly smoothed her hair. "Will Balae be alright?"

"She seems better." He sat beside her and watched as the crew moved about the deck carrying on their duties. Gwen sat up at the helm with a young blonde crew member that was perhaps five years her senior, they sat in comfortable silence as they piloted the ship. "She's young to be a captain," he mentioned off handed. "Braxeus was telling me that her father had been captain and the respect they carried for him spilled over to her in his passing. He was murdered. The crew wants revenge, they trust her to bring it to them."

He looked down at Danica who previously was unable to sleep through any conversations much less ones directly above her head. "Did you cast a spell on her?" He teased.

"No, she's just that tired." Savane stared at her then looked toward Abarris, "Dayin do you think it was isolated, do you think this rider was coming for something in Abarris?"

"Oh Lady, I think to believe that it was isolated would be too naive." He looked down at her, his eyes filled with sympathy, "whoever this rider is, it is only the beginning. Shamus warned us that it was coming, you were fortunate that you heeded what he said and learned what he taught you. I have spent a great deal of time going over what happened that night that he escaped, and I know he never intended to harm you, you were his student, I think somehow he knew what was coming."

Savane knew what he was saying was true but inside there was a nagging that uncovering the book and revealing Lelandra's Tear had set into motion a great war. That had she minded her father, married the prince, she could have stopped it all. Her eyes reddened with the thought of all the dead at the hands of the rider and she choked on the belief that it was not even the beginning much less an ending.

"Do you still believe that?"

The Empress had slipped into a melancholy that I was certain she must have suffered before. Her smile had faded, her eyes were glassy. "Throughout my life I second guessed every decision I made because of that one. I wondered had I not been vain enough to believe that I was born to do great things that I could have lived a life of peaceful joy."

"You did do great things." I heard my voice react to my heartbeat rising in my chest. How could this woman who changed history and bought us our peace feel that her path had been the wrong one? She placed a hand on mine.

"Sir Rolen, I assure you, there were moments, but they were fleeting, and most never knew I had them. Only my closest friends."

"We sailed for what felt like forever, we stopped

in the Port of Denalin and sought audience with the Duke there. He was one of the oldest families in the land and he had one of the greatest armies. I felt it only fair to warn him and perhaps see if there was anything he could do to aid us."

"The castle was ancient but meticulously maintained. The walls had been reinforced and the design, because it was so old, was foreign to most. There were said to be great passageways that ran beneath Denalin and that the Dukes son and daughter were the only two truly familiar with them all. I remember how I trembled as I approached those walls. As though some one had a grip about my shoulders and had rattled me like a child's toy."

"He was a great monster of a man, with wild hair that was strung in oddly placed braids. Where his hair ended and his beard began was impossible to know. In his prime, he had been the greatest of his father's warriors. His family believed that the right to rule was earned at the end of a sword. His brothers relinquished their rights to the duchy when they were defeated in combat, though they served on his war council."

"His daughter was very much raised as I had been. She was elder to her brother and his favoured child. While her brother, slight and small of frame had been ill as a boy and sought for approval from him, although he never quite reached his father's expectations. Their mother had been a soft-hearted woman who had been part of an arranged marriage to a warlord. One day when the grief was too much, she hurled herself from the tower of one of their Northern castles. No one in the family ever spoke of the Duchess"

The Empress looked up at me and then seemed to look back into her memory. "The great hall to his castle was very much like the one to this castle, cold and over-sized. It had the most amazing tapestries running the walls and I remember the braziers burning in intervals along the walkway to his throne. He had massive dogs at his feet and many off his men had been in the room at the time."

"Lady Savane of Abarris" The Duke went silent as did his people at her announcement, his eyes narrowing in suspicion.

"Young Lady, you are calling at a very strange hour. We are half into our spirits and I received no word from your father of your intent to visit."

"My father is unaware of my presence here Duke, although I am here on his behalf."

For whatever reason, the Duke snorted at her in contempt and then eyed his daughter, who stood only a few paces from where he sat. "Were my daughter to act on my behalf without my say it would mean I were near enough to dead that she could do it herself."

Savane allowed a moment of silence to gather her thoughts. "My father has barricaded himself within the walls of his estate in an effort to survive an attack from invaders. They killed all of the nobility."

The room had taken on an eerie silence, all eyes were upon her as she spoke. "They were marauders from the north. Four of them. They road in and slaughtered the villagers."

"It sounds to me Lady that your father may have been idle when he should have been attacking."

"I did hope that you would be able to provide

some men meant to aid my father in deposing such a villain." Savane cringed as outright laughter filled the room. She drew a deep breath and straightened her spine before she spoke again.

"Sir, I came to you of respect for both your rank and your army, the people face a true danger and you mock me."

The Duke's posture changed and resonated power and confidence.

His voice clear and harsh. "You come to ask me for help, when you are nothing but a girl. I have no time for you or your cowardly father in his guarded estate. Kaleb show the Lady to the door; we can make amends for laughing at her at least."

"I need no escort; I can find the door well enough Duke." she played out the proper courtesy and turned rigid on her heel to go face to face with the Duke's son. He was no longer the small sickly boy that many of the stories had led Savane to believe. Instead he was easily a foot taller than Savane with hair as wild as his fathers. His childish physique had been transformed into the warrior his father would be proud of. His eyes were focused on her and he watched her gather herself before stepping passed him. He fell into step behind her and walked the remaining length of the hall.

"You know this danger is not only to our land-lord Denalin, it has the potential to become a true threat to your father."

Kaleb's eyes narrowed with the use of his title. He took the cloak that a servant offered him and placed it around Savane's shoulders.

He held them there for a moment before turning her around to face him. He paid little attention to propriety as he tied her cloak around her shoulders. Though the way he did everything seemed gentle, there was a coldness to him that left her feeling very threatened.

"We will fight," Savane drew in a breath and let it out as he continued, "When it is at our door-step."

Savane bit her lip so hard she could taste blood. Kaleb's eyes held no emotion as he seemed to acknowledge it. He turned on his heel, "I can assume you know your way out."

Savane was back on the ship and vibrating with anger when Theries came in and sat across from her. She noticed him take a seat and was near biting more holes in her lips when he spoke.

"What in all of the realm were you thinking to go and speak to a man such as Denalin? He is the lowest noble in all this broken little empire. Others only leave him alone because there is not a single army that could outthink his war council."

"And that is why I went to him. If we are on the fringe of war Theries, I wanted him to hear me out."

"In case he wanted to take the side of a Lady with a poisoned land and a coward for a father?" Savane's eyes flashed with pain for a moment before she gritted her teeth and stood across from him.

"Perhaps I am not the strategist you are Prince Verentine, but I am aware that this war is coming. As sure as it has poisoned my land it will snake its way to you and your father. So before you snap your forked tongue at me, and think me and my land a lost cause, I would ask that you consider if you have alienated everyone around you, how you will save what you do care about."

She turned on her heel and opened the door, the air suffocating her and burning her eyes. She stood on the deck in the still night air looking out over the water. Her breath coming in short, sharp bursts as emotion constricted her. She scanned the horizon in the dark where her home should be lit up but there was only darkness. The fog and death that had consumed everything had taken the light with it. A sound from behind her drew her attention to Danica, standing an arm's length away. Savane started and tried to hastily wipe away tears that had once again found their way down her face.

"You must think I cry a great deal." She had instinctively spoke in her Northern tongue.

"Because you weep for the death of your home?" She walked over and stood at the handrail next to her. "I cried too. Tears are not a sign of weakness Savane, giving up is. What did you call that?"

Savane looked to the red tear that seemed to be just above them in the sky. "Lelandra's Tear."

Danica caught herself as she made Urrie's clicking sound in her throat. "If a goddess can shed a tear for fear of what is to come, why can you not shed a tear for what has passed?"

Savane drew in a long, ragged breath. "How did you know I needed company?"

"I heard him speak to you as he did and knew

that he had upset you. He has that effect on you."

"He does." She watched the water lap the side of the ship. "I don't know how he is able to do that, but whenever we speak it is as though he knows exactly what to say to anger me."

"I would not spend much of your thought on him." Danica shifted and then leaned on the ropes, noticeably uncomfortable at sea. "He does not see your strength. That is all. You are very brave. he may be a prince, but I see a leader in you that he cannot. Rulers who rule by fear are not worthy of tears, just as the rulers who do lead are worthy of blood."

Savane stared at her in silence. Her heart racing.

"You spoke once of your blood Danica, what is your gift?"

Danica's eyes shifted from Savane's gaze, they scanned over the horizon and settled on the castle.

"My eyes are not limited by distance as yours are, my ears, not confined to the room I am in. I can see the people of the castle still moving about despite the late hour. When we were waiting outside the walls for you, I heard how the Lord spoke to you."

Savane stared disbelieving.

"You see, they think you mad right now. They think themselves better learned then you. That it is impossible for a young noblewoman to know something that they do not. You must let them think you mad Lady, there will come a day when the truth of what is, will meet the truth of what you spoke of. When that day comes, as terrible as it may be, you will be their leader." Danica shifted her cloak on her shoulders before turning toward the lower decks.

"Do not let small minds set the limits by which you learn."

Danica was gone, Savane sat still on the barrel she had leaned against. Her heart still raced, her mind trying desperately to keep pace. Her tears had dried and for the first time in weeks she was found. She closed her eyes for a moment and then made her way to the lower decks to find Dayin, and rest.

Chapter Fifteen

The return to Abarris was over clear waters. Savane spent the majority of her time reviewing her mother's book and the notes that she had compiled regarding the mythology behind the blood. If there was any truth to the assumption that Dayin and Danica were drawing about the rider gathering the bloodlines, then one could only ask who it was that he was gathering it for? The question of who these champions that did the killing were and what were they trying to accomplish was going to need to be solved. She was pouring over pages and pages of information in search of answers when she was made aware that the coast was visible again, and that they had only a few hours before landing once again in Abarris.

Balae had returned to the living and even made an effort to walk on the deck. She was nowhere near fighting strength and would be unable to for some time.

Savane stood and reached for her cloak. She went still as Dayin stood to do the same. He wrapped it around her shoulders and reached for the book they had spent the morning trying to decipher. Pages that covered the battle on the bone fields and the different factions in the war. "My mother makes reference to Lynstrom's sword on more than one occasion. That it was his sword that struck down Vetis and ended the battle. If such a weapon were to exist, perhaps there would be a way to stop the rider." The door opened and Gwen looked in. "We have docked. Your friends are prepping to leave." She turned and made her way down the narrow hall and up the steps.

"Now the daunting task of seeing my father."

Dayin reached for her and pulled her cloak over her hair. "We don't know what condition the people are in." She nodded and made her way down the hall.

Danica looked childishly excited as she eyed the ground, disembarking quickly when Savane reached the deck. The others were already on the dock below. Gwen swung her legs over the rail and climbed the ladder down as Savane and Dayin used the gangplank.

Theries looked up at Savane and nodded toward her hood. "Keep that in place. It seems the riders are gone, but the people are very suspicious."

Balae looked toward the Estate and took a deep ragged breath. "Time to go pay our due I suppose."

Braxus looked at the estate and then to Balae. "Do not overestimate your healing. You are still weak and have much to mend. You may be able to start a fight, but you are in no state to finish it."

"That is good advice, provided my brother heeds it and stays out of trouble. Words will never be enough a thanks for what you have done for me." Braxus put a hand on her good shoulder and smiled.

Gwen looked at the lot and shook her head, "We sail for Osmadante if you need to make a clean getaway. I can take you anywhere in between." She turned and started to make her way down the docks to see if the dock master had survived.

Everyone stood still, seemingly waiting for another to take the first step. Danica looked toward Savane, "To the estate then?"

Savane nodded and took a deep breath, "To the estate then."

The road to Savane's home was empty. Merchants weren't lining it, selling their wares, calling to the passersby. The guards were still held up in the estate, no one patrolled. The silence that had settled, replacing what was once an area of such energy, left Savane horribly alone. They took the road in silence and when they reached the gates, they opened without request.

Driedger, her father's personal guard stood in the entrance way. His eyes held none of the softness he had reserved for her in her youth. He instead went from Savane to Dayin with equal disdain.

"Driedger, Is my father well?" He eyed Dayin, his posture calm but carrying a hint of angst.

"Your father has nearly lost his mind with worry over what you have done. You left him nothing to tell him where you were going, what you were doing and why I have no doubt he will want to throw the lot of you in the prison for an extended period."

Theries stepped forward, an egotistical gleam in his eyes, "He is welcome to try."

Drideger bit back and adjusted his stance. "I am certain he would not assume to withhold you Prince Verentine."

"Well, if the Lady disappeared in the night it is

because I took her. Her father and I can discuss the details of my misguided decisions at a later time then. Now, if you would take the Lady to her father and leave your judgments of your superiors to the barracks, less one might think you a traitor and see you hang for your loose tongue."

Savane's eyes had snapped to Theries at his defense of her and stayed trained on him as he spoke. When he finished and Drieger had started walking ahead of them, she saw the slightest smile curve the corners of his mouth.

"You just enjoy the conflict, don't you?"

"No Lady, I enjoy the victory."

Driedger led them down the hall to where her father's library was guarded by two men. He stopped where they were and then motioned for her to take the lead.

"He has been unwell for days Lady, demanding we leave him alone., He won't eat and hasn't been caring for himself at all."

Savane opened the door to the great library that she had spent her life in. First crawling on the floor, then reading in the window seats until she was often behind the great wooden desk ensuring that everything was running smoothly within the estate. All those memories rushed through her mind as she looked at all the books thrown about the room and her father in what appeared to be a mad frantic search. Pages were torn and littered the floor while very few books remained on the walls. Savane stood in the doorway, her eyes widened and bewildered by a man she had never seen lose his temper much less become so completely unhinged. His eyes had darkened and lines along his brow had become chasms of desperate worry.

A knot tied in Savane's stomach, she passed back the bag that held her mother's book to Danica who stood just behind the door. She folded it in her grasp and removed herself from the Dukes view. The sound drew his attention and he froze in his search, his eyes, orbs of madness.

"Savra" Savane choked as he addressed her with her mother's name. "The book Savra, where did you put your cursed book?"

"Father, it's me, it's Savane." His hesitation as she stared at him, filled her with dread.

"Yes, Savane. You left, you left, and your mother came back."

Savane looked back to Theries who stood in the

doorway, his brow raised at the sudden change in the Duke. Gone was the strong commanding presence, leaving behind this unwashed haggard man.

"Mother is dead, father." She stammered, her voice barely a whisper.

"No, Savane she's back and she wants her book."

"He's lost his mind." she heard Balae whisper from behind the door, "say nothing of the book."

The Duke seemed to become despondent, as though listening to another voice in the room. Savane could feel the hair on her neck start to rise, Dayin shifted behind the wall, suddenly uncomfortable.

The Duke turned his attention back to Savane, his eyes dark with exhaustion. "You have her book." he spat with vicious accusation.

Savane felt a hand tear her from the room as Theries pulled her down the hall. The others close behind. "I am not certain what has happened to your father Savane, but that is not he, that man reeks of death."

Darkness crawled along the walls lengthening their shadows. Dayin held Savane's hand as the others followed with the sense that they had been led into a trap. Behind them they could hear the crazed shouts of the Duke demanding that they be arrested or killed. Dayin drew his sword and took the lead while Danica swung to the back of the group, her weapon slack in her grip.

The close confines of the hall would be awkward for her, having never fought inside in her life, she swung the flail in a close trail arc as the first of the guards rounded the corner. The power behind the practice swing was enough to give them pause. Only a moment, before the rage of the Duke overrode the fear of the Northerner.

Dayin turned in the hall as Drieger stepped out of the doorway. "You showed such promise Drake, in exchange for the admiration of a girl you stepped away from your duty. A moment of praise for doing what you were obligated to do, and you faltered."

Savane gripped his hand and whispered, "Don't listen to him." Theries seemed to watch for only a moment before giving Savane to Balae, insisting they move down another hall. He moved in very close to Dayin, his hand on his sword hand and whispered "Dayin we are getting out of this madness. Do what you have to do to rescue Savane, you already know it is bigger than this petty little castle."

He turned his eyes to the captain of the guard, "Do what you're obligated to do."

They could hear Danica fighting down the hall and guards coming from another. Theries turned from Dayin moving down after Savane and his sister.

Dayin turned his attention to the captain of the guard and postured, his sword low at the ready. The two collided as they had for years on the practice yard. Dayin had only one thought as he stood off against the man who had been his mentor. Just give them enough time to get away. They exchanged the first few strikes, testing each others range.

Then it became a barrage of constant attacks and blocks. It was only one hit though that ended it. A lucky hit through the defenses of the senior guard that barely nicked his shoulder, but it passed through armor into flesh and bled. Within moments the man fell to his knees. Dayin froze in confusion, the man should not have collapsed from a nick. His blade had been poisoned.

Danica came up the hall from where she had been battling, covered in blood from unknown sources and looked at Dayin's victim on the ground. "No time." she spat in southern tongue. Others had turned down the hall and were running after them when she yanked him into motion. The two raced to catch up to the others, having to fight to make it.

They had all been separated from each other. When they finally made it to the docks, Dayin saw Savane being helped up on the ship. She seemed incoherent and unable to use her legs. He knew just by the sight of her she had once again over stretched her magic. Balae had reopened her wound and was bleeding through her clothing. Danica was covered in blood, none of which belonged to her. Theries meanwhile was remarkably clean.

Gwen looked up from where she sat on the rail and looked past them. The estate seemed to be preparing to follow. They were trying to mount horses, but at the same time seemed intent on fighting a very aggressive horse. "Braxus, the gang plank"

The giant took only a moment to swing it out, drop it to the deck and tether it to the ship. The horse that had been fighting in the courtyard had broken away through the corral and was racing after Dayin and Danica. Theries had already arrived at the ship and helped his sister board while Savane stood weak and wobbling. Her face dirt covered, and tear soaked, her hair pulled from its loose braid. The wind threatening to knock her over as she waited to see if Dayin would make it to the ship.

The horse, she suddenly recognized, was Dayin's Seraphic. Now, he forced himself through the men to free Dayin from the danger ahead. Seraphic bore down on he and Danica. Dayin grabbed a fist full of mane and pulled himself up, turning the horse once to swing Danica up behind him. Without the safety of the saddle Danica, paled at the notion of riding the beast. Dayin held her long enough to ensure she was on securely before turning again and racing toward the ship.

"A horse" Gwen shouted, "you think you are bringing a horse?" Savane turned her purple gaze to Gwen and for a moment Gwen felt as though she were a mother denying her child. The tears had made Savane look tortured and lost. Gwen threw her hands in the air. "Prepare the brig for our four-legged guest." She turned her gaze to Savane again, "My crew is not responsible."

The horse road up the gang plank without a moment of hesitation. Dayin lowered Danica to the ground dismounting while the crew of the ship quickly embarked and prepped to sail. Savane threw herself into Dayin and all the emotion she had held inside broke open. She sobbed uncontrollably against him. He held her for a moment, his breath caught inside, fearing the moment when propriety outlasted consoling.

"You have the book?" She nodded her head in his shoulder as he gently pulled himself free. "Danica, take her below please. See that she is not left unattended." Danica nodded and took Savane by the arm, disappearing below deck.

Dayin turned toward Gwen, "You have my gratitude Gwendolyn, thank you for waiting, and for making accommodations for my horse." He watched as they lowered his horse into the brig. "We will do our best to keep you from regretting it."

Dayin turned to Balae who sat with cloth covering her arm that Braxus had already looked at. "You should get below deck as well and get some rest." Balae stood looking at the noticeable tension radiating from Dayin toward her brother. "Is that wise?"

"I would recommend it," Theries replied dryly.

Dayin waited until their group had banded below deck before turning on Theries, who truly believed he was due to be struck.

Dayin's posture and expression denoted nothing less, instead he took a very deep and controlled breath.

"Let us be clear about one thing Prince Verentine. I do not believe in poison nor do I consider coating my blade, saving my life. The next time you're feeling magnanimous, please understand that I will turn this poison on you." Dayin turned away from Theries, the anger he felt inside tied knots of grief and left him sick to his stomach. His mentor had been an incredible soldier and to die from a nick in the shoulder. Dayin grit his teeth. He took another deep breath and moved to the bow of the ship. He watched his home consumed by fog as they sailed further out to sea. Below deck, he could hear the sounds of his horse nudging the makeshift stall and the sounds of the crew adjusting to once again having guests on their ship.

"For what it is worth, because he corrupted the deed, does not take away from who you are." Dayin started at the sound of Gwen's voice. He paused and closed his eyes.

"I poisoned my mentor, he died with a nick of my blade."

"He would have killed you leaving no one to protect Savane. I have not been with you all long enough to judge or really even have the right to speak to you in such things, but Theries seems like a very complex person that has ulterior motives. Whatever reason he did what he did. You were only the delivery of that fate."

His body stayed rigid and closed. "Why were you willing to do so much for us?" They both stared to the coast where the frustrated remnants of Savane's father's forces amassed on the fog covered shore.

"Well, you needed it. Her father had no ships, so the risk was minimal. Had I not been willing to take you, you would have had to run by land. Although her father has no ships, he has an entire army of military and reserve units not to mention mercenaries that would take the bounty to bring his daughter back. Executing any who stood in his way. That may still be a concern."

Gwen scanned the horizon; her red hair being pulled free of its braid by the same wind that carried them to the safety of open waters. Her blue eyes focused and unafraid. Dayin turned his gaze to the sea and watched the calm of the water.

"When I was a girl, my father sailed this ship as a pirate and stole from Resnick's men. The people loved my father, but his choices caught up with him and got him killed. The same may happen to me, but like my father I couldn't stand by and watch you meet your fate. Not when it was in my power to change it. Perhaps your Prince is no different than I, it is just my sacrifice is easier for you to negotiate then his."

"You should not put yourself in the same light as Theries."

Gwen raised her eyebrows and turned on her heel. "I would be careful young knight; your small group is all you have in this world. Trust me," her hand swept out in an arc to encompass the ocean before them, "It has far more shadows then light." A voice called from the upper look out. "Capt'n a ship."

"Colours?"

"Too Soon Capt'n"

Dayin watched Gwen's posture. She had been sailing long enough that the mention of an oncoming ship left no cause for alarm. She made her way with swift even strides to the helm and stood next to a very young man, perhaps four or five years younger than Gwen and put her hand on his shoulder. "Perhaps it's time to relinquish the helm Mr. Bowen."

The young man nodded with a grateful smile. As her turned to leave the deck, a tall wiry young man with wind burned, sun darkened skin landed on the deck from nowhere. Dayin scanned above to see the mast had a narrow platform the man must have been seated on. He carried a certain confidence that most would call egotism as he eyed Dayin, there was a sense that he was trying to weigh him.

"Mr. Stiele, I want to know who that is." At the command, the man was instantly focused. Dayin was amazed at the level of control this young woman had on her crew. Each member had a task and had set about it without direction. Catapults were being loaded and secured.

"Capt'n they're preparing to fire." Gwen narrowed her eyes and then shook her head, "Stand down." The crew instantly obeyed though there were a few odd looks. "They are too far out to hope to hit us, they know that." As expected, the ballistic fired way off course plunging harmlessly in the water. "It's Konrad."

"Konrad?" Dayin questioned. "An ally. We were to meet two days ago. It seems I am running late, and he came looking."

Dayin watched Gwen's face as she watched the

ship drawing near. He looked back out to sea at the oncoming ship. "Have you known him long?"

"Aside from my crew, he is my greatest friend. He has saved me more than once and has always managed to show up just when things are at their worse."

"I'll leave you to it then. I'm going to speak with Lady Savane." He turned with the dismissive nod of her head as she watched the oncoming ship. He was almost to the stairs when Gwen seemed to have recalled the conversation they had been having before the ship had come into view.

"Dayin, what Theries did seems beyond horrible to you. I would ask you what led you to that moment. Just because he poisoned the blade Dayin, you still stood to face him, you still fought with honor. It wasn't you."

"Thank you, Captain. I understand your message and I am grateful that you spoke your thoughts. Now, go greet your friend. I am better for our conversation."

Dayin walked down the narrow corridor of the ship's hull to the rooms that lay beneath, slowing in the dim light when he saw Theries. Dayin felt his spine stiffen and knew that Theries saw it. "How is your sister?"

"She's hurting but will be fine, I am certain. She has always denied injury when we were young." Theries watched Dayin as he looked in at Balae. Her head was cast back against the wall with her eyes closed. There was a slight tremble in her hands that seemed completely involuntary as her body dealt with the pain.

"I know you didn't approve, but we would have all died and your Lady would have been at the mercy of that madman."

"Why does everyone think that that is a consolation for compromising your beliefs. If Lynstrom had willed our survival, we would have made it out?"

"We did. It wasn't Lynstrom, it was me." Dayin snorted in disgust as Theries closed the door to Balae's room, blocking his sister from Dayin.

"You can say all the prayers you want Dayin, in the end, faith is a matter of obligation. Your god sets you on a path, perhaps. But he will not send the hosts of the house of Gods to rescue you if you fail, he'll just set someone on another path. Look at your Lady's mother. Did you ever consider that perhaps that is the very reason I am with the lot of you? I will always do whatever it takes to end this as I believe it is meant to end. I will never let anything compromise that." Dayin shoved past Theries his heart pounding with anger and frustration. For the first time, he felt Savane's anger toward Theries.

Dayin stood outside the door to Savane's quarters for a few moments, letting the anger fade and his breath return. He tapped lightly on the door and was greeted by Danica. Her eyes were focused, but her face was blackening from her battle. She had easily faced five or more men in that hall and all she had to show for it was a heavily bruised face and a slight limp on her right side.

"Are you well Danica?" She nodded and turned her attention back to Savane who sat listless on the floor. Her eyes had taken on a ghost-like expression as she stared to the ground.

"My lady?"

She started, her eyes snapping up toward him. "They tried to kill you all. I led you into a trap."

"Did you?" Her eyes took on a hurt expression. "It was a trap set by them, but you my lady, were only going home."

She leaned forward and reached up to him. He drew in a deep breath and knelt down to her. "I don't want this Dayin, this book, this mantle, this path," she choked on her words as he embraced her, holding her in his arms. She felt his strength wrapped around her, seeping into her. She felt a moment of shame as the tears once again stung her eyes.

"No more tears Lady, this is a new day and you must stand. From here on, move forward knowing that there is no way to go back. Whatever the reason, whoever we are to become, take a breath, and let us become it."

He smoothed her hair as the tears that had threatened to fall dried in her eyes. "In the beginning I had serious doubts about this tale you were weaving, the Scorched God returning and who he may be, but my reservations have been silenced. We have no choice but to believe that what that book says is truth."

Savane took a deep breath and stepped back from his embrace despite her desire to stay forever within it. "What do we do now?" He smiled down at her and tugged lightly on her braid. "We follow your book."

Chapter Sixteen

The Empress had a soft smile on her lips as she idly combed her hair with her fingertips. I was certain she didn't even realize that she had stopped her story. She was so lost within it. To watch her in that calm, when I was beginning to understand the panic that her life had been, was peaceful. So, I stared at the statues before me and enjoyed the silence. The air had warmed and filled the garden with the sense that winter did not have the hold we thought it had. The sun however had once again begun its decent and soon the air would chill, thoughts of warmth would be banished into the night.

The Empress returned to herself and looked to me with a smile that may have been tinged with embarrassment.

"It seems I was lost a moment there, Sir Rolen, my sincere apologies."

"No need. It was relaxing." She placed her hand on mine as I placed the quill down. "Perhaps we can have dinner now?"

She nodded as I stood and helped her up. She wrapped her furs once again around her shoulders and we made light conversation on our way to dine.

Every moment I spent with this magnificent woman filled me with a sense of purpose. She carried herself and shaped her conversations in such a way that you felt more than yourself having spoken with her.

When we finally settled back to speak of the past, she seemed lively and energetic. I put the parchment on my lap, pulled the quill and uncorked the ink only to see her watching me with most peculiar smile.

"What is it?"

She shook her head softly, motioned toward the parchment. "Let's continue."

"We spent a fortnight sailing to Osmadante. I spent nearly all that time reviewing pages upon pages of notes detailing what I thought would be the next challenge in the puzzle. My mother had found a man who had a map that was said to lead to a vault containing godly treasures. She had circled it as though she had intended to travel there. I remember feeling as a dog chasing his tail and felt that were I to mention it to the others they would not hesitate to tell me so. As it would have it, we would all be willing to chase our tails together."

Danica spent each moment we were on that ship in my company below deck. She had still no love of sailing and was very content to conceal that weakness from the crew.

Everything I thought about this journey I poured out to her and she listened with such calm understanding. It was she who made me tell the others of the hunt I wanted to undertake.

Savane sat at the end of the bench in the galley of the ship. She could hear the crew above deck and the horse in his stall. The water lapping against the frame and the people in the rooms adjacent to the galley talking, planning. She looked to Danica who sipped at her soup, knowing that it would not be the last time she would be seeing it. Savane eyed her with sympathy. "Can you truly hear things far away?"

Danica nodded miserably and then looked up suddenly. "Yes, I can." She blurted. She took on a look of concentration. "I can hear land." Savane smiled at the ridiculous grin Danica revealed. "How far?"

"That, I don't know, but it's close." Her smile was infectious. This woman who never showed emotion, seemed so awkward with her blatant excitement for the land. Savane stared at her with a smile of her own. Moments later they heard the call of land from the crew and within hours the two ships were docked parallel in the harbor of Osmadante's capital. Only a short distance from where Gwen had grown up.

Konrad and Gwen went to the dock hand as easy friends. She spoke and he listened with a warm satisfied smile. They were comfortable in each others company and the hard exterior she had displayed on the ship melted away in his presence.

The ship's crew finished docking the ship and helped Dayin's horse out of the brig. The beast remained still and passive as Braxus hoisted it up with the deck crane. Danica seemed more impatient with getting off the ship then the horse, Dayin watched her and looked back at Savane.

"Seems she is anxious to get earth beneath her feet." He smiled. Savane nodded and made her way to the ladder that Danica stood next to.

"Don't wait for us Danica." She looked over the side then back to Danica who wore the look of an excited child. "We'll be along in a moment.

Danica threw herself over the ladder and climbed down, jumping the last few steps to land gratefully on the dock. Savane watched as the thoughts seemed to pass through Danica's mind. She began to smile again as she made her way to the end of the dock to where the ground was solid.

"If we put her on another boat again anytime soon, I think she will rise against us." They smiled at each other before gathering the last of their things and making for the gangplank where Theries stood looking out over the water as he waited for his sister. He regarded Savane with his cool gaze and watched where Danica had gone.

"What are your intentions now?"

She looked at him a moment. "I have an idea of where I am going, you need not feel obligated to maintain the illusions you have over the past month Prince. You owe me nothing." He stared out over the winding dirty streets of the port city and seemed pensive. In that moment without the darkness that usually consumed his face, he was so handsome.

"Ahhh, My Lady, you owe me." Just like that he returned to himself and stepped off the boat and onto the gang plank.

"Why try?" Dayin whispered. Savane shrugged and placed her book bag over her shoulder before taking steps to follow the others.

"There are moments that it seems that it is all an act and that beneath, he is no different than you or I. As though his father has demanded something of him that he feels he cannot achieve without the hardened exterior, the mask he wears."

Dayin watched as he and Balae walked together down the dock. She spoke and he listened with a lingering smile that he seemed to reserve for his sister alone. Even when she casually touched him, he would behave in a fashion that one would expect from a brother. To all others he was entirely different.

"I would not expect him to deviate far from what he presents to us M'lady, he is what we see. If you allow yourself to believe otherwise, you may perhaps be hurt more when he displays his true intentions." She adjusted her shoulder strap and stepped down onto the gangplank following the rest of them.

She was just coming up to Danica when the young man from the ship raced passed her and skid to a stop at his captain. Whatever he told her drove Gwendolyn's eyes to the horizon and to a ship that was making to dock at the end of the slip. It was a great hulking ship that in the light of the day appeared to have canons and ballistics along each end of the ship. The figurehead portrayed a beautiful woman whose body and face were ravaged by death. Bones peaked through torn ribs, her clothes tattered to the point beyond modesty and her tortured eyes were cast to the heavens in silent plea for mercy.

Dayin stared at the ship, its crew busily scurrying about the deck in preparations to dock.

"By Lynstrom, that ship is…"

"It's the Reaper, Dirk's ship." Gwen had resumed composure and stood behind them on the edge of the dock.

"It is the largest ship on any of Shoanne's seas and by far the deadliest. We need to finish up here so that we can make our way to the front end of the city before they come ashore. They won't stray far from the docks."

Theries seemed intrigued by the expression on Gwen's face and watched a moment as she seemed very intent on the crew of her own ship. They were busy on the deck before they all seemed to disappear below.

"Should we be concerned?"

"Only if you plan on staying there." She turned on her heel and started into town, Konrad and Braxus on her heels, trying to keep up with her determined pace.

"We seem to be developing a bit of a knack for getting into troublesome situations." Theries looked toward Balae and fell into step beside her as she followed the pirates.   "Where are we going Gwendolyn?" Savane called.

"To an inn. I want a bath and a hot meal. I'll worry about that..." she hooked her thumb toward the Reaper, her voice laced with annoyance, "...after."

The road that they traveled on was crowded with merchants and traders all calling out their wares with excited voices to draw people in. Were it not that the memory were so fresh, the road would have reminded Savane of home. She kept close to Dayin who marched in silence with his horse tethered to a lead. He had insisted that Balae ride. She had already ignored the priest once and he was certain she would again. He tried to at least increase her idle time as best he could. The fact that the whole town was built on a steep incline to protect the upper-class homes from flooding notwithstanding.

The inn they stopped at was a massive old looking place that towered over most of the homes close to it. It had a beautiful carved staircase with knot wood balusters at the base. The finish gave it a regal feel that seemed to carry on to the interior. The hay on the floor was fresh, the air smelled of food and spices instead of the smoke and urine that Savane was unfortunately becoming accustomed to.

"Ensure you select rooms on the lower levels, we may need an exit strategy." With that the Pirate and her first mate and the charming Konrad slipped into the dining hall to sit together for a meal. Savane stood next to Danica and Balae as they waited for Dayin to return from stabling the horse.

"Where are we going to find coin to stay in taverns and stable horses? We have nothing." Balae shook her head, don't worry on that." As though planned Theries produced a small purse of coin that he dropped into his sister's hand. "Where did you get that?"

"I exchanged one of my gems." He said with indifference. Savane looked at the bag of coin and stared up at the prince's' sister. Theries had already wandered inside when Savane's expression made Balae turn to her with one raised eyebrow.

"No matter how you feel about him. He will have his way in all things, so stop trying to make it harder on us will you. He has very little value for coin and therefore will not consider this a debt."

"Who won't consider what a debt?" Dayin came in squinting from the sharp contrast of the bright day outside to the dimness of the inn. He carried the faint scent of the stables and horses on him as he took his place beside the ladies.

Savane looked toward Theries and motioned toward the purse in Balae's hand.

"It seems the Prince is funding our expedition to follow my mother's clues."

Danica looked to Dayin and then nodded her head to Savane, "You watch your Lady, I will watch the horse."

"I've paid for the horse." Dayin protested.

"I'll get it back." Both Dayin and Savane flinched as Danica walked out of the Inn.

"Go with her Dayin."

Danica was only a few paces away when Dayin fell into step beside her. "Get the money back for the horse and pay for her room." Dayin shook his head.

"Danica they won't give back the coin." She turned her gaze toward him but kept an easy pace to the stables. "Let's see."

Dayin walked in the stables and looked to the stable master.

"I seem to be leaving sooner than expected." The man was an older slovenly looking man with dark greasy hair and crooked eyes that made Danica instantly question his bloodline. She had heard of the dark gifts of Vetis and how it could appear in malformations of the body. He regarded Dayin with a calm smile and nod of his head.

"I'll saddle him for you." He turned away and lumbered toward the stall he had put Dayin's horse.

Danica watched. Moving around the stalls to keep her watchful gaze on this man, who busily set to the task that was asked of him. He spoke in a calming voice to Dayin's horse that set Danica at ease, if this horse was calmed by this abomination then perhaps Danica was wrong to judge.

Within moments she had reassumed her place at Dayin's side. "Why do you look shamed Danica?"

"I swear he was a concern, but it seems your horse is a better judge than I am."

The man made his way from the stalls with Dayin's horse saddled and ready to go.

"I'll fetch your coin sir,"

Dayin watched him leave and looked to Danica, "Perhaps you frightened him." She narrowed her eyes and focused her hearing, listening to the man as he walked to the front of the stables to where a girl, a young woman counted coins to him.

"Why must you take back the coins," She muttered, "The knight isn't staying." His voice was calm and quiet. Not laced with the anger that Danica thought he would carry.

He returned counting the coins from one hand to the other that he had wiped on his pants, which were none to clean to begin with.

"Here you are Sir, I am sorry to have kept you waiting, you have a beautiful horse." Dayin took the coins and looked to Danica. She still had an intent gaze upon the man as though he were a monster hidden in the dark that she was trying to see. He tugged on the reins and nudged Danica at the same time to break her from whatever trance he had leveled on her and the two left the grimy stables behind.

"So why do you want to take my horse and stay in the wilderness that you do not even know, with an animal you are not even fond of?"

Danica looked to the trees that surrounded the city. There were no walls, no high gates like the castles she had been to in Abarris, but the city itself was a prison. Her ears hurt from all the voices, her nose burned from all the smells and worse of all the ground beneath her feet was a mix of heavily compressed earth and stone. Here in this place she could feel nothing of Peiashchic, that all by itself was reason enough to leave.

"I will wait for you outside this city. Your horse

will be safe with me and should you need to leave quickly as the pirate said, this way you need not go back for him. See the tree that stands taller than the rest? I will wait there till dawn, if you have not made your way there by then, I will find you."

"These are Resnick's lands. If you hunt you will be tried for poaching." He scanned the docks below for stocks and spotted a man hanging in a cage, his bones protruding beneath his thin sunburned skin. Life clinging to him in a painful mockery.

"There," Dayin motioned for her to note the method of punishment in Resnick's lands. "He's an unscrupulous overlord, capable of monstrous acts of cruelty." Dayin's voice was barely a whisper. The wrong ears would condemn him.

Danica eyed the man being guarded by a soldier. "He has him guarded for fear someone may try to free him?"

"No, he is guarded to prevent others from putting an end to his misery."

Danica watched a moment, her jaw clenching in disgust. "He seems a coward to me."

They stopped outside the inn that Gwendolyn

had selected for them to stay at. The only vision of anything beautiful in an otherwise dull and dirty street. The dust and haze shadowing its lovely presence.

"Never underestimate a coward Danica, in your lands your enemies are plain and out about it,"

"Not all of them," she interrupted, "here they are all your allies until you are no longer of use. Be careful you are not fooled." Danica eyed the man in the cage and then looked to the hand that held the reins of the horse.

"I shall go, you go and pay for your lady's room and food, do not allow her to further in debt herself to the Prince. He casts a long shadow and I would rather she not stand in it."

With that she turned and made her way to the center road that led out of town to the heavily forested lands that outlined the city border. Dayin replayed her words in his head as she had said them. Theries did cast a long shadow. What a perfect way to relate how he felt to words. He stared at Danica as she disappeared into the throngs of people. None touching her as she walked. Some even going out of their way to avoid her. He shook his head and entered the inn. What a strange time that they were caught in that he trusted this tribal barbarian over a prince from his own lands.

Danica watched the people dart around her with an ever-growing amusement. None spoke to her and none offered her their wares. It was the most silence she had experienced since arriving in this rat-infested city. She watched as dirty children ran past her with none of the fear of their elders. Stopping only after they had passed and staring at her sunburned skin and dark auburn hair tied in thin braids around her head. She was unlike the Southerners and she knew what they saw. All the stories their parents had told them came to life in her visage and they ran.

She walked next to the horse with calm confidence as she drew closer to the edge of the city. Guards stood in small coteries at the ends of the streets.

They were the ones making her skin itch with caution, the ones whose heartbeats were pounding from their chest with anticipation of a battle. Their scent was a whole other revelation. They watched her with wandering eyes. Danica assumed that killing the few that surrounded her would be easy, but the number that would come to claim "justice" would be another matter. She watched the guards gaze at her from the corner of her eyes and winced inwardly as a small group began to follow her. She was not

even a few paces from there when she was surrounded. There were eight in total, half of which
seemed uncertain of their choice.

Danica stopped the horse and stayed still. She
watched the one who instigated the delay. He
smelled unwashed and of days old wine, women
and other filth. He was dressed far better than
the others in his command but had only the
smallest hold on the men in his company.

"What are you doing here barbarian. Are you
lost? It would seem the southern sun doesn't
agree with your northern skin." He drew closer
to Danica, assaulting her senses further. He
stood so close that she could smell his rotten breath and the wine he had drank to hide
it. With so little distance between them, the
guards that surrounded her had no idea the
weapon she was holding to the officer's man-
hood. He was brazen enough to place a hand on
her shoulder and lazily let it fall along her front.

"What are you doing here I said?"

"Unhand her." The voice behind her was commanding and unfamiliar but it stilled the blade
that was about to be embedded to the hilt in this
one's eye.

Danica did not move to see who it was that came

to the guards rescue, instead she waited until he fell into her line of sight. He was of a medium build with all the pretty features of the south. His clean brown hair was tied back but falling in wavy curls around his face. His clothes were rich looking though worn often and at his side was a weapon Danica was certain was a sword only it seemed more a sewing needle with a wide ornate handle.

"I am on my way to tend to Lord Resnick at the wedding, should I inform him that his guards are accosting the lords and merchants' servants now? Stand down sir, thank you for the fabulous job you are doing here in the city."

The guard was bewildered as the other man started to walk next to Danica. The two walked in silence for a few paces before he looked at her and smiled.

"My apologies, not a very good first impression. My name is William and I intend to see you out of this place, else you may find yourself in a similar situation. It wasn't always thus. It was once a very good city." He eyed her carefully a moment then seeing no interest in her eyes fell silent beside her. "You do speak the southern language do you not?"

"Yes"

"So why are you still silent? The threat is gone."

"I was not in any danger William,"

"They would have hunted you for killing their men."

Danica stopped the horse and looked at him. "You are wanting gratitude?" She said flatly. "My lady would be happy that you prevented the unwanted attention, she would be grateful."

"Perhaps I will go see her then to stroke my ego, as it seems you are not willing." Danica turned on him a moment trying to identify the words in her language. William put his hands in the air, "An expression Northerner, not an insult."

Danica pulled away, suddenly aware of several people in the street whose hearts raced with the moment she had confronted him.

"You have your own men." She said flatly. He looked bewildered a moment at her acknowledgement of his concealed people.

"I never travel alone, that is true, but I mean only to see you out of this city without Resnick's men taking you to the stocks."

She watched the men that walked around them in a distant circle along the streets. One of which was a woman whose expression was familiar to the look Balae wore, perhaps even Danica herself from time to time, one of protective fearlessness.

"Where are you going in these lands? You are far from home."

"I am where I need to be." she breathed.

He let out a free-spirited laugh that drew Danica's attention.

"I suppose you are little wolf."

Her eyes snapped wide toward him, startling him. "What did you call me?"

"Little Wolf, you are a child of the north are you not?" The confusion in his face and the sudden concern made her return her gaze to the forest. William looked at her a moment then stopped, "Good Luck, if you find yourself in need in these lands, speak to any of the commoners the name I gave you and you will find aid. Stay away from the large village north of here, however, there is a wedding filled with all the snakes this nest of a city has."

The woman who had been walking a short distance from William took Danica's place as she moved on.

"That was curious, why help her and risk being discovered like that?"

"It is the cowards that hide from the salvation of common people that have brought these lands to ruin. In truth she was right, I did only save the soldiers' lives this day. She had the lot of them dead in her mind already."

"Are they not all twisted, the Northerners?"

"Well she was a beauty so unless seduction is her weapon, which given her disinterest in me I don't believe it is, I would say the stories of the tainted legion are vastly exaggerated."

Danica tethered the horse to a low hanging branch in the forest that surrounded the village. The slope of the land let her see all the way she had traveled, the coast with its ships, the merchants and their squabbles, the Inn and its fine wooden entrance way. From where she stood, she was a perfect sentry. The noise at least had calmed, and her head was becoming clear. She sat against the tree and pulled the moss into a pile to lay against. She stared up at Lelandra's tear which seemed to be almost directly above them, though perhaps it was north, where the snakes were congregated.

Chapter Seventeen

It took Dayin a few moments for his eyes to adjust after he entered the Inn. Savane, Theries and Balae sat apart from Gwendolyn and her small crew. Savane reading her book while Balae drank ale and Theries seemed to observe everything with catlike perception. Including the purse at Dayin's side that had been refilled with the coin from removing the horse from the stables.

When he joined their table, Savane brighten with the sight of him. "Is our Northern companion perched safely on the hill?"

"By now I suspect so. She was very intent on not staying here." He made eye contact with the Innkeeper and motioned for service.

"Not so strange, I would think our walls feel like prisons to her." Savane closed her book.

"She knows more then she lets on. She seems to have a great understanding of things in the south." The Innkeeper set food before Dayin and smiled. He was a kindly looking man with reddish brown hair that was turning gray at the sides. His beard was well groomed and his clothes though worn and stained were clean. "Will you be staying the night, Sir?"

"The Lady and I require a room please." The inn-keeper nodded and made his way back to the counter to fetch the keys. He stopped several times to talk to his patrons and refill their tank-ards before he returned.

"That is a man who truly loves what he does." Dayin smiled, admiring the easy presence of the man.

"It is a rare sort that are so content in this place." Balae retorted. "If you think my brother a prick, you need to meet the man who claims regency over this land. He makes the indifference my brother expresses look like genuine love "

Dayin let his eyes scan over the room until they fell on Gwen and her two companions. Despite Braxeus obvious mixed blood the inn seemed accustomed to him, for none in the room eyed him with caution. The two ship captains seemed to talk endlessly and only stopped to ac-cept more ale and food. It was a comfortable room that felt like home. Gwen had already said this place was corrupt, yet they were all so con-tent.

"Why the furrowed brow Dayin?" Balae took a bite of her stew-soaked bread.

"Curious about how they are able to enjoy this place so completely when they're in a town that bears the scars of oppression, yet this place is untouched."

Theries sat down and placed a glass of wine before him.

"This place is untouched because the owner is the uncle of the regent, and a silent supporter of the man who his nephew absconded the regency from. Of course, most people do not know the true regent as he is only just coming of age. Nearly every southern port town and domain has been at one time wrestled from the true blood lines and been divided for the powers who serve the tyrants. Osmadante, Ashmore and Seneen, they are all ruled by lesser nobles with great ambition. That, Sir Dayin is why I say the Gods falter. Even their blood has failed."

"Once upon a time, it was enough to be gifted the Gods-blood to sit upon a throne, but blooded people became complacent and acquired a sense of entitlement. They have forgotten that they won those thrones on the battlefield and by using their blooded gifts to make them leaders. Gods died to make them kings." He took a sip of his wine and a melancholy smile surfaced "It seems now that kings are dying to rebirth a God."

Savane's head snapped up from the book on her lap.

"Did you read that in my book?"

Confused, Theries looked to the book then back to her eyes. "No, I am merely assuming that is the case."

"My mother says that very thing."

"Well then, it would seem we are on the right path, what does she say we are to do next?" There was a tone in his voice that Savane could not decipher, mocking or supremacist either way she chose to ignore it.

She watched the room and then turned her attention back to the Prince.

"She writes about a map to a vault that contains Godly treasures. I am not certain what things are there. She refers to the weapons used in the battle on the bone fields, but I can only assume that if she had intended to venture there that perhaps we should."

"Godly treasures? Are you not thinking that it seems a little too much like a child's fairy tale?"

Savane shook her head and turned to the page in the book, images, renderings of a sword, a dagger and several other small weapons or charms lined the pages.

"Most of the weapons belonged to the warriors themselves. When their essence was transferred and they became Gods, they were collected off the battlefield and stored in a vault. But this sword," She tapped the drawing, "this was Lynstrom's. My mother believed it had the power to sever the tie of men from their Gods, including that of the new Gods from the old, it would have the power to render Lynstrom and all the new gods mortal. With the exception of one."

Balae's eyes darkened, the room around her seemed to shrink with the single thought of him. She felt the throbbing in her shoulder and rubbed it absently to restore feeling. "Can he truly have that kind of power? That he can not only rise from the deadlands but breech them and restore himself to his godly existence?"

"Perhaps not on his own, but those riders are blooding the nobles for some cause and we can only assume that it is this." Savane eyed Balae as she absently rubbed her shoulder. "Does it hurt?"

Balae shook her head, "No, but I think the memory is still too fresh and brings about an odd sensation with the mention of him."

Theries stared down at the book. His eyes scanning over the writing and searching for any clue on which direction to take from the thief infested port city in Osmadante.

"What about the prophecy we are currently following? What relevance does this union that we are chasing have? "

The excitement fizzled out from Savane's eyes. Dayin looked at her perplexed before looking back to Theries. "That star is in the heavens for some reason and finding the cause or its meaning may have to wait. This," he placed his finger on the sword in the middle of the page, "this is important."

"We are less than a day away from this wedding. We'll investigate whether it is the blessed union so spoken of, or if it is another false hood with no relevance to the challenges we face." Dayin watched the captains as they spoke to each other at the other table. Gwendolyn had an odd posture as though she were being told ill news, but there was no way to ascertain what words were spoken without the gifts that Danica possessed.

Dayin looked to Savane and excused himself from her company. The two captains and Braxus seemed immersed in conversation when Dayin approached the table fell silent.

"Sir Drake?

"Gwendolyn, may I have a word?" Gwen glanced to Konrad in apology and stood while he sat back nonchalantly in his chair, continuing his conversation with Braxus. He had an easy presence with a warm expression that put Dayin at ease about who he was.

The tavern was loud and boisterous so the two walked to the hall and sat upon the staircase to the inns second floor.

"What can I do for you sir?" He glanced around the room from where they sat and satisfied that they were in privacy he folded his hands together then looked to the floor.

"We are going to the wedding North of here and then planning to pursue something that may require a great deal of travel. I am not certain we will be able to get the head start we require when we leave this place. Can I trust you to wait for us?"

"Ask what you want to ask Sir Drake, better yet, let me tell you what I know you want to ask. By now you must have questioned how a woman can maintain control of a crew of men at sea. My crew have a great of loyalty to me. As I mentioned before, some years ago I acquired my ship and my crew when my father, the previous captain of my ship, was murdered by the man that captains the Reaper. He is a horrible man who follows the orders of Lord Resnick and does not hesitate to elaborate on those orders. He is a dangerous man Sir Drake. So, if Resnick is at this wedding in the North, I can only assume it is why his dog has come to port. I intend to go with you to this wedding Dayin and it maybe I who requires the head start you speak of."

Dayin looked into the eating hall and watched the table that Konrad and Braxus sat at, "and Konrad?"

A smile crossed the captain's lips as her gaze followed Dayin. "I remember the distrust you feel. I once felt that for everything and everyone I met. Konrad changed that for me. He has been my friend and ally in my search to destroy Dirk. We all have our reason for standing against tyranny and in my case, it was what Dirk did to my family. In Konrad's case it is what Resnick is capable of doing to his. Resnick has Konrad's daughter. We don't know where, only that he does. We know that Dirk is the only other person that knows where she is. Resnick uses her as leverage to control Konrad. You need not worry about his loyalty."

"Are you not afraid Resnick will set the two of you against each other?"

Gwen's strong presence relaxed and Dayin could see the emotion underneath the anger and rage "I was just a little girl when Dirk killed my father, they left my mother and I, raped, beaten and broken, ready to die, I am certain that Dirk has no idea who captains the Angry Maiden. The ship was renamed and changed from my father's days. To him I am just another ship on the water."

Dayin's disgust with Gwendolyn's circumstances darkened his features to the point that Gwen almost laughed and placed a hand on his shoulder. "You see sir knight; you may think that you are not significant in this game and that your life is less important than your honor. But I can tell you from being on the other side of men without honor, that you are what stands between them and her." she motioned toward Savane.

"Do not ever assume she will be fine without you."

Konrad stood with a smile taking a bag of coins that Braxus had offered to him and patted him on the shoulders before walking to where Dayin and Gwendolyn had seated themselves at the stairs. He had a grace about him that was born of confidence. His long hair was tied back. Though they had been at sea for some time, his care and consideration for his attire was evident. He could easily have been mistaken for a noble. He stopped at Gwen's feet on the stairs and looked to Dayin. "Can I sweep her away now?"

Surprised and a little uncomfortable with being asked, Dayin nodded and stood. Before he could offer a hand to Gwen, Konrad had scooped her up and made his way up the stairs. "Good night Sir Drake. Rest well, you'll need it." He watched them ascend to the first landing and listened as laughter came through the door they had secreted themselves behind.

Dayin watched for a moment longer before he turned his attention back to Savane's table. He walked over and stood at the end of it. "If we are leaving in the morning, we may want to consider an early night. This is not likely to be a good night's rest." Dayin looked at the lively state the tavern was in, all manner of the city's people were gathered in good spirit and laughter.

Savane looked up from her mother's book and watched as the room around her seemed so happily cloaked in ignorance. "Fair enough Sir Drake." She closed the book and looked to Balae and Theries. Who both held their drinks in their hands, Theries lowered his as Dayin made to pull the chair for Savane. "Just because we are a long way from Abarris that does not mean that thieves would not be happy to find out what value she holds. Do not tempt fate." The high arch in Balae's brow told Dayin that she agreed with her brother. With a deep sigh he conceded and resigned himself with simply carrying her book instead. Savane stared at the siblings and tightened her cloak around her shoulders.

"The two of you can share a room this evening Theries, rather then you enjoying one to yourself. Since we are all such common folk, no need to play at propriety." Balae choked back laughter as she swallowed her ale and looked to her brother. "You are long passed proper Savane." He smiled and sipped the last of his wine, his amusement glittering in his eyes. Savane turned incredulous and started up the stairs with Dayin on her heels.

The rooms on the first level had balconies that led to the streets below. From where she was Savane could see the docks alight with nightlife at the bottom of the road they had traveled and a glance in the other direction she could see the forest that surrounded the city. "I wonder if Danica can hear and see me now." She stared into the trees in wonder. "You know that she can." Dayin stood behind her at the threshold.

The air had cooled in the last few days. He looked to the North where Danica had gone and wondered if she would be warm enough and then almost laughed when the realization of where she was from dawned on him.

He wrapped Savane in her cloak and then leaned against the wall. She glanced back in gratitude and pulled her hair free of the braid that had been thrashed by the winds at sea for days. She gently tugged at snarls and tangles, her mind drifting to Lyselle and wondering where her Lady had gone, or even if she lived.

Dayin watched her posture change and looked up at the sky to Lelandra's tear.

"The world we know is changing Dayin and I am afraid of how I will change with it."

"The world we know is gone my Lady and you have already become stronger for it. Everything will work out. Come get some sleep." Savane turned to go back inside, she glanced over her shoulder toward the trees. "Good night Danica, sleep well."

The horse snorted in the trees drawing Danica's attention from Savane on the balcony of the tavern. From where she stood against the mossy tree, she could see everything. From this distance the ocean beyond the coast looked like the vast empty waste land that she called home. In the darkness Savane was a warm shadow to her eyes and Dayin behind her, warmer still. Her blood was still revealing its gifts to her and she was still unsure that she understood them all.

The one thing that was without a doubt going to take getting used to, was the dreams. The voices, the screams and cries of her village, her keen senses were no less acute in the throes of sleep. All of what had transpired a lifetime ago for her was still as profound and left her unwilling to succumb to sleep at all. Bouts of unconsciousness on the ship were easier to endure, but on the ship, there was little need for mental clarity. Now on land, every moment they were in this port there was the possibility of danger. Danica watched the shadows moving about the port, leaving the tavern and stumbling along the road to home from overindulgences of all sorts. Her people would find their weakness to brewed ales amusing no doubt.

Danica leaned back, pulling her fur over her shoulders and watched the red fire tear streaking in the sky over head. She could only watch for a moment or two before its intensity was too much. But in the moment, she looked away, there was such darkness that she almost felt calm.

A sound in the distance drew her attention, she opened her eyes, still poorly adjusted from staring at Lelandra's tear. She heard the sound of panic and violence, then silence. Danica stood and blinked trying desperately to focus on the origins with her ears alone. But the violence had ended and who ever had been in danger, was no longer.

A shadow crept from a room. Moving with agile grace. There was no colour to whomever it was, only blackness. They were several doors down from Savane's room and further still from the room that Theries and Balae had taken.

The shadow moved along the walls with the confidence of a street rat. Knowing every turn and rail, knowing exactly where they were going. Danica felt her limbs tighten. An awareness that had the threat been to Savane sleeping in her room, she would never reach her in time. So, Danica watched in silence, her jaw clenched and sickened with the realization that she would be helpless to save any one from where she was, perched on the hill. The shadow jumped from one balcony to the next landing on Savane's and Dayin's, lingering long enough to peer through the shutters and watch before moving to the next window and out into the ally below. They know her, Danica thought, why else stop on that balcony.

With the shadow long having disappeared into the dark, Danica felt the fatigue grip her and pull on her eyelids. The last of the streetlights of the city had gone out and with the total darkness her gift of sight was gone. All that remained was the red glow from Lelandra's Tear. She could still hear the voices and from somewhere far away, the lapping of the water along the coast. Suddenly, there was a sound behind her. The sound of trees and branches submitting to boots as someone approached from the North.

They had managed to avoid detection for longer than Danica was comfortable with and when the shadowed figure cleared the trees, Danica froze in silence. The Northern gatherer was tall and wiry looking, his limbs were cords of muscle with the tattoos and scars common to her people. His gaze had an intensity that held Danica in her place as he approached. Her muscles clenched but would not respond to her urge to reach for a weapon. He knelt on the moss beside her, his hawkish features focused as he stared at her.

His breath washed over her like a cool breeze as he whispered to her, "This is mine," he placed one hand against her chest and Danica could feel nails biting into the flesh above her heart. She screamed and felt the cold of his presence recede as nightmares gave way to daylight. Dayin's horse stood above her, his velvet nudging her awake. The city below had come to life and the sounds filled her with relief that not only had day come, but that the presence of the northern gatherer had been her dreams; new nightmares to hound her.

Savane woke to the light streaming through the window. Her eyes focused and watched as Dayin knelt in prayer at the open window. The holy symbol that she had given to him clasped between his hands and his eyes closed while his lips moved in recitation of prayer. She loved to watch him when he didn't know that she did, when he was riding or when he was talking with others. His smile was so warm that she could feel herself smile in return. But this was new, she had seen him in prayer, but he always stopped when she entered the room out of duty or obligation. Now there was none. She stayed as still as she could to avoid disturbing him, watching the sunlight in his long, unbound hair. The scruff on his face had nearly become a beard and examining his face, she was certain that he had grown wearier in the most recent days. His eyes looked tired and his posture, though still impressive, had slumped if ever so slightly. His lips stopped moving. Savane closed her eyes not wanting to be caught gawking at him in so vulnerable a state.

When she heard him rise and gather his things, she stretched her arms above her and opened her eyes in the most convincing display she could manage. If he suspected deception, he said nothing.

"Good Morning My lady," He placed the holy symbol around his neck and walked to a tray of food he had acquired from the kitchen below.

"Real food?" Savane sat up excited. Dayin sat behind her and re-tied the braid that she had loosely gathered the night before. "I am going downstairs, ready yourself and we'll be off. The sooner we leave Osmadante the better. This place is corruption at its core." Dayin stood and walked toward the door. His hand rested on it for a moment as he watched her, motionless in the sunlight. "Did you sleep well?" Her fingertips trailed along her hair where he had braided it. "I almost forgot where I am" he smiled a sad smile and pulled the door open. Savane watched him go before turning her attention to the open window. She got out of the bed and pulled her riding clothes back on. There was a time when she would have cringed at the thought of wearing those clothes, but she had grown fond of the softness of the fabric over the confines of her corsets.

The sky outside had become a beautiful blue, but the air had the crispness of fall. She ate her food while leaning against the balcony casement, staring out into the city that for whatever reason had Dayin so uncomfortable. Her focus was far away in Abarris when a figure on the street below caught her attention. The girl staring up at her must have only reached her tenth year or so. She stood staring at Savane on the balcony, her eyes taking in Savane's surroundings more than she herself. When Savane realized the girl was looking at something above her, she stood on the balcony and turned around. She took a deep breath in when she realized that someone had painted her casement with a red streak that bore a resemblance to the comet in the sky out of blood.

The door to her room opened suddenly, just as she was about to re-enter and made her jump. Her relief must have been apparent because Dayin moved swiftly into the room to gather her and her belongings. The speed to which he moved made Savane sick to her stomach. "What is it Dayin?" She could barely find her voice. "What has happened that you seem so..." A whistle from outside made Dayin look to find Danica, and his horse waiting in the grounds below, an intent look on her face.

"Talk after. Leave now." She called.

Obediently, Savane let Dayin pull her cloak over her hair and pull her from the room. Balae and Theries were also on the move and Gwen and her first mate stood at the doorway while Konrad followed them down the stairs to the door. Savane wanted to yell at them to explain. She felt that sickening memory of the nobles being corralled in Abarris. When she got outside Dayin hoisted her onto his waiting horse and mounted behind her. For the first time since they had been together there was very little concern for propriety. No judgments from Theries came, who seemed to be in the process of concealing himself in his cloaks with his sister and walking a different way than the horse was headed. With a heavy kick, Dayin's horse lunged forward throwing Savane into Dayin's chest.

Savane craned her neck to see what had all of them working so synchronized. The window from the room they had shared was still wide open, the wind blowing the heavy curtains, the blood mark of Lelandra's tear above the casement. Laying dead in the balcony room above were a man and a woman. Their hands clasped in a last attempt to remain united in affection even in death.

Savane felt the panic rise back up inside. Her eyes wide as she stared at Dayin who didn't return her gaze. He knew she was seeking comfort and reassurance, but until he was clear of this city, he had none to offer. Instead he drove the horse harder. He could feel it too. The sense that someone had not only placed the markings over their window but ensured that the two were killed in the room above them. They had sailed for days after they had left Abarris, they had only been in this city the one day and yet someone had found them and knew what they were looking for. Two lovers that would birth the freedom from the darkness.

The pace did not slow until long into the day, the city was far behind them. Dayin had settled into his saddle and Savane leaned miserable against him, her eyes cast to the red fire tear streaking across the sky. Theries and Balae had re-joined them on the ride after procuring horses for the lot of them. Balae watched him as they rode, searching for some sign of emotion or concern, but as always, his face was a blank slate to her.

"You keep staring at me Balae, has travel lost interest for you that you must stare at me instead of where we are going?"

"I am merely aware that there is someone on our heels and wondering why you are unaffected by it."

"If I allowed my emotions to be read upon my face, I would not be an effective king when and if, it ever falls to me to lead my father's kingdom. You see, even the Lady Savane is learning the value in this lesson."

Balae looked to Savane, her eyes cast on the sky, where tears would have once left stains along her cheeks, her face was dry and unmarred.

"It is a sad day when you become that girl's teacher Theries." Theries made a mocking gesture of having been wounded by his sister's words. His horse whined and everyone halted. Danica had crouched down ahead of them and held her hand low to the ground for all to follow. Gwen brought her horse to a halt and dismounted. She watched the direction that Danica was looking but approached Dayin. "The wedding is by invite only," she produced several coins, all of them with ribbons tied to them.

"Your invitations." Dayin stared a moment at the ornamental coins, wondering who they were that they had coins minted for their wedding.

"Settle in here and get ready for the wedding, not all of us are attending."

Savane threw her leg over the side of Dayin's horse and slid into Gwen's arms. "Who do you intend to leave out of this?" She knew Dayin's mind well enough to know that he had no intention of letting her walk right into a wedding that had Resnick and potentially his other nefarious relations.

"You aren't leaving me here?" Theries was already starting to ready himself for the wedding, donning a clean cloak and cleaning his boots smiling as he listened to the exchange between them.

"In all honesty Dayin she is a perfect cover for you, her ability to talk should provide us with ample distraction." Savane absorbed the slight with minimal expression. Balae watched her brother for a moment with a lingering smile. It was his first attempt at doing something nice for her. Even his acts of kindness were mired in insult.

Gwen looked at Braxus, "You, are unfortunately unable to blend," he nodded and took the reins to the horses.

"I will stay with the horses and await your return." Danica watched the grounds of the manor, her eyes scanning, and her ears taking in the music and talking of hundreds assembled within the manor. She looked to Savane and then back to the manor. "I will stay with Braxus. I will listen, if you must depart quickly, look for us there." She pointed to the south western gates of the property which were linked to the estate's temple and cemetery. Savane nodded. "Be safe."

Danica watched as Theries, his sister, Savane and Dayin, Gwen and Konrad walked down the hill. Braxus sat on a rock tethering the horses together to graze. "Will you be able to hear them through the others?" Danica looked down at the hulking giant sitting passive. Pockets and pouches of healing salves and potions across his torso. In the North he would be a normal sight, no one would be afraid of him, but here he was terrifying to any common people. "Their voices are known to me, so easier to hear." She responded. "Why are you a healer?" Braxus smile was a toothy grin that showed his lower fangs. I heal because Shoanne saved me when I was born. She saw fit to let me live, so I help others who need her." Danica thought back to Balae's shoulder and for a brief moment had wished that he had been there for her brother after the bear. "Can you restore life to the dead?" Braxus' smile drifted away from his lips and he took on a lost expression that Danica recognized as regret. "There are healers that are so closely tied to the gods they serve that they can commune with their God and yes, have power over life and death. The practice is grueling and takes its toll on both the one working the spell and the one returning. Some do not survive the spell, while others are haunted by the shadows throughout the remainder of their days. I am not so skilled." He watched the horizon and closed his eyes as a breeze swept across his face. "Is it not an honour to die in battle among your people?"

It was Danica's turn to be stung with regret. "To die in battle, yes, not to be left behind." Danica traced the scars that ran the length of her hands. They were such different hands from the beautiful graceful hands of Savane. She clenched her fist. "What do you know of the tainted bloodlines?" Braxus looked up and focused on Danica's expression. He searched her face a moment for something that Danica was unable to understand then resigned himself. "Is that how you are able to hear the voices of our companions? How you were able to save us back at the tavern before the guard arrived?" Danica nodded her head and let her gaze fall to the ground. "Well, there are two ways of looking at it. The blood in your veins may have the power of a dark God but he, like the other gods, is dead and their essence was transferred to people like you. Some would believe that you can do as much good as you wish only to have it undone when the darkness calls to you. You will defile all that you have fought for in surrendering to the power in your veins. I believe that you are not only made up of blood Danica, there is so much more than just that."

Danica sat beside Braxus, letting his words sink in and the world around her drift away so she could absorb everything that was happening around Savane.

The invitations that Braxus had been able to obtain worked perfectly to let the six of them in. Savane and Theries, against both their wills, played the part of themselves. As though their wedding had taken place, complete with their entourage while Gwen and Konrad fell easily into the role of merchants and traders.

The court of Osmadante contained an obscene

abundance of wealth that was flaunted in every conceivable way. The food was laid out in vast amounts. More than the attendants could possibly consume, and the dress and decor left even Theries appearing middle class. Savane watched the expression on Theries face as he circled the room of people, trying to gauge what persona to adopt to avoid his viperous retorts. With Dayin and Balae playing as the noble couple s escort, she was at a loss of how to behave. Theries was talking to the guests as though he truly had a place among them. Learning about the bride and groom with the most subtle queries and never to the same group of people. He moved in and out of groups watching for who shied away from conversation with whom. "You have a gift for hiding in plain sight Theries, it's remarkable to watch." His gaze fell to the floor as it often did between them and then he lifted his dark green eyes to her own.

For a moment there was a softness in his eyes. Savane believed that he had never received a genuine compliment that he sought to hear. He raised her hand to his lips in husbandry fashion and then the cool ego returned to his gaze, leaving her fully aware that he was the master of playing the part to attain a goal. Most opportunities to banter back and forth between them were seized by Theries at every turn. This silence left both Dayin and Balae wondering what

Theries was trying to learn while communicating with the people in the ballroom.

It was shortly after the dinner had been served that Theries leaned back to his sister and whispered something for only her to hear. Savane watched as she blanched and then a smile whispered across her face. She stood back beside Dayin and Savane could hear them discussing their departure. Theries noticeably leaned forward to watch as Resnick was greeted by two well-dressed, but sun weathered individuals, that were very much in line with the look of Gwendolyn's adversaries.

Danica sat forward on the rock she had occupied for past hour while listening to the exchanges between Theries and the members of the wedding. Braxus started with the sudden movement then stood. "What is it?"

"They recognize Konrad, they know he wasn't invited." She grabbed his proffered forearm and stood looking balefully at the horses, knowing that she would once again be forced to ride one.

The moment that Resnick spoke with the two men, Gwendolyn was already excusing herself from the company of men surrounding her. She slid her arm happily into Konrad's and the two were walking for the door when Resnick sent guards to intercept them. Savane felt Dayin reach for her and started as she and Theries were pulled apart by Balae and Dayin trying to maximize the targets. They turned down one hall while she was certain that the prince and Balae went through the servant's kitchen. Dayin's familiarity with the way an estate was run made it an easy escape into the western grounds and cemetery. Dayin waited for the others, or guards in silence, but they remained alone.

Balae turned down a corridor with her brother casually following behind. His manner, calm, as he adjusted the cuffs of his tunic. "You slide in and out of personas like they are clothes to don. How are you so calm?" He placed a hand on her sword arm as a guard ran past them in the corridor. "Because I think of who I am in moments like these, while you think of who Resnick is. Be calm sister. Our door is right there." He looked ahead and heard the voice of the guard returning. Theries stopped in a hallway and put a finger to his lips for her not to reveal his location. He all but disappeared in the darkness of the doorway while his sister remained visible.

"Where is the man you were with?" he looked further down the hall. "My Lord? He was meeting with a girl. He didn't want his wife to suspect." Balae was unsure how Theries had managed to get behind the soldier but the moment

325

he knew, it was too late. Theries blade was deep in the man's lungs from under his arm. Balae stood in awed silence as the man died silently before her. "Because he didn't see it coming, doesn't change its necessity. The door." The two slid through the door and down the stairs into the courtyard below to Savane and Dayin waiting in the cemetery.

Gwendolyn's heart had already started to pound the moment they were discovered, but she didn't think it would be Konrad that gave them all away. They ran through the staircases, using the panicked guests as obstacles for the guards in pursuit. At the base of the rounded stairs was a small gathering of the pirates from Dirks crew in the center of the gathering was Dirk. Gwendolyn's throat clenched as she held her breath. "He doesn't see you yet." Konrad whispered as he passed in front of her to draw Dirk's attention.

"Well, well privateer, I don't remember you being on the invitations."

"I could only assume I had been forgotten, so I saw to obtaining my own invite."

"I thought that was your boat in the water. Is this your Maiden? The Angry Maiden perhaps?" Konrad stepped in front of Dirks line of sight. "Come, come, Konrad, I thought we were friends. Not going to share?"

The sound of shouting down the halls drew Dirks attention for a moment. "Well, your guest can depart Konrad, but I was looking for you anyway so I would like to have a few words with you." Gwendolyn's hand tightened around Konrad's. "No need for her to delay in her departure, unless you would like us to be better acquainted?" Konrad drew her in and kissed her forehead before releasing her hand with momentum that forced her to the door. "What did you want to discuss?"

Shaking, Gwendolyn was fifteen years old again and her mind grappled with the thoughts of killing him. It would take only a moment to kill Dirk, His crew would kill her for it though and most likely Konrad and his daughter would also pay the price. She walked through the front door to where she could see the cemetery to her right. She walked as though on hot coals, every step as the child that had been so horribly wronged. Her chest pounding and air feeling too thick to breathe, making her vision cloud as she desperately sought for her anchor, her brother. Braxus could see by her stride that the weight of her past had been dropped upon her. He took a few steps away from the group to allow Gwen to see him and only him.

Dayin watched the exchange between the giant and the captain while keeping between Savane and the entrance to the Manor. Dirk was still watching Gwen walking away with absent interest, as though she were a fleeting thought that he was trying to catch. His eyes narrowed and turned cold as Konrad stepped in front of the view once again.

Gwen reached the horses and placed a steadying hand on Braxus. The giant held the moment long enough to give her strength before hoisting her onto her horse. Danica handed her the reins and met her gaze, her face a mask of concentration as she reached beyond the current conversation to hear Konrad. "He knows who you are. You need to ride now! He's sending riders after you. You can't stay here, he figured it out as you walked away."

"What of Konrad?" The pleading look in Gwen's eyes reminded Danica what it was to live completely for someone else. "He's acting surprised and pretending that he never knew who you were to Dirk. He's not in any danger."

"Go! Braxus and I will hold them off."

"I can't let you do that," Gwen was out of breath and shaking.

Danica met her gaze, "They are mounting their horses, there is no time to argue. Protect your crew."

Danica turned to Braxus and the two mounted their horses and veered off the path to get behind Dirk's men as they would assuredly pursue the road ahead. Dayin led the other five down the road as fast as their horses would take them. They would have to make it back and set sail before the crew of the Reaper returned. or they would never clear the harbor before her cannons would send the Angry Maiden and her crew to Shoanne's watery depths.

Chapter Eighteen

Gwen paced the docks, her blue eyes scanning the horizon for any sign of Braxus and the Northern warrior. Relief washed over her as the dust rose up, two horses racing through the streets. One overly large and the other, an inexperienced rider. As they got closer, she called for the crew to ready, watching as Theries finalized the sale of the horses they were riding. He raised his hand to Danica who barely controlled the horse into the awaiting corral. She pulled herself off the horse and eyed it with vehemence. She and Braxus jumped the wooden gate and strode for the docks, meeting Theries along the way. Gwen took a deep breath and climbed the rope to the ship. Theries scanned the horizon, his eyes intent on the roads they had taken before he turned and followed her aboard.

Danica stood on the docks calculating how long a walk it was to their next port. She looked resentfully at the ship that would take them safely back out to sea.

"Are you going to board or just pray for flight" Braxus stood behind Danica on the dock. His large face made less threatening by his large toothy grin. "I would be grateful if there was something in those pouches you wear to induce a slumber while we sailed." Braxus' smile widened as he reached inside to produce a root. "Chew"

The relief on Danica's face brought forth a burst of a laugh from the giant that made her smile as she took the rope ladder, one dreaded step at a time.

Balae sat at the edge of Theries bed watching as he meticulously cleaned weapons. Her eyes trailed along the length of the dagger he had used to kill the guard. Her memory of the way he moved in behind the man and the smooth motion it took to kill him. There was no hesitation, no regret, as though it were practiced hundreds of times. She recalled in their youth, the few times they were together, the torture that lived in his eyes. That look that had endeared him to her and made her the guardian over him even to this day. He had never confided in her the reason behind the ghosts in his eyes. Now, having full awareness of the man he had become, she was beginning to suspect that there was more than training to be a king in his studies. Her eyes regained focus, leaving her memory in the past, he was watching her with his usual intensity.

"Where were you?" She blinked and sighed a deep breath. "When" she responded "Not where, when. I was leagues away at home watching the look in your eyes as a boy."

Theries brows rose, and he paused in the oiling of the blade. "That boy is gone." Balae leaned back on the bed, propping herself up on her arms. "I hope not. He was my brother."

Theries took a breath and met her gaze, a softness replaced his aloof expression. "I will always be your brother Balae, no matter what you may think in the future. That and all it brings with it, will never change."

Savane watched the coast disappearing as they caught the winds in their sails. She watched as the crew busied themselves, including Gwendolyn. Her intensity as she prepared to head out to deep waters had induced calm in her. There was no sign of the panic that she had felt back at the manor. Savane admired her strong will and understood why the pirates of her crew were so easily lead by her. There was no sign of discord as they followed her demands despite being rounded up from whatever pub they had been yanked them from. Now, most of them were focused and content as they worked, oblivious to the threat of Dirk in their wake.

Savane felt a cloak slip over her shoulders as Dayin sat next to her against the barrels. "Do we know where we are going?' "Right now, I think her only priority is clearing this port and disappearing into the ocean. For us, there is a Port city west of here that should be where we find the individual my mother said she entrusted the map to." His eyes scanned the horizon, scanning the seas. For now, it was clear. The bright sun was beginning to dip into the ocean, turning everything a bright gold before them. Dayin stood up and adjusted his cloak around her shoulders. "I'll go talk to Gwen, see if we can get us as close to that port as possible. Do you know its name?"

"Fairhaven" he nodded and turned, swaying slightly with the lurching of the ship and moved toward where Gwen had disappeared behind the captain quarters.

The captain's quarters were littered with books and maps Davin noted as he approached Gwen's quarters. He walked into the room quietly and waited patiently. Her eyes lingered a moment on the pages of the book she was reading before she met his gaze. "Dayin, how is everyone?"

"I was going to ask the same of you. Has your heart settled and stopped racing?" Gwen eyed him a moment. Had it not been Dayin, with his sincere gaze, that asked she may have assumed he meant to mock her. Instead there was a warmth that let her sit back in her chair and nod her head, offering him a seat across from her. "So, I am assuming you are wondering how we are tied together then, now that we are sailing away. Where are we going?"

A smile surfaced as she read his exact purpose for his visit. "There is a port West of Osmadante that Savane believes we need to go to, Fairhaven?" Gwen nodded and took a deep breath, "I know the port. Not a fan of pirates there but that being said, it is a good place to go to put some distance between the Reaper and the Angry Maiden. It's got a narrow harbor pass that limits who comes in and out. They have canons at the pass, Dirk never takes the risk. So, I don't mind the opportunity for peace of mind, and who knows perhaps Konrad will look for me there." Dayin placed his hand on Gwen's shoulder to try and bring her comfort. His grip was gentle, Gwen smiled in the sudden awareness that after a lifetime of guarding herself, his touch didn't cause her to flinch. She met his gaze and let a smile set him at ease. "I am fine Dayin, I can see the concern on your face, and there is no need. I know Konrad, he isn't in any danger, nor would he ever do something to place me back in Dirk's sights. It'll be dark soon Dayin, any chance they had of seeing us on the water will fade with the daylight."

Dayin nodded and left the captain's quarters. He walked down the hall and stopped briefly at Balae and Theries door. The silence within made him carry on down the hall, he tapped on Savane's door and entered. "We are bound for Fairhaven." Savane looked up at him from her book, her eyes were glassy and tired looking. "Why don't you sleep, I'll stay with you." He took her book from her and closed it, placing it beside her hammock.

"You know you are not responsible for everyone's lives."

"I think back to the Duke of Denalin and how he resisted what I had to tell him. If I don't behave like I am responsible for saving their lives, who will?" Dayin softened, "I don't disagree that you have to try, but so do they. You must also take care of yourself, or they don't stand a chance."

The Empress took on that familiar distant look that always came when she had a memory floating in her thoughts that she had not yet shared. Thankfully despite the long day of retelling all she had lived through; she was not yet interested in ending the day.

She pulled her gray furs around her delicate shoulders that had once carried the empire upon them and heaved a breathless sigh. Her eyes focused on mine and a soft smile took her lips.

"Fairhaven, as its name suggests was a port free of pirates and all the scoundrels of the sea..."

Its narrow pass was laden with rocks and sheer cliffs that encompassed the city port. The view from the ship was breathtaking for everyone that had never turned into the concealed pass that ferried you to the city. It had massive ballista that were positioned at each of the more prominent narrow passageways. Each post had a cadre of men guarding it. Their towers evidence of their presence on duty at all times. Each tower was affixed with signal fire pyres that also lined the long cliff that served as a backdrop to the city. Ancient rock carvings that had fallen to ruin along the walls were the only indication of the citadel having ever experienced an attack. Every other wall and building seemed to almost glimmer.

Danica took a deep breath and looked to Savane, "You certainly know how to make your stone prisons beautiful."

"Why do you always leave us and sleep in the forest when we stop for the night, even in small villages and towns."

"Where I come from there are no stone structures, everything is huts and shelters, only the chief's home was made of wood. Even then, the wind could still be felt moving through it. These homes that you build are too far from the elements for my liking, it makes me feel trapped within it. The sounds are louder without the land to dampen it and the smells are sometimes choking without the air moving them. The forest floor to me is safe and feels powerful whereas the stone reminds me that someone else held the power to construct it."

"We must seem weak to you." Danica stared at her a moment reliving the death of her slave in the north. "I do not measure a person's strength by their origins Savane, I, like you have found far greater meaning in our deeds and actions. I have known greater weakness in the North than in you." Savane smiled and watched as they sailed passed the great walls that surrounded the city.

"Welcome to Fairhaven," Gwen called as she climbed the stairs from below deck. She was dressed in proper attire and had her hair piled atop her head, hanging in long red tresses. "I have friends in this city, but we have to look the part. Merchants, can be as ruthless as the next pirate when they smell competition." She looked toward her youngest crew member and with a nod of her head he slipped over the side of the boat and painted over the Angry Maidens telltale script.

"Mr., Steale, would you be so kind as to guide us through the rocks as only you can."

"Aye, Maiden," he called. He swung himself along rigging and landed like a cat on the navigation deck, barking the orders to cut the sails.

The man was unlike any of the others on the crew. He had the sun bronzed skin of the crew, but his dark brown hair was perfectly tied at the base of his head. His intense blue eyes were trained on the nose of the ship as though he could sense its path and whether or not it was safe. He had an air of confidence about him that bordered on arrogance. He wore it so well that even Savane found herself watching his concentration as he navigated the channel. She wasn't alone in her interest, Balae too watched the pirate, though Savane was certain she was less focused on his level of concentration than she was on his appearance.

The crew busied themselves in preparation of docking as Gwen searched the horizon for any sign that Dirk had pursued them. Savane followed her gaze and shook her head. "He didn't have time to get back to his ship Gwen, it will be alright."

Gwen lowered her gaze and looked at Savane, her purple eyes still filled with naivety and hope. It brought a smile to Gwen's lips as she placed a hand on her shoulder. "Do you know what you have to do here in Fairhaven?"

"There is a map that we need."

Gwen laughed and scanned the city with a wide sweeping gaze. "One map, in all this?" Savane furrowed her brow and looked above her to the fire comet that had stopped being a trusted source of guidance as it was no longer over land but instead had burned a path across the horizon and was leagues out to sea. "I will find it." Gwen shook her head with an amused smile on her lips, "I believe you Savane, I most certainly believe you. I have a friend here in Fairhaven that deals in odd treasures, perhaps he knows something. It's worth a shot."

The port docks were extended and had room for more ships than Savane had ever seen in any one city. The city was beautiful and resonated splendor. The crew moored the ship as Savane gathered her belongings and met with the rest of them to enter the city. Gwen helped bring Dayin's horse up from below deck to give it much needed time on solid ground. She was walking him down the gang plank when Stiele noticed the harbor master making his way over to her.

"Captain?" She looked up at Stiele then followed his gaze to the approaching paunchy, silk laden man with his well-groomed beard and hair. Stiele tossed her a silk purse that she caught out of the air just in time to turn and face him.

"Good afternoon Hagrim, I see the port life agrees with you these days. Are you keeping the place clean?" The man leaned in to embrace Gwen, to Savane's surprise, was welcomed into an embrace as a father would be.

"Doing my best maiden, doing my best. What are you doing in Fairhaven? Finally decide to work for your uncle?"

"You know better Hagrim, I loathe the solid ground after about two days of being locked in the stocks" she winked at him and handed him the oversized purse. He let out a burst of laughter and put the purse beneath his robes before turning toward everyone else. "Can I assume you are staying at least a day or two? Your uncle will be happy to see you." Gwen nodded and motioned for everyone to join her, "Keep an eye out for eels Hagrim, and take care of my ship."

"Eels?" Savane looked over the side of the dock.

"I'm referring to deadly things in the water...Pirates...more specifically Dirk. Hagrim was one of the many people who helped me when I took on my father's crew. He knows that I am more of a transport captain than a pirate. I have more forgiveness than most that come here."

"And your uncle?"

"Vin is everyone's uncle, he's not really my uncle. He's the one I said we would go talk to. I have some errands to run first so, why don't you find a tavern and get some good food. You won't encounter the usual hostilities here that you did in Osmadante. This place loves company." Gwen separated from everyone taking Braxus with her. The two disappeared down the street.

Dayin stood next to Savane and watched her watching where Gwen had gone before turning her attention to the taverns that lined the streets. There were none of the usual types of noisy taverns that Savane had grown to loath. Instead they were clean and smelled of fresh bread. "I feel like someone tidied up before we came."

Dayin laughed and guided her into the first tavern. Danica and Balae followed but Theries looked to his sister and motioned for her to go in on her own. Then turned without objection, other than the one in her eyes, and walked alone down the crowded street. He was soon gone from sight and a nagging feeling sunk in the pit of her stomach. Danica watched the emotion on Balae's face and looked where Theries, still clear in her sight, stopped at merchant tents and shops.

"In my land you have to bleed to become a man. A king without scars is not a king, he's a manipulator. If you will fight every battle he is faced with, you will be King, and he will be a shadow." Danica slipped passed Balae and entered the tavern. Her senses aroused with strange music and beautiful foods. Balae followed in silence and only took a moment to fall into Savane's excitement about eating "normal" food and not smelling urine.

It wasn't long before a few of Gwen's crew found

them all seated, the table got longer, and the conversation got louder. Balae was content to get to know Stiele, who seemed equally interested in getting to know her. They sat side by side and Savane smiled as Balae's laugh filled the tavern. It was such a warm full sound that made her wonder why she had never noticed it before.

The sun was just setting when Gwen and Braxus returned and joined them at the table. The tavern keeper seemed to recognize them and brought them each a drink, then busied himself with lighting the lanterns and candles that lined the walls. Gwen's smile was genuine as she took a sip of her drink. Savane watched them all and for a brief moment let go of all the fear of the book and Lelandra's tear. She took a piece of her bread and dipped it in the stew broth in front of her, and quietly enjoyed the peace.

Danica watched the room as everyone enjoyed the food and mood of the tavern, they were all content. When Theries slipped in, no one noticed. He sat on a stool at the bar watching everyone with an illegible expression that Danica tried to decipher. His breath was steady and even, as it always was, his entire body was relaxed. His manner was the same as so many of the warriors in her tribes. He possessed the quiet confidence that came from knowledge and power. Her focus on him drew his attention to her and their gaze locked. He watched her for a moment then lifted his glass of wine to his lips and let his gaze fall back to the room. Gwen seemed to notice Danica's gaze and then Theries. "If everyone is done, then, it's time to go meet Uncle Vin."

The Streets after sunset in Fairhaven were illuminated with oil lanterns suspended on wrought iron posts that were twisted in unique patterns and designs. Each one different and often depicting various themes depending on the district of the market they were in. The oil lantern itself swayed in the breeze that made the light flicker and dance. The cobblestone streets were patrolled by the city's guards. Danica couldn't help but note the significant difference between the guards in Osmadante and these men. Each in uniforms that were cleaned and polished, a custom that bewildered her until now. Each member embracing discipline that Osmadante had never witnessed.

The most distinguishing feature of Fairhaven, however, was not in its illuminated streets or ample military presence. It was in the feeling that every road had purpose. They all funneled to the market that made up the center of the city. Even in the still of the night the city center was alive. People drank and ate and celebrated. "Is there a festival?" Savane called to Gwen over the minstrel's playing. "It's the summer song. It's just what they do here, they celebrate artists, musicians and life. It is a mixture of different races, humans, elves, half-elves and even half ogres." Gwen placed a hand on Braxus shoulder. "It is one of my favourite cities."

"Fairhaven dates back to before the fall of the first Gods and many of the statues you saw as we entered the cove were built then. Because of how well guarded it was however it never fell to the armies that ravaged the rest of the empire. Many of the elves that live here have never left, their families still reside within these walls free of judgment. They are also free of the connection that makes their kind less trusting of humans and of course, free of the magic their people are so well in tune with.

Savane watched as a minstrel sitting on a rock played. His eyes were closed. he seemed so completely lost in the music that she stopped to watch him a moment. His shoulder length dark hair hung closely to his face and pale skin seemed to almost glow in the firelight. His eyes opened to reveal a deep brown that carried a sadness that Savane recognized almost instantly. He stopped his song, a look of recognition on his face as he looked at her. Danica watched him closely as he stood face to face with Savane. He was perhaps only half a foot taller than she and his soft features lead Danica to search for an Elvin lineage, but he was human. Just fairer than any she had ever met before.

"Do I know you?" Savane whispered to him.

"No, M'lady, I don't believe we have met, for I would remember so kindred a spirit as yours I believe."

"Kindred Spirit?" Savane adjusted the satchel on her shoulder that carried her mother's book. "How can you be certain we are kindred in spirit?"

"I recognize the loss you have suffered, there is such sadness that lingers in your beauty." he paused to set his lute beside him on the rock. Like everyone they had passed so far in Fairhaven he had finer clothes, a long leather riding coat and high boots. He took Savane's hand which issued a ripple of caution from Dayin and Balae. Danica raised an eyebrow at the two before returning her gaze to Gaelan. His eyes flashed to them only briefly before he proceeded with a soft kiss to her hand. "I am Gaelan, I am a minstrel and storyteller. I hope to meet you again." He let Savane's hand go and stood, collected his instrument and drifted down the street.

Gwen's eyebrows had disappeared into her hairline watching the caution that the group had collectively displayed over the show of gallantry from Gaelan.

She took Dayin by the arm and started him back into motion down the road they were initially bound. "You know, were you in any other city, any other city," she repeated, her eyes intense and focused. "You would have just put a price on Savane. Be more careful Dayin, Savane is not made of glass like the lot of you believe her to be."

"We have experienced odd things, in Osmadante with the couple that was killed in the room above us. I guess we all feel as though there is someone following us, and when he spoke of familiarity it seemed that it might be him."

"He's a storyteller Dayin, it was poetry." He took a deep breath and settled. "It's okay you're better to be cautious, just don't let others witness it." She patted his shoulder and motioned down a walkway that lead to a beautiful villa with large open pillars to beautiful gardens just beyond. "We're here."

"This is Vin's home?" He paused to take in the view beyond the walls, a large pool of water with lush beautiful greenery and lanterns hanging over the water to reflect them back. The stone walkway was winding and opposite of the pool were large trees with branches that drifted overhead and sung in the breeze. Everyone walked in awed silence until a petite sprite of a woman stood in the path. She was a young woman, but her eyes were somehow older. Her hair was a dark glossy black pinned neatly around delicate flowers with fragrance that lingered in the air. Both she and Gwen smiled warmly at each other before they embraced each other in a warm greeting. "It has been too long Gwendolyn Bannier." Gwen nodded her agreement and looked to the friends that surrounded her. "These are my friends; I've brought them to meet Uncle Vin. This is Yabensi, Vin's first wife." Gwen smiled as Savane's eyebrows raised. "He takes a new wife every year."

Balae poked Theries in the ribs, "And you couldn't even handle one." Theries eyed her a moment, not sharing in her amusement.

"How many wives?" Savane tipped her head to Yabensi in greeting.

"He has eight. In Fairhaven they are almost royalty." Vin was a poor man with great ideas, now he's a rich man who knows everything. He tied Fairhaven together and because of this, fathers offer up their daughters as wives. He takes them if they are willing to wed him. They learn to read and work as leaders in the city in various trades. Yabensi, however stays here in the villa."

"Not all accept the proposal?" Yabensi looked to Gwen who returned her comment with a wink and a smile. "Not all, no."

"He is expecting you." Gwen motioned for Yabensi to lead and turned to follow her.

Balae extended her arm to her brother letting him fall in behind Dayin and Savane. "When you're king, you can have eight wives too Theries, won't that be amazing?"

"I'm more likely to ban the practice of arranged marriages, right after I have you married to Vin."

Balae stifled a laugh as they all were brought into a large room with dim lighting and a massive red wood round table that sat low to the ground. Oversized fluffed pillows were arranged around it and at the back of the room on a pile of pillows was what everyone assumed was Vin. He was a large portly man covered in silks, his hair pulled back in a tail and his beard oiled and smooth. He sat contently sucking on a long pipe, exhaling out the smoke when he saw Gwen enter the room. His smile was such a genuine show of emotion that it made Savane smile in return. A warm laughter burst out of him as Gwen made her way to his place at the table. When she reached him, she knelt at his side and he caught her in a warm fatherly hug that seemed to diminish all her cares for a brief moment.

"Where have you been, my beautiful angry maiden?"

"I'm sorry I've been gone so long, I got caught up in life." She looked back to everyone behind her. "Are these people, the 'life' you've been caught in?" Gwen smiled and stood helping Vin to his feet. "Vin this is Savane, Dayin, Theries, Balae and Danica."

His eyes froze on Balae for a moment longer than everyone, shifted to Danica before returning to Balae. "Have we met before?" It was Theries turn to choke on laughter then mask it by coughing and clearing his throat. Vin raised an eyebrow but returned his gaze to her. "You are from Ashmore are you not?" Balae shook her head, "you must have me confused with another. I am from the east."

"I don't believe so." his tone was filled with confidence that made both Theries and his sister glance at each other before he shrugged it off and looked to Danica. "And a Northerner. My Gwen, you are caught up, aren't you?"

"Savane is chasing a prophecy that her mother tried to unravel before her death."

"Sounds like a very dangerous hobby for a noble woman to undertake." he looked to Savane who despite her common clothes he had already identified as a noblewoman. Gwen had been accurate in her statement that he was a poor man that knew things, he had already stripped their secrets down.

"Does this have anything to do with Lelandra's Tear in the sky?"

Baffled Savane stared at him, "yes it does. We're trying to find a map, Gwen thought that you might know where to start."

"You're looking for the Last Gods House. It was a temple that stood before the fall of the gods and the birth of the new ones. It was a map that I once had in my possession. Enderie, my third wife, however, was the daughter of a skilled sage who was writing memoirs on the old Gods and wanted to map out their fall. Sadly, he was robbed recently, and the map was one of the things the brigand took. For now, he's in the next port, in Ilvaran. The last I heard he was living at the Heckling Whore, a tavern on the west end of the port. He's a monstrous savage that would meet the eyes of your brother Gwen. He motioned for Braxus, he's a savage one that lacks any manners whatsoever and I would question whether he has any devotion either."

Savane stared at the man for a moment and realized that everyone had the same dumbfounded look on their faces. They hadn't expected the map to be real, much less that Vin would actually have been the one-time owner. When she regained her focus, Vin was smoking his pipe and listening to Gwen and Braxus talking about some of their recent events before they had joined up with them. Balae looked lost in thought and Theries seemed to be watching her, searching her expression for what Savane couldn't tell. One thing she knew was that they had to make their way to Ilvaran and find this monstrous man there and located whatever she was meant to find.

The warmth of the summer night led to conversations and humor. When they made their way back to the inn after much protest about staying at the villa, Savane was so tired that she fell into the bed and started wrapping her blankets around her with closed eyes. "Did you find his attention to Balae alarming?" Dayin put his sword down and removed his cloak. He looked down at Savane who seemed to have shared that thought with the last bit of wakefulness she possessed. Her hands were gripped around the blanket, her eyes closed, and her breathing had become the steady rhythmic breath of dreams. His mind drifted to Gwen's assessment of her strength. He took his holy symbol from his chest, twisting it back and forth between his fingers on the chain. He took a deep haggard breath and closed his eyes.

Danica in the room next to Dayin and Savane was in a similar state of thought. She sat in the center of the floor and let her ears absorb all the sounds around them. There was no more music, very little talking and the sound of hundreds of small hearth fires and braziers keeping the darkness at bay. "Danica?"

Her eyes opened to Dayin's voice from the door. She stood and opened it. He was in his clothes as she was, rather than the armour that they had become so accustomed to travel in. She opened the door and let him in. For the first time since they had met, he saw her back exposed and all the scars that ran in long strips from the wolves. He said nothing as he sat

"Can't you sleep?" She whispered.

"No, not since Osmadante, not well anyway." Danica thought back to the figure outside the room and closed her eyes slowly. When she opened them, he was focused on her. "I saw the figure enter the room that night. I heard him kill them. I was too far to do anything about it. It was a man, slight and expertly trained, he walked the railings like a bird does. He knew Savane was in that room. He stopped at the window." She could hear Dayin's breath and heartbeat struggling to remain calm.

"Why do you hide your feelings from each other?" Danica took a sip of water before meeting his gaze. For a moment it looked as though he were going to deny it, instead the weight of carrying it in silence dissolved and he seemed somehow relieved. "We can't keep much from you can we, Danica? She is of noble birth and I am not, there is no world in which we can be together, I understand that. Far better than she, I think."

"What does this mean noble birth? All birth is noble."

He smiled at her. He shook his head and corrected himself. "She possesses the blood of the Gods, because of that she must marry into another noble family."

"You have Gods blood Dayin."

"Many of us do,"

"No, you all do. Balae, Theries, Gwendolyn, you."

"Balae and Theries are siblings their bloodlines are the same and mine is far weaker than any of them."

"You are wrong." his eyebrows raised, and a smile formed. He loved the way she cut through diplomatic conversation with harsh truths. "In what, am I wrong?"

"All of it, Theries and Balae, you are not far weaker than they are. Different but not weaker. Savane is by far the strongest and Balae is a close second. Theries is a different kind all together as though he has a different source. You and Gwen both resonate with it as well."

"How do you know this?" he hadn't noticed that he had sat forward in his chair.

"I just do. It's like a scent that seems more like a memory that lingers on you. I see it in everyone, whether they are, or they are not blooded by the Gods"

Dayin was frozen for a moment, his mouth gaped

and the holy symbol in his hand hung loosely. "It's not just about the smell then that drives you to the forest at night." She shook her head, "It is so very much more."

"In the north it was far weaker, but whether it has gotten stronger with age or if it is being here that has made it stronger, I am at its mercy. I see it all in swirls of colour, in scent, in the drums of everyone's heartbeats."

"How do you focus? How can you live with that and not go mad?"

"How do you have the feelings you do for your lady and keep them silent?" he took a deep pained breath.

She rescued him from his thoughts "It is what we are accustomed to do that we become good at. At first by the fires in the Borderlands when I could feel Kazmir's blood, I thought it a curse of my bloodline, but I have learned to use it."

Her eyes had become soft as though she felt she had told him enough and that he couldn't handle anymore. He sensed it. "What aren't you telling me?"

"Theries. He isn't what he seems Dayin. He isn't just a prince from the east. I haven't figured it

356

out yet, but there is so much more to him and I can't see it. His breathing seldom changes, his heartbeat never races. When he runs or exerts himself yes, but never when his feelings should make it race. Never anger or rage, or excitement or want. He is still, like a blanket shrouds him." Dayin watched her expression, the frustration that whatever it was lay just out of her reach. "It's alright Danica. We'll keep her safe." She smiled, one of the rare times in which she had. It faded quickly as she looked at the sky that was brightening outside. "You need to try to sleep Dayin, tomorrow is coming, and we haven't let today go just yet." He got up from his chair and walked to the door. "We sail sometime later today for Ilvaran."

He closed the door behind him, Danica lay awake just long enough to hear him slip into sleep. The last of the bodies around her to fall away into the dream world. Their breath, their hearts rhythmic and calm. All but one. His heartbeat never changed, never showed excitement or fear. But unlike everyone's it was not confined to a bed, it wasn't still. He was awake.

Gwen woke everyone in the late part of the morning with threats of leaving without them. Knowing that once they were clear of the harbour, they would be free to sleep again, made embracing the morning less daunting. Savane sat on the deck of the Angry Maiden re-braiding her hair. Danica had taken up her usual residence at the middle of the ship, poised for her stomach to wage war against the tide. Dayin had already disappeared below deck as had Balae and Theries. A whistle came from the docks, Savane looked out to see Gaelan, his mandolin strapped to his back.

"Gaelan? What are you doing here?"

"I want to come with you." Gwen walked to the gunwale and looked over the side. She eyed Savane a moment and then looked to Danica who had stood and made her way to where they were. She looked down at Gaelan and back to Savane who seemed to be waiting for her to answer. "It is your journey; I am just your guardian."

"But he is one more thing you may have to guard me against."

Danica shook her head, "No, not him, he is what he says he is. He really just wants to come with you." she turned dismissively and made her way back to the place she had claimed.

Savane looked to Gwen, whose eyebrows were raised. "He's another mouth to feed and doesn't look like he can handle combat."

"Why do you want to come with us? It's dangerous and there is no reward for what we are trying to accomplish."

"Vin said that you are trying to resolve the comet." the air rushed out of both Savane and Gwen. They exchanged a glance before looking back him. "Well, I guess you're coming." Gwen called. Savane looked back at her, confused. "If Vin made sure he caught the boat, he's getting on the boat."

"You trust his judgment that much?"

Gwen reached down and took Gaelan's forearm as he boarded the ship. "Yes" Gaelan landed on the deck between the two women. Feeling the tension, an uncomfortable smile raised his features.

"I promise, I'll carry my weight."

Gaelan stayed above deck for the departure from Fairhaven, his eyes scanning over the beautiful city as it began fading from sight. There was still that look of loss on his face that she had identified the night before. "What do you know of the comet?" Savane asked as she settled next to him. He looked at her then back into the sky.

He seemed reluctant at first to speak, but after a moment of gauging her he said, "I was once in love with an elf, and she with me. Elves that live among the humans are far different from the elves that live in the forests, Ghenhilde was the latter. Her father was high in the Elvin hierarchy and in the beginning, he believed his daughters affection for me to be childish curiosity. When she refused a marriage on the grounds of our love, things became more threatening. We made promises to each other that we would escape at all cost and we chose a night to run, and run we did. We thought we were clear and stopped to rest by a stream. She held me close to her in the most beautiful embrace I had ever felt before we were both struck by the same arrow." He pulled his tunic to reveal a wound over the right side of his chest. "You can imagine, from my wound where her wound was, she crumpled in my arms. Death was kind to her and welcomed her instantly, while mine dashed away as I tumbled down stream. I was carried unconscious downstream and in a state of delirium. I was standing before the most divine beauty I had ever seen. She had fire red hair that seemed like a halo around her head and she wore the earth like a garment. She stood before me and kissed the wound on my chest. She said that I knew true love but that it was the loss of it that would be my strength. The wound washed away with the water and her eyes were the last thing I could remember seeing. Tears formed in the corners of her eyes and as one fell across her cheek. My eyes opened and I could see the red fire streaking across the sky for the very first time. It sucked the air from my chest. I was alive, but Ghenhilde was not. Her blood and mine had mixed across my chest, but I could feel her slipping away. But the tear in the sky, Lelandra's Tear called to me like a ghost. When Vin said that was what you were trying to resolve, I felt that I had to join you."

He handed Savane a cloth that he produced from beneath his tunic. She looked at it having not realized that she had tears in the corners of her eyes. Danica had also listened from her perch against the side of the ship. She too had felt a tremor of loss in her heart as the storyteller had spun his story. But it was no story, his heart had pounded with each painful part of the memory and his breathless airy voice verified his suffering.

"I guess we were meant to meet then. You know that we have had pirates after us and very dangerous people on our heels the whole way?"

Gaelan looked up and back at where they had come from.

"Is it too late to go back?"

"Yes." Smiled Savane sensing his humour. "Then I guess we are going to have to find a way to keep me alive." he winked at her and they both smiled.

The trip to Ilvaran was fast. In the time it took to make their way down the coast the clouds had moved in and rain threatened. Danica was overjoyed when she heard Stiele call for the sails to be cut.

Arriving in the port was a complete contradiction to arriving in Fairhaven and even the weather felt a need to show its disappointment in the notorious settlement. Where Fairhaven had been bright and musical, Ilvaran was dark and odious. There were no guards patrolling the streets and the taverns that lined the waterfront looked vile. Savane stood next to Dayin and Danica on the deck, after having spent a small amount of time making introductions to Gaelan and explaining her reasons for entertaining his request to join them. Gaelan had already settled in with the crew and opted to stay aboard with them rather than be an additional room in the tavern.

Gwen walked over as they lowered the gang

plank and looked to Dayin, "Remember what I said back in Fairhaven, this place in a nest of the unscrupulous sorts. If you think even for a moment that you are in a bad spot, it's likely too late. They are truly selfish people in this place."

Dayin nodded, "Are you sure I can't convince you to stay aboard the ship with Gaelan?" He looked at Savane who shook her head. Dayin sighed and made his way down the gangplank with the others. Seraphic had been left in the stalls during the time in Fairhaven, was now hoisted to the deck for a chance to be free in the forests beyond with Danica.

"Will you be alright?" Dayin took Seraphic reins and handed them to Danica. "I think I am more likely to be alright than you, this place smells of filth."

A look of annoyance lingered on Dayin's face. "Well you enjoy then. See you at Dawn?" She nodded and started down the road.

Savane watched as Danica disappeared down the street with Seraphic. She was certain it was more of an escape than a return to nature. The rain that had started to fall was mild for now, but the horizon promised a stronger storm. Many members of Gwen's crew stayed behind to secure the deck and minimize the storms impact. Theries and Balae had already left the docks and wandered only a short distance behind Danica, while Dayin finished up a conversation with Gwen before she turned back up the gang plank and drew it back aboard the ship.

"If you have not already noticed the difference between the ports Savane, this is not the city to explore. Gwen has warned me more than once to ensure you stay close."

There was something in her that made her want to tell everyone to stop treating her like a child, but just as the thought crossed her mind she watched a fight break out between two merchants. One overpowered the other ended up being thrown off the docks and into the water with a wound to his midsection. He floundered for a few moments before grasping at a rope ladder and clinging to it.

Savane's mouth had opened to protest, Dayin smiled at her as it snapped shut. He knocked a finger under her chin playfully and guided her off the docks into the streets where the Heckling Whore Tavern was and the mercenary that was to lead them to Yhamkari.

The tavern was undoubtedly the worst place Savane had ever had the displeasure of entering. Even Dayin, with his patience of all people, wrinkled his nose at the smell. "We are not eating here!" Savane glanced around the tavern, trying to see through the smoke of whatever plant the locals were smoking. There was no sign of the mercenary Vin had spoken cf. Savane looked bewildered at Dayin, he let his shoulders rise up and walked over to the woman behind the tavern counter. She was a portly sort with frizzy red hair and glowering gaze that made Dayin hesitate before asking after the mercenary.

"That miserable bastard is the reason my tavern is in such ill repair. He comes in here and buys up my ale and picks fights. He tries to convince my whores to work for free and more oft than not gets his way. The brawny bastard, if you see him, you tell him he owes me for last night. They took him off this morning when he was still face first into his tart."

Savane's eyes widened as Balae moved up beside her, an amused grin on her face. "Did she say tart? Do you think she meant the fruit kind?" Savane scolded her with a gaze and turned to vacate the horrible establishment feeling light-headed and nauseous. "They came to get him. A person can get arrested here. For what? We watched a man nearly kill another in the streets and the magistrate decides to take the only reason we came to this lavatory?"

Balae let out a laugh and placed her hand on Savane's shoulder, "I'm sorry but you are most certainly in need of a return to Fairhaven. We'll find him Savane. Don't unravel just yet."

Savane took a deep breath and looked to Dayin who was using the steady falling rain to wash his face. She let Balae's amusement at her discomfort settle in, a smile returned to her lips. "Now I know why Danica all but ran from here." "We need to find a place to stay the night if we're going to go looking for magistrates."

The four walked through town and stopped at the only inn that didn't appear louche. They paid for their two rooms then made their way to the magistrates. The sun had been hidden by the cloudy skies and relentless rain all day. It was evident that it had begun its descent and the pleasing rain showers were becoming a pelting surge.

They found the magistrate just as he was closing his office. He was an abundant man with a jewel on every fat finger. His hair flattened to his head was an odd combination of red and gray. His clothing, like his jewels were fine and delicate. Though he seemed concerned about their condition, he was more concerned with Theries as he moved in behind him.

"Good Evening Magistrate," Theries purred, "It seems you have someone in your custody that the Lady here would like released."

"Tomorrow" he snorted, "Come back tomorrow," Theries flashed Savane a silencing look as she was about to protest. "You see this is rather important. We've sailed some distance to come here and the knave needs to be returned for justice. I'm certain those rings you wear could be augmented with some Eastern stones, perhaps a green emerald?" Theries produced one of the many stones that were in his purse. The magistrate's eyes lit up, with ample reason, the gem was worth a fortune. He eyed it cautiously then turned to the lock and once again accessed the office and the prisons where the mercenary was supposed to be held. The moment he was inside, they could hear the cursing and shouts of the man they were seeking.

"I'd be making sure your weapons are drawn if you're wanting to retain him as a prisoner. He's monstrously strong and no dunce with a weapon."

Balae opened the prison gate and made her way down the small staircase that led to the prison cells below. The bottom was flooded in water rushing from the streets above. When she fell in sight of his cell, his shouting and battery of the cell stopped.

Boeden was as tall as Vin had described. He was similar in size to Braxus, though perhaps not as tall as the half-ogre, easily as well muscled. His hair was rain soaked and plastered to his bearded face, was wild and poorly kept. His armour was mix matched pieces of whatever he could afford. His eyes had a touch of crazy that Balae recognized from her days training with mercenaries.

"So, what are you gonna do, stuck here in this rotten place?" Balae grinned, leaning against the bars.

"Well I was hoping to break out and kill as many of the bastards that are trying to hang me as possible. Did you have a different plan?"

"We are looking for a treasure map you are rumored to have claimed from a sage, in Fairhaven. We have a ship, the means to get you to your treasure. All we want is a few small items that according to legend are among the items in that treasure. Do we have an agreement?

"Can I fit you somewhere into the arrangement?" Balae smiled her charming smile, "You're currently knee deep in rainwater and whatever else has floated down stream. I think I hold the high end of the bargain."

"Are you planning on leaving me in chains?" Balae chided and waved a finger at him, "No," she mused, "Are we good? Do we have a deal?"

"You break me out of here and we have whatever you want."

Balae waded through the water and stopped at Theries who produced the keys the magistrate had given him. She looked to Dayin and glanced again at the magistrate with a look of warning, "I know his type, you best be between him and this giant or Theries is going to get his gem back."

Theries looked at his sister with quiet resentment as though it were already something he had anticipated. Balae flashed him a smile and winked before disappearing back into the cells below.

Boeden was at the bars when Balae returned. He watched her expression in a way that made Balae grin, "What stops me from taking what I want from you and running free?"

"What you want? What you want is a belly full of ale and fat coin purse and I suspect, a fight to keep you feeling alive now and again. I know you could get all three from running me over and defeating my comrades at the top of the stairs, but you will have to work for your treasure and work for your coin. Don't forget you are a wanted man in Ilvaran, so you would have to work for your freedom." She slid the key into the lock.

"Stay with me, aligned with me, and I promise you will always have a battle to fight. Fight more than you wanted, and you will have much more than you are currently worth." The lock made a grinding sound as Balae turned the key and pulled on the bars. Boeden stepped forward and towered over Balae. "Let's go find a treasure."

He took the stairs with ease and when he got to the top and saw the magistrate. He paused, watching Dayin and Theries. His eyes lingered for only a moment before he stood to his full height and without a weapon disarmed Dayin and held the magistrate in a vice like death grip. Balae came up the stairs to Savane letting out a startled cry before rushing to Dayin's side. The barbarian whispering something that made Balae wish that Danica was not so far away. The Magistrate was a horrid shade of red and blue when Boeden let him loose and fixed his tunic. Dayin had righted himself and raced across the room to where Boeden had thrown his sword, leaving it planted in the wall. He retrieved the weapon and turned to face Boeden as he looked at him. "We all learn to pick our battles knight. We learn it when we win, and we learn it when we lose. Which is it gonna be today?"

Dayin changed his posture from the crouched battle posture. He stood and guided Savane away from Boeden, who seemed to just notice the blooming lady under Dayin's protection. His smile made Dayin clench his teeth and cast Balae with a woeful glance. "So, are we going treasure hunting or are we going to stand here and shoot each other romantic eyes?" He winked at Savane playfully.

Dayin stepped in front of her and Boeden shook his head, "I don't play with boys, No matter how pretty."

Balae had a mix of amusement and horror on her face as she slid past Dayin and opened the door to the pouring rain outside. "Time to go."

Boeden walked out smiling, he glanced at the streets and back to Balae. "He's a touch sensitive, isn't he?"

Balae glanced at Dayin's sword and then to him. "Let's go. This is much bigger than us Dayin."

The sun had already disappeared below the horizon and the streets had become dark. With the beating rain the city watch hadn't bothered to light the oil cressets along the road leaving the streets cloaked in shadows. Savane could barely make out the shapes of everyone running ahead of her when Balae came to a slow pace before stopping at a fork in the road.

"Are you lost?" Theries shielded himself with his hood and stopped beside his sister, who was watching as two figures had taken up posture in the centre of the street they were meant to travel.

"Thieves?" Balae whispered, Theries shook his head and glanced back at Savane and Dayin. "Ready yourself," he eyed Dayin.

The two figures were mere shadows, but when their stature and weapons became evident Balae's eyes widened. She almost instantly gripped her shoulder and eyed the streets for the other rider. "It can't be them" Balae growled as the ogre gatherer took a few lumbering steps that broke into a run. His great spiked mace arcing in the air as he advanced. The other, Balae remembered with his iced eyes, was a ghost in the dark of the streets that seemed to disappear in the mist and rain. Balae could already feel her stomach knotting and it made her feel like a child. Her weapon suddenly heavier than she was able to bear, her shoulder echoed with pain in a way that made no sense to her. It wasn't until Boeden, who had no idea who he was running to meet in combat, raced under the ogre's brutish weapon and slammed heavily into his oncoming charge that Balae regained her focus and gripped her weapon. The ogre slammed his fist down on Boeden and raised his knee to kick Boeden's ribs as he fell against the power of the blow. There was a monstrous noise that came from the barbarian that sounded like a wild animal seething against restraints. From his crouched position he reared and lifted the ogre off the ground. Again, the ogre regained his balance and swung his mace into Boeden. To a normal sized man, it would have knocked him down or even killed him, but Boeden was enraged and oblivious to whatever injury his body had taken. Balae refocused her attention to the other gatherer. He stalked toward she and Dayin with his eyes alight with iced hatred.

"Where is the last one" Balae called, her voice dampened by the force of the rain and the battle between Boeden and the ogre. Dayin eyed the streets before returning his gaze to the approaching threat. This gatherer was narrow in build, but solid. Dressed in armour that shifted and moved with the same agility that he seemed to possess. His weapon moved like an extension of his arm, his every footfall was precise and disciplined. Where Balae's fighting style was based on force and fearlessness, he fought with calculated grace. He parried and dodged every attack that both Dayin and Balae tried to land. There was no room for error as they returned each foray. Balae felt every slice that ripped through her armour. Before long she felt lightheaded and fear set in as she noticed that Boeden seemed to be losing against the ogre. Dayin wore the same look of exhaustion and had multiple wounds.

Behind her she could barely make out what sounded like Savane speaking in rhythmic low tones.

Theries had pulled Savane back and watched as she chanted, much like she had done on the night of the emergence of Lelandra's Tear. She drew shallow breaths and magic ripped out of her in a pulsing wave. The ground beneath them seemed to heave slightly and cough out a fog so thick as to cloak everything it touched, spreading out across the ground and engulfing everything.

Balae and Dayin pulled back, disappearing from the combat, bringing forth frustrated growls from the gatherer. Boeden seemed less willing, but even he had reconciled the experience gap between he and his opponent. Theries barely noticed Savane collapsing under the weight of the magic that had left her. He spun around and caught her, sliding his hand under her head just as she folded to the ground. He looked up to see Dayin trying to peer through the fog to find her. Theries grabbed Dayin, side stepping his blade.

"She's there." Dayin crouched despite the wounds everywhere on his body. He lifted Savane into his arms and slipped away in the fog and darkness.

The weather had kept most of the people home and the tavern was uncommonly quiet. Boeden seemed unaffected by his monstrous bruises and punctures. He leaned over the bar to pour a tankard of ale before taking a key, then took the stairs two at time and disappeared behind a door. Dayin was only just setting Savane into a chair when Balae closed the door behind her and shook off the rain.

"Is she alright?"

Theries looked to Savane and then back to his sister, who while under the wet of rain had seemed in better condition than she was now, that the blood was beginning to pool on her skin and clothes. "She's exhausted from whatever she did back there, but will be fine I think, better than you and Dayin."

The two exchanged looks at each other's wounds, then sat in the chairs next to where Savane was.

The innkeeper took keys from behind the counter and brought them to their table. He glanced at Savane who appeared to be sleeping. He shook his head, "The lot of you are leaving blood on my floor." Theries took one of the keys, helped his sister to her feet and the two disappeared behind the door next to where Boeden had gone.

Dayin sat back and watched over Savane. In part, he was ensuring they weren't followed, but mostly it was a reluctance to move. All the thin slices through his armour were clotting and he knew the moment he moved they would open all over again.

When Savane's eyes opened, there was the same confusion that had happened when she had awakened in the hut on the borderlands. He watched her focus on him with the hint of a smile that faded when she saw the blood.

"Dayin?"

"It's alright. We're all fine, the fog saved us. All of us." She sat back in the chair she was in and took in the wounds that bled through the armour.

"We should tend those." He nodded and gratefully took her hand when she stood and offered it to him. She steadied herself as he leaned on her to get to the stairs. They took the stairs slowly and opened the door to the room that Savane had been so reluctant to occupy when they first came to the Ilvaran. Now, the room seemed more than acceptable as both of them were exhausted.

Savane helped Dayin remove his chest plate and took in the crimson shirt that lay beneath it. He glanced at her, as a sharp intake of air asserted her fear of his wounds.

"It's not as bad as it looks Savane." Her eyes drifted to his eyes then back to his wounds. "Let's clean them and see." She took her wine skin from her things and drained the water into a basin. She unrolled bandages and carefully blotted away blood.

"Do you have that thread and needle still?" Her eyes widened. "You want me to stitch your wounds?" He put his hand on hers as it rested on his shoulder.

"I'll be fine if you do and perhaps not if you don't."

Savane took a deep breath and threaded her needle with shaking hands, she took a deep breath and set to closing his wounds. True to his word, Dayin didn't move under the pain of the needle. His eyes had closed and Savane listened as he began to pray. His hands ran over the chain and along the medallion. She was certain that Balae was in the same state and that it was Theries stitching her wounds.

"What of the barbarian?" Savane whispered as she began washing her hands once she had finished. Dayin pulled a clean tunic over his head. He took a deep breath that Savane knew was because he had already made his opinion of Boeden. "I'll check in on him. Had he not been there, Balae and I would not have made it."

"They are incredibly powerful foes. Fearless and calculating. I thought there was three when we were in Abarris." "There was, the third was a northerner"

Dayin went to the window and looked outside. The rain was still pummeling the streets and the darkness was absolute. He muttered a quick prayer for Danica and then turned his attention to Savane. He pulled his cloak off of his pile of belongings on the floor and lay it over the bed. "Here, you get some rest and I will check on Boeden." Savane looked at his cloak and felt a moment of guilt before the gratitude set in of not having to sleep on the beds in this place.

Dayin paused only a moment longer at the door to make sure she had settled before he walked down the hall. He stopped briefly at Balae's door and could hear whatever conversation they were having and decided to leave them. Whatever the prince's skill sets, there was more to him then he was willing to admit. For the moment that was just fine.

He stopped outside Boeden's door and was not surprised to hear snoring from the other side of it. He checked to the lock on the door and sighed to find that the latch didn't line up and so the lock didn't work. He opened the door and was about to say Boeden's name when he realized the snoring had stopped. Despite his apparent slob like appearance in the prison, there was no disputing that before all else he was a man of war. His weapon was already in his hand and his eyes had already regained focus.

When Boeden recognized Dayin he sighed and waved him away. "I told you knight I don't like boys." he groaned as he lay back in the blood-soaked bed.

"Savane was curious if you needed any of your wounds tended."

"She was asking after me, was she? I knew she would." Dayin decided to ignore the comment as he gauged the severity of his wounds. Boeden watched him a moment and grinned. "Tell the vixen I'm bleeding out and need her to come and kiss me goodbye." Dayin noticed that the puncture wounds Boeden had he had stuffed with bandages and most of his injuries seemed to be bruising around his torso.

"I'll tell her." Dayin closed the door and took a deep breath. He walked down the hall and stopped outside of Savane's door to scan the tavern below. Fire light danced below but there was no movement, no sound. He pulled the handle of the door and glanced at Savane, who had already slipped back to sleep. He took the creaky chair from the corner of the room and sat in it, propping his feet on the edge of the bed. He rolled his holy symbol back and forth between his fingertips and slipped back into prayers before he slipped off to sleep.

Danica breathed in the forested surroundings of Ilvaran and closed her eyes. Not even a full day of sailing was the difference between the most beautiful city she had ever seen to the greatest hub of thieves and pirates congested in one detestable place. The ship had only been in port a few moments when the smells assaulted her and made her anxious to return to the nature that shielded her from it all, the looks, the smell, the noise. The power that she had once considered a gift had begun it's decent into burdening her. Standing too near to someone meant that even their heartbeat and breath were a sound she had to try to drown out. The taverns were a torture of noise and chaos, smells of every kind assaulting her in waves of stagnant putridity.

The forest, with its moss and ancient trees dancing in the ever-moving wind was peaceful. Even Seraphic was a welcome and grounding scent. She had grown accustomed to the horse. She pulled her furs off the back of him and laid them out. With the sunlight waning behind clouds that threatened rain she built a fire and settled into the peaceful reprieve.

As the rain started, Danica caught movement from the edge of the camp she had settled. A great bear lumbering in a clearing below shook in the rain. His posture was guarded as she watched him. He raised his head and sniffed the air before making eye contact with her and holding her gaze for longer than Danica felt was natural for a wild animal to do. She scanned the air for his scent, searching for a den but there was nothing in the air.

Until there was.

Seraphic snorted, he and Danica caught the scent. Faint as it was in the rain. It was familiar to Danica, but the strange sort of familiarity of a waking dream that lingered. She turned away from the bear and scanned the trees. But the Northern Gatherer cleared the trees opposite to where Seraphic was tethered. His hand raised in a fist that seemed to deny Danica the ability to move. He only glanced at the horse before kneeling on the ground in front of her. His eyes focused and intent. "Why do you run to the surrounding forests Danica, are you too far from home?" He leaned forward, the smell of leather and steel washed over her.

Svetovid was a tall northerner and up close to Danica he was easily a foot taller than she, with hair that was tied in braids around his head and loose down his back. The rain had drenched it and it lay flattened against his beautiful face. His blue eyes had an intensity that left Danica feeling exposed. His hand raised against her cheek and trailed along her ivory skin to her dark hair.

"Why are you so far from home?" The memory of Karra's betrayal was poison that rushed through, Danica and made him stare even more intently at her, as though her deepest thoughts were an open book to him. He drew nearer to her, his body now shielding her from the flickering fire light and casting her in darkness.

"This is not your world child of Vetis, you are the Mother of Shadows, the Blood Bringer." Danica could feel his breath and felt as though her own blood was moving toward the words he spoke.

"You have tied yourself to them and I must unravel you. I have something to give you."

His hand washed over her face and Danica felt all the fury and heat that her blood was. Memories of her home, wars and hunts, her brothers and finally Karra. The blood that she sought when she killed Urrie, the aggravation when she could not pull his blood as she had witnessed Danica do to the southern slave. His voice returned like cool water amid the fires of hatred. "Only you can save them Blood Bringer, but to do so, you must let go. You don't belong here."

Svetovid pulled her into him and let whatever enchantment that held her in place go. She felt the freedom return to her limbs and reached for her weapon. A smile danced across Svetovid's face telling her that he expected the fight. He met it with his massive blue hued blade. Her glaive struck his sword and the two jarred against the blow. He was monstrously strong and accustomed to pressing the advantage his height brought him. Each strike was blocked. And each exchange with his sword seemed effortless. Danica felt the rage boiling inside, the memories still so close to the surface, poured out of her. Deep inside the fire, she could feel a yearning, the blood refusing to be denied, answering Svetovid and drawing her into his world. She could feel her lungs burning as the battle began to take its toll on both of them. The rain had become heavy but did nothing to cool her. His effortless defense had more purpose and Danica's rage had made her attacks more danger-ous until the first drop of blood was spilled.

They both froze, rain mixing with sweat drip-ping down their faces. Despite Danica's moment of success, she stopped and stared at his split skin. An upward strike that had barely caught his upper chest and collar. The blood drib-bled out splattered on the mossy carpet beneath them. Such a strange sensation that washed over her, like pain or regret that she had wounded him. She felt her will dissipate beneath the draw of power in him. This time when she closed in on him she dropped her weapon and thrust him against the tree behind him. Their lips locked and hands tied together, all the while a voice in her head screamed against her.

Svetovid let her stay in control as they tumbled to the forest floor, their clothes and armor aban-doned. His skin was as white as hers, scared like hers, Northern like hers. For the first time since she left the north, she had found something familiar. He matched her intensity although her mind and her body were at odds as she felt rapture enslave her. He fell above her, his breathlessness matching hers. His face so near to hers, his forehead in the cavity of her neck. "He wants you Danica, but now you're mine." Just a whisper that should have been threatening but instead made her remember her home, her father and brothers, they all claimed their women. She closed her eyes and traced scars across his back with one hand and twisted a braid between her other fingers. Somehow laying there in the company of someone who should have been her enemy, she found sleep.

When Danica woke in the morning, Seraphic snorted his obvious disapproval. His head danced against his reins. He had broken the branches around him and was now stuck to branches that had become entangled from the one she had tied him to. Svetovid was gone. Any sign of him having been there was gone. All but a symbol drawn in his blood across her abdomen. A figure made up of two lines with arms held above her triangle head a circle in the center of what would be her stomach.

She untied Dayin's horse and sat in the mild warmth of the morning mulling over how she allowed what had happened to her the night before. Whether Svetovid had done something to control her, if the bloodlines were so potent that Vetis blood was just seeking to be empowered by aligning them. He was the very thing they were fighting against. She gathered her clothes walking barefoot across the rain-soaked forest floor and stopped at where she saw the bear the night before. There was no sign of him in the daylight, no broken branches from his passing, no residual scent, and no footprints. Had she dreamed him, had he been her longing for the North, or was he Peiashchic warning her of Svetovid's coming.

She made her way down to a small river that wound its way around the outskirts of Ilvaran and waded into the water. Her body ached from the jarring of both the combat and what had followed. She had never been with a man. Were it not for the blood she would have questioned whether last night was a dream. Everything about it left her standing waist deep in the water, confused and feeling betrayed by him and by herself. She stared down at the symbol he had drawn on her stomach and with a handful of water she washed it away. At first with tenderness then as the realization of what she had done, set in she vigorously scrubbed until all that was left was raw clean flesh.

As dawn broke, the bright, warm sun woke everyone. The rain had moved on and only the sounds of it dripping from rooftops left any indication that it had been at all. All of Dayin's injures screamed to life as his eyes opened. He took a deep breath and tried to relax. Savane still slept and it was easy to watch her do so. Before long however she stirred, her eyes opened to find his gaze. "Are you well this morning?" Her voice was still wispy and soft. "I'm well enough." She sat up and pulled the tie from her braid. Taking a moment to run her fingers through it she separated all the strands and then began to reform the braid. She watched Dayin as she tied it off and then wrapped her arms around her knees. "Boeden was alright?"

"He is very familiar was the toils of war and had his wounds bandaged before I went in. You should be wary in his presence Savane, I am not sure he can be trusted where you are concerned." She nodded and threw her feet to the side of the bed before getting up and taking Dayin's cloak with her to the window. She shook it vigorously and then watched the street. "Dayin, Danica is here." She gathered her things and only then noticed how slowly Dayin was moving.

"You aren't well, are you?" His brow knit together as he sat forward in the chair. "I will be.

You saved us last night, thank you." She placed her hands out for him and helped to support his weight as he stood then she gathered their things and opened the door. "Let's get back to the ship, you can rest in a far better place than this."

When Savane came outside, Danica was standing in the street beside Seraphic. Her hair freshly tied, her posture relaxed and calm until Dayin came out of the tavern. Savane couldn't understand the look that passed over Danica's face, it was more than concern, a mix of concern and rage. She left Seraphic's side to take Dayin's armour from Savane. Dayin shook his head. "I'm fine Danica"

"The others?"

"All of us are fine, Balae, the barbarian and I all took some injuries, but it seems we had all the help we needed." He shot a glance to Savane that made her lower her head and blush. Danica glanced at her for a moment before she looked back at Dayin.

"Who attacked you?"

"Those riders from Abarris, the gatherers." Savane tied Dayin's armour onto his horse before turning to face her. "The three riders?" Savane shook her head. "Only two of them. You weren't attacked, were you?" Danica felt sick.

She shook her head.

Savane nodded and took Seraphic's reins, "let's get back to the boat and set sail before the light of day brings those two back to finish what they started. I'll get the others." Dayin made to protest but Savane swept past him and back into the tavern. He eyed Danica for a moment in a way that made her feel that he knew but a tired smile found its way across his lips and she settled into guilty silence.

The Empress was still. For some time, she was silent, the pain of that memory lingered on her face. She looked up at me as though I had startled her. "I'm sorry, I was lost for a moment. That night was, that port was when everything changed. We sailed away from it with complete ignorance of the weight of what had just happened, or what was about to happen'. She looked at me. In the time I had been with her there was always a levity in her eyes that amazed me with all she had endured. That moment had passed, and I could feel the weight saddle her as she recalled the events in preparation of telling me what came next.

"The coastal waters were dark and from where we set sail the shadow that was the imperial city loomed on the horizon. From Ilvaran however, the island we were bound for was north west, we would sail for days in calm waters. To our surprise, is was as though for the first time since it had lit in the sky, Lelandra's Tear, was leading us.

Danica sat at her usual post but was to be introspective for the whole sail. I was becoming familiar with my newest companion Gaelan, Balae was content in training with Boeden, who despite his extensive bruising seemed content as long as he held a weapon in his hands. He was a child of war that Balae recognized, not as a friend, but as a weapon. He was a weapon, one that would have to be minded or it could be turned easily on its wielder.

Dayin and Theries had spent the majority of the sail below deck. Dayin recovering from wounds and Theries intent on knowing what Savane's mother had meant in her book about Yhamkari. He knew by the book that there had once been a land mass between the imperial city and the island. That when the God's died, the citadel had collapsed to the ground. As we drew nearer to it, the island was ghostly. It was dawn when we heard Gwen call to cut the sails, and the island was lit with the red light of Lelandra's Tear and the early shadows of dawn. The pillars that had once been the entrance to the land bridge on to the island, were poking out of the water as a warning more than a welcoming. Many were collapsed and invisible beneath the shallow waters, but the pattern of those that were still visible made them easier to predict. Gwen wasn't taking chances with the possibility that there was more beneath us. She anchored and we prepared to row to the island with our small company, Braxus, Gwen, our new friend Gaelan, Dayin, Balae, Theries, myself and our guide through the island, Boeden.

The empress took a deep breath and settled in for what I could feel was a part of the story that even after all this time was a burden on her. It seemed almost an unwelcome memory among all the challenges and victories of her past. So again, I prepared as she began to speak.

∞∞∞

Savane stood on the beach after they had landed on the shore. For a moment she could feel a pulsing in the ground as she stood still. Everyone else unaware as she felt magic receding back into the island. This place had been untouched for generations as ghost stories and legends frightened away countless rogue's intent on stealing the riches of the God's house for themselves. Gaelan watched her for a moment, the longing on her face as she could feel the magic dissipating. "You feel it too, don't you?" She whispered when she noticed the look on his face as he watched her. He nodded his head. "I have a limited understanding of magic, but even the smallest amount lets you feel it."

The others had caught up to them and Boeden had already started talking about which direction to go. His axe already in hand as he trudged through forest growth that hadn't been disturbed for hundreds of years, now surrendered to his garish presence.

Danica walked through the trees, her weapon loose in her grip, apathy settling in on her as memories stirred her stomach. She watched as everyone ahead of her looked to the highs of the island while she herself could barely bring herself to level her gaze. They cleared the crest of one of the islands many high points and the wind picked up. It was then that Danica's downcast gaze lifted. The smell of death poisoned the evergreens and hardwoods that surrounded them. Her grip on her weapon tightened signaling to the others that they were no longer alone. "What is it Danica?" Dayin ahead of her pulled his sword. "Death." she scanned the horizon, as far as she could see there was nothing but stillness, no birds, no life. "Why?" Savane stood next to Danica, her hands tingled with the magic that hung in the air. "When the God's died they birthed new Gods so why does this place wreak of death?"

"Because we aren't alone here." Danica could hear it just on the very limits of her hearing. It was like a presence holding their breath waiting for the moment to go undetected. Beyond that Gwen's crew still on the boat were talking of an oncoming vessel, "You're crew is hoisting anchor Gwendolyn and sailing for the North Eastern shore of the island," Gwen nodded, "that was the plan if they saw anything on the horizon, to keep our presence here secret." She looked to Braxus "The question remains, who is on the horizon?"

Boeden watched a moment, "well your treasure trove is this way, the faster we move here, the quicker we can fight whatever is out there." He turned and started down the steep decline that led down to the deep forest. Pillars that had stood for ages were moss covered and looked like trees with no branches in the dimness of the canopy shaded floor. Boeden stood at a well in the center of what looked like a court-yard though it was hard to envision something so overgrown having ever been The Last house of the Gods. The ground and grade of the whole island had been forever changed in the death of the gods.

"Where is the door?" Savane looked to Boeden who raised an eyebrow at her. "We gotta take the back-door Lady"

Balae's eyes widened as she looked to Savane to see if she grasped the lewd implication, but she was blessedly unaware and instead returned her gaze to the wide opened well with a pool below. "Have you been down there?" Boeden shook his head, "Nope. I said I knew where to go; I didn't say that I knew whether or not the treasure was real." Balae looked down into the well while stripping her heavy boots off. "How do you know the well leads inside?" "Cause I've seen the map, which despite my inability to read, I can interpret a picture well enough." He got down to his pants and tied his axe to his back before heaving the ships rope into the water. He gave the end to Dayin, "find a good strong tree and tie it off will ya?" Savane watched a moment before starting to place her things on the ground. Balae stopped her and looked down into the well. "You aren't going down there."

"What do you mean, I have to go down there." Perhaps, but not till I've been with Boeden and we know how far it is underwater before there is air. I know I have to keep reminding you, but you are the heir to lands and title, you don't fling yourself into danger. You fling others in your place." She winked at her brother and pulled herself over the well wall, took hold of the rope and started her decent with Boeden only a few feet below her. Dayin watched as a sigh escaped him, Savane looked to him before returning her gaze to the rope. "Why the sigh."

"Because I don't like that I am placing a friend in harm's way, I like even less who is leading her there." Balae let out a concealed shriek as she entered the water. "its cold, that's for sure." with that, she took a deep breath and followed Boeden into the water below.

The light that bathed the well faded quickly underwater and it took Balae more than one attempt to find her way through the darkness. Boeden each time following her back to make sure she made it. "You can't keep coming back when you want to go forward." "It's blackness beneath and I have no idea how far we have to go." Boeden swam over to where they tread water in a small pool with enough room for them to steal air. "I know, just stay with me, and don't turn back." Balae nodded and took a long slow breath. He took his and the two sunk back beneath the surface and swam. The pulsing of the water in front of her as he kicked was all she could feel. Her lungs tightened and she could feel panic starting to creep back in, each second passing, each pull with her hands, and then spots started to swirl in her vision. Suddenly, Boeden's hand grabbed hers and reefed her from the water. Air rushed in and Balae's head instantly stung. "There you are, a swordswoman and brave."

"Swimming in the darkness made me brave?"

"No, trusting your life to me. That made you brave." he winked at her and pulled her up out of the water. It was in that moment that Balae realized she could see, there hadn't been anyone here in hundreds of years but there was light.

She ran her hands through her hair and looked around at the stones that surrounded the pool of water they had surfaced in. They were all of the same size cut in crude indications of each of the early gods. The stones emanated a dim glow that combined was enough to see the marble walls and a sconce along the entrance of the hall. Balae walked over and dragged her hand along what looked like a black line along the otherwise perfect walls, it wasn't a black line but a carved hollow that within lay pooled oil. Boeden took her sword off her back and struck it with his axe. A few attempts produced a spark that caught the reservoir and within the span of a breath, the room was bathed in light.

Boeden tied the rope to the center stone god and looked to Balae, "Well, can you get them all here in one piece?" She waded back into the water and braced herself for the journey back.

She took a deep breath and took hold of the rope, pulling hand over hand she easily found her way back to the reservoir. Without the panic of uncertainty, she easily held her breath back to the base of the well. When she broke the surface, Savane was hanging her face down in obvious concern. "She's back!"

"Take only what you need, it's a bit of a distance, the rope is tied to something on the other side. I'll go first, Savane and Gaelan you follow and then Dayin, Theries and Danica. Gwen, can you and Braxus stay with the things?" Gwen nodded and started helping Savane down the rope. "Be careful." Savane nodded and felt fear of being underneath the water. As if reading her expression Balae looked at her and re-tied Savane's hair. Hand over hand and don't slow down. I promise you'll be fine. It's blackness and there is one spot to stop and breathe but you will make it." Balae looked to each person. "All ready?" Before any could answer, she went under. Savane fearing too much distance between them followed without thinking.

Gwen watched the last of them disappear beneath the wells surface. She looked to Braxus and sat back against the well. "Do you think it's Konrad?"

Braxus smiled that despite all of what had happened in the past hour she was still hanging on what Danica had said about a ship approaching. "It is possible that he decided to follow the tear to see if he could find you. Knowing that we had been following it as well."

"I want to go and see."

"Danica also said that we are not alone on this island, I am not sure that going anywhere alone is wise, but I can see by the look on your face that nothing I can say will dissuade you."

"No, you're right, I'll wait." Braxus' eyebrows rose up.

"Are these people talking sense into you?" Gwen shook her head, "I saw her face when she said we weren't alone. She didn't give me confidence that whatever is out there is inconsequential." Braxus put a hand on Gwen's shoulder, I know you are concerned, but we will find him."

Danica was the last to break the surface of the first breathing space, Savane, she could see hung over the rope trying to catch her breath while Balae checked on Theries by moving past each person. "Is everyone up?" Danica called out, "I can see everyone, and they are all here."

"You see even in absolute blackness"

"I couldn't in the beginning, but it seems the more I use it the better it has become."

She saw Theries turn toward her. She didn't have to see the features of his face to know what he was thinking.

Balae moved back along the rope, "everyone ready themselves, and let's go." She took in a deep breath and one by one they all followed.

Danica broke the surface the second time as everyone else was pulling themselves from the water. She pulled herself along the rope, Theries was standing in her path.

"You said that the blood only strengthens the gifts when you follow the path of Vetis,"

Danica put her feet on the ground and stood in the water, her height easily a foot above him. She adjusted her weapon as she met his gaze. She looked down at him and took in the scent of a man without fear. Someone who she knew she couldn't intimidate. "Theries, a man who surrounds himself with swordsmen and women and doesn't wield a weapon of his own, yet still, is never afraid either is a fool or believes himself stronger than those around him. Which are you?"

From behind Theries, Savane called for Danica. She looked past him before going to step out of the water. "You aren't the only one that can smell when something isn't right Danica." Theries whispered, "And I don't need a God's blood for that."

Danica stepped around him and squeezed the water from her hair and clothes. She walked over to Savane and looked her over. "You're okay?" Savane nodded and looked toward Theries, "What was that?"

"That was the prince and I disagreeing on what makes a person dangerous."

"What does he believe makes you dangerous?" Danica looked back at him and then returned her gaze to Savane. "The ability to see him."

Savane smiled at first before realizing that it was not said in humor. She looked back to Theries. "Why do you dislike him Danica?"

Danica thought for a moment before she looked back at him, "I like an enemy that declares that he is a threat."

"Danica, he isn't our enemy."

Danica let her shoulders fall, closed her eyes and sighed. "It is only a feeling that he is hiding something that made me speak so harshly, you are right."

Savane looked to Theries and then back to Danica before making her way back toward where Dayin and Boeden were discussing the path forward. The oil reservoir lit the hallway that wound its way through where Gods had once spent their days. Savane could feel the magic still lingering as she had felt on the beach, a quick glance at Gaelan affirmed that he felt it too. His eyes were glassy as emotion gripped him. She was uncertain how recent his loss was, but there was evidence in his demeanor that revealed it not having been too far in the past.

"Are you alright?" She whispered to him as they started down the long corridor. "Do you feel it?"

"I am not certain if what I am feeling is the magic of their lives, or the magnitude of their deaths." Savane looked at him suddenly aware that the feeling she was experiencing was distinctly reminiscent of the ache of loss.

The first branch in the corridor led to a set of stairs that had once gone up into what would likely have been the grand entrance. There was no way to ascend, as the entire staircase of stone had crumbled in on itself. Fractures lined the marble walls in every direction. Rubble and forest growth along the ground was hindering how quickly the group could make their way through the halls.

"Did the map say where it was in this tomb?" Theries looked to Boeden, who seemed throughout the hall to be the only one treading with confidence. "It's this way."

He turned left down a corridor that split in two directions and paused in front of a large serpent skin that lay against the rocks that blocked the majority of the passageway. The rocks formed a V as though something had burrowed or cleared enough room to proceed. "Well, that wasn't here before."

Balae spun on him and slamming him into the wall, her hand holding him against the rocks, "I knew you had been here before. No one can remember so clearly from a drawing. What aren't you telling us?" Theries had closed the distance between where he had been to behind his sister and had a knife drawn concealed by his hip. Savane took at deep breath at the effortless transfer from silent onlooker to dangerous protector.

"Easy now girl, you'll rip your stitches." He grinned and closed his hand around Balae's hand on his bare chest, "Not that I mind the intensity, perhaps we can save it for another night, hmmm?" She slid her hand away from his chest and glanced back at Theries, who had already begun to recede from his sister's side.

"Yes, I've been here, but I can't get in."

"What do you mean?" Savane felt panic rise up in her that they had come for nothing."

"I mean it's locked, there are no doors in." he looked at the confusion on everyone's faces and shrugged, "let's just keep going, right." Balae looked to Dayin and Savane, her eyebrow raised in question. Savane sighed and waved her hand in resignation, "Lead."

She watched as Boeden pulled himself over the rocks and freed what was left of the enormous serpent skin from the hole. He moved through the opening without any hesitation while everyone else seemed more concerned with whatever left the skin behind.

On the other side of the rock wall, Balae slowed her pace to keep time with Theries. "Did you run to my defense big brother?"

Theries expression remained aloof, as he watched the hallway end in staircase down. Without a word he met her gaze and then turned his attention back to the stairs that disappeared beneath more water.

Savane's eyes widened, "More water? Are you out of your mind? Did you see the size of the snakeskin?" She could feel panic rising up and snatching her confidence. "It's the last thing that stands between you and the room that has no doors that I told you about."

"How far are we to travel under water then?"

"Less than the first, it's a strait swim, just trust me."

Savane's eyes widened. Savane looked to Danica who was crouched by the pool of water. She took a deep breath and dropped into the water. Boeden grinned and followed her. Savane stared at the opening and recalled the spell that illuminated her hands. She uttered the words with ease where they had once stuck in her throat and exhausted her. They now flowed freely, and her hands glowed a bright luminous yellow. Without further thought she followed them in. The path was as Boeden described, a strait shot that dropped into an opening and resurfaced into a great opening. The light that Savane had wrapped her hands in, revealed a dark chasm below. Her heart raced at the thought of what lay beneath it beyond the reach her light provided. Danica pulled her free of the water on the other side and watched the glowing of her hands dissipate. She took her hands for a moment and then returned her gaze to her eyes. "When did you learn to use this?" "It's coming to me a little bit at a time. My mother's book mostly, and the lessons I learned from..." she stopped not certain how to explain who Shamus was to her, "someone I used to know."

"Where I come from, magic is forbidden, I have never seen it used as you have used it." Savane looked at the room they stood in as the others, one by one emerged from the pool. Once again Boeden lit the braziers along the walls bathing the room in the warm glow revealing a great room.Images crudely etched into the walls of battles that had been waged five centuries before. Five metal swords broke up the images in the circular room standing off the walls and hinged at the base in a fashion that made Savane think they could be moved or turned. All of the images, depictions of those that walked the earth during the battles at the bone fields, the humans, the Elves, the tribesman that became the tainted legion and the Gods themselves.

"My mother believed that all of the Gods weapons from the bone fields were collected and locked away by the new Gods themselves, in hopes that they could avert the cataclysm that once destroyed the entire pantheon." Savane stood in the center of the room and looked around, the images showed a battle with mages encircled by blades and the blood running into the ground.

Danica spun as she looked up to what looked like the comet. "Is this the past or the present?"

Savane followed Danica's line of sight to the comet which seemed to be the only part that was out of sequence with the history Savane had become so familiar with.

"The swords on the walls, Balae can they be moved?" She lifted her eyebrow and walked over to the first of the five blades, she pulled at it and felt it groan and fall outward to land pointed at the center of the room. "All of them. Do it to all of them." Suddenly very confident that she knew how to open the door, she stood in the center as everyone pulled the blades into place off the walls and aimed at Savane in the middle of the room. Savane started to chant the spell that had awakened Lelandra's Tear. Her words rising and falling with the magic's intensity.

Gaelan watched Savane, his brow knit together, "It's not working," everyone watched in silence, almost holding their breath until Theries scanned the room, his eyes frozen on an image. He moved toward Savane suddenly. Danica moved to intercept him, but she was a moment too slow as Theries dagger was dragged across Savane's out stretch palm. So immersed in the spell, she barely acknowledged the pain as Danica watched the blood pool in Savane's hand and then fall to the ground. There was a loud exhale from Savane as she crumbled to the ground and the room shifted as though the floor itself dropped a level and a door revealed itself. "She did it!" Boeden shouted.

Danica stared at Theries from above Savane. "She was missing something in the spell." He said dismissively. Danica took a cloth and tied it around Savane's hand, to his credit Theries had controlled the depth of the cut and it was just a superficial wound. Dayin closed the distance and helped to get her to her feet. His teeth grit as Theries receded back to where his sister waited by the newly revealed door.

Savane took a deep breath, "Did it work?"

"Yes, it worked. Though you really need to stop doing that. If you push too far, some day you may not wake."

"Are you an authority on magic now Dayin?"

"No but I would like to think I am getting to be on keeping you out of harm's way." She smiled a weak smile and put his cool hand on her own forehead. "I admit, that was a tad uncomfortable."

Savane looked up to where the swords surrounded the room above them. For a brief moment she wondered how they would get out, but for now she focused on drawing the energy to stand and enter this new room. The group drew closer and to their surprise the room was unlocked. Dayin pushed the door and it swung open to reveal a dark chamber within.

Danica moved along the dark rooms walls and pulled torches down handing each of them to the others to be lit. Once lit they put them back in the holders on the walls. As the room filled with light, statues revealed themselves in a large circle. The shadows receding from their faces to reveal the most detailed rendering of the Gods who had once been men and woman on the bone fields. Lynstrom the God of Justice, successor to Adua. Shoanne the Goddess of the Sea, wife to Lynstrom and mother to Viserra. Amhuinn the God of Nature and his wife the Goddess of Fortune, Silke, their daughter was the young goddess Lelandra. The last of the gods was Aaehil the God of Magic and his wife Senna the Goddess of Light. Their son Bromwynn, was the battle driven God that all who entered the battle fields would ask for strength and guidance. Finally, the northern Gods who were born of Vetis' bloodlines, Peiashchic and Valiechic.

Savane marveled at the detail and intensity on each of their faces. Dayin's God Lynstrom stood tall and dressed in full armor. His gauntlet clad hands rested on top of the pommel of a white hilted sword. The scabbard concealed the blade, but the outer condition of the weapon was immaculate. Danica was frozen in the center of the circle as her eyes found who could only be Peiashchic. His northern features were instantly distinguishable. It disarmed Danica to see a resemblance between Peiashchic and Svetovid. Peiashchic held no weapon, no armour, and Danica found herself wondering if anything had been collected on the Bone-fields from her god until she saw it. Tattoos that were painted on the statue each a rendering of great beasts, the bear, the wolf, the eagle, tribal tattoos had their beginnings long before the bone fields. Peiashchic was deadly in the art of them and the mastery of them had slipped into obscurity since his induction. She traced the image of the bear that ran along his stone arms, her heart racing. Her mind drifting to moss laden forests and the great bear that had tried to lead her away from the camp that Svetovid had found her in. She reverted to her northern dialect and whispered to him, "I am sorry I betrayed you." She let her eyes fall to the ground before looking to his side where Valiechic stood. The Winter Witch she was called in her home, ruthless and uncaring of anything save Peiashchic. She had always been depicted as an old hag in the lore, but as Danica stared at her visage, she was reminded that the two had been lovers and her beauty was evident even cast in the stone.

Her statue was clad in furs and her long obsidian hair looked wild.Her eyes were wide and fierce, like Peiashchic, there were no weapon in her hands, only a bracelet made of white stones. It seemed so odd a trinket for one such as she. Danica touched the stones but instantly pulled her hand away, somehow feeling she was wrong to do so. "We have the blade, we should leave."

Theries had found the slight figure concealed in a row behind the first circle. The Gods children, who in their own right were gods but not present on the Bone Fields. Born after the battle, Viserra, the goddess of Shadows was a capricious self-serving deity. She was slight of figure and the stone she was carved in was black obsidian. Her hand was drawing a long thin dagger from its scabbard.

Theries took a moment to ensure he wasn't being watched before he drew the dagger from her grasp and sheathed it in the place of his own. He watched the statues face for a moment, before stepping back to the center of the room. Savane had found Lelandra, much as Theries had found Viserra, in the back of the room behind her father.

Her hands were clasped together, her face was wet with tears. Savane touched them and pulled her hands away. She had felt a sense of something powerful, magic pulsed around the statue enough that Gaelan looked up. "Savane, don't!" his warning came too late as Savane again touched the face of Lelandra. The tears went from clear water to red. Savane shuddered as images washed over her. Gwendolyn was racing down the beach, chasing Dirk. Savane pulled her hand away, "She is going to get herself killed. Dayin, take Lynstrom's sword, we have to go!"

Boeden looked at Balae, frustrated, "There is no treasure?" Balae looked to him then back at the room they were in, "I'm sorry, can we talk about this after?" She turned and brought one of the torches from the wall. Boeden looked down at the bracelet on Valiechic's wrist, and he ripped it off and put it under his belt before running to catch up with the others in the center of the first room. "What now?"

Savane was shaking, she didn't know if what she saw was the past, the present, or a glimpse of what was coming, but it felt urgent. "If we don't reverse the spell, we leave this room and all its contents exposed." Gaelan looked at Savane, "try and cast it again, just as you did to open it."

Balae looked to Dayin who appeared as though he had been struck dumb. He held the sword in his grip but there was a definite oddness to his face. A lack of opposition to Savane casting a spell that had already been enough to drop her to her knees. "Are you alright?" He nodded his head and placed the sword across his back, he seemed breathless but walked over to where Savane stood, "Try."

Savane started the spell as she had the first time, her hand still trembling she pulled the bandage away, reopening the wound and let the blood flow. She refocused and the words flowed more easily until she felt the ground shift. The circular room was raising back to its original place. Savane looked to Balae when the room finished moving waiting for the fatigue to wash over her, but it had only made her dizzy this time.

"The swords Balae, right the swords." Balae went around the room with Danica, putting the swords back into their upright positions. Before returning to where the pool of water led back into the dark below. The water however was no longer a still pool, instead it seemed to be pulsing, vibrating, a slight tremor started under their feet. "It's collapsing,"

Each in their turn jumped into the pool, following Boeden to the staircase. There was no light from Savane's hands this time and the memory of the darkness beneath made Savane s chest heave as she neared the surface. Her lungs on fire as she burst through the staircase and was pulled out by Dayin in front of her. "It's alright, we're almost out."

"Only two more dark pools of water to endure." She sighed and wrung out her hair as the others emerged from the dark pool.

Dayin grabbed her uninjured hand and pulled her into motion, "No time, the rocks are collapsing, we still have two more dark pools to clear." Savane's eyes widened, remembering the underwater path from the well, all rock and collapsed citadel.

Boeden had already cleared the collapsed rocks in the hall and Balae and Theries were right behind him. Each in turn made their way through the passage until it was just Danica. She glanced back to watch as a man began to pull himself from the submerged staircase, Danica stared wide eyed as the man's legs revealed instead a massive serpent's tail as he pulled himself from the water, he lunged forward at her. "You are not meant to be here child of Vetis." She pulled her weapon from her hip, watching his face. His words were more thought than spoken and she was confused for a moment. Unable to focus, her weapon went slack in her hand as he approached her, slowly slithering across the ground as it rumbled and groaned. He drew closer, his face a mirror image of Urrie. The closer he got the more he resembled her brother. She ran to him, her arms open as he embraced her. "I have missed you so much Urrie, Peiashchic sent you, and you're here?" Urrie looked at her softly holding her tear-soaked face in his hands, "I won't leave you again."

Dayin got Savane to the corridor that led to the well and stopped, Boeden had already submerged and Balae was behind Theries and about to go under when she looked back.

"Danica!" Balae looked at the faces as they made for the water, "Dayin, it's crumbling around us."

"Go, I won't leave her here. Balae, take Savane." Panic set in on both of their faces as he turned back. Rocks were already starting to fall into the water. "Come on," Balae growled, looking to Savane before returning her gaze to where Dayin had gone back for Danica.

When he found her, Danica was wrapped head to toe in the serpent's coils. The colour of her face and her heaving breath made Dayin panic for a moment as he climbed through the hole left by the crumbling hall. "Danica!"

"She is almost gone, son of Adua, let her go, she has betrayed you. The serpent's eyes were fixed on Dayin, but his coils stayed tight around

Danica. Dayin reached for his blade and thought better of it. He pulled Lynstrom's off his shoulder and watched as the serpent writhed, and loosening its grip on Danica, she heaved a breath.

"You are an old one, aren't you? Calling me child of Adua, I am a servant of Lynstrom. This sword is said to sever the ties to the Gods, are you tied to the Gods serpent? Would you be mortal if it cuts you? Dayin swung out, the serpent retreated with Danica still in his coils. Her face had regained colour, but her mind seemed locked in a memory. Dayin lunged again, as the serpent seemed content to drag Danica under with him. He moved toward the pool that lay beyond the staircase. Dayin grit his teeth and threw the sword through the air slicing the bulk of where Danica was weighing the serpent down. The coils released and unraveled almost instantly. Danica's mind was freed from whatever illusion he had created for her. Urrie disappeared and the serpent was revealed. He recoiled into the water, knocking the blade in behind him. Danica dove for the blade, falling in she grabbed the weapon. Not having recovered from the constriction, she felt her lungs ache with the lack of air. As her hands gripped the weapon, pain rushed in, they felt as though she held fire. Despite the pain, she held on until Dayin pulled her up. She took a deep ragged breath when she surfaced. Sobbing as he pulled her in to him, he had never seen the hard-exterior crack. Despite the danger of the stone groaning its protests, he let her recover a moment before he looked to her hands. They trembled and vibrated as they gripped the blade. He pried her hands open to reveal severe burns along her scared hands. "Oh Danica, it's okay, I have you. Up, you have to get up."

The two stood and broke into a run once they cleared the wall. They arrived at the pool with the iridescent stones and Dayin looked at her hands again and the rope they were going to have to use to pull themselves along, "I'll manage," she growled, and just like that the woman he had come to admire broke through the grief and sadness and took the rope. He cut the rope, freeing it from the stone it had been anchored on and dove in. Pulling himself along until he felt the rope being pulled from the other side, the rocks around him crumbling. When his head broke the surface, he reached down and pulled the rope the remainder of the way. Danica surfaced and took a long, controlled breath. Dayin pulled up onto the rocks. His body heaving from a lack of air and the weapon that seemed to pulse across his back with an incredible amount of power. Unlike anything he had ever felt before, it churned his stomach. Savane looked down at Danica, her unshakable ally who was silent leaning against Dayin for comfort. Her hands turned up at the wrists so that they wouldn't touch anything.

"I'm sorry," Danica whispered, "I'm so sorry." Dayin wasn't certain if she was speaking to him or not, "You have nothing to be sorry about, it was just magic Danica, a trick of the mind." She said nothing, her eyes just took on an inconsolable gaze as Dayin made to climb the rope. "Dayin, we have to hurry, Gwen and Braxus aren't here." Savane called. Dayin closed his eyes as the realization gripped him that whatever Savane had seen, when she touched the tears of Lelandra, it was most definitely not from her past.

Chapter Nineteen

Gwen and Braxus sat with their backs against the well where the others had disappeared. Gwen stared at the sky, the tear leaving its red stain on the heavens. "Do you think that there is any truth to what Savane believes about that damned comet? That a goddess has placed it in our sights to warn us, or guide us to protect anyone?"

"I think that she has had the answers to almost everything you have asked her, nothing she has led you to has been false. Each step is another in the journey and that I think you are no longer an unwilling participant but a full partner in what whatever destiny awaits them." Gwen lolled her head away from the comet to meet Braxus gaze, "When you choose to believe in something, you most certainly go all in, don't you?"

"That is what faith is." Braxus smiled and looked out into the forest, the trees moved in the breeze, but it was the only sound he could here, no bugs, no birds. He furrowed his brow. "There is an oddness to this island Gwen, it seems it was not just the Gods that once dwelt here that died, but they brought all that live here with them in their passing."

"Danica said that she thought we weren't alone. A ship on the water that moves our crew and an unknown entity with us, making everything frightened enough to leave on the island. Can we just go back to being pirates?"

Movement in the trees drew Gwen's attention. She felt her nerves rattle as Stiele broke through the clearing. Blood on his forearm and head, blinding him as it flowed down his face. Braxus got to his feet and ran to Stiele before he crumpled to the ground. "What happened?" his deep voice rattled with concern as he pulled bandages from the pockets around his chest and started to tend to him. Gwen's weapon was already draw as she waited by the clearing he had emerged from, "Who did this?"

"I've made my enemies in this life," Stiele said, "but how they found me here, I do not know."

"Enemies? Stiele you look beaten senseless. What are you even doing off the boat?"

"There was a ship on the horizon, at first we had hoped it was Konrad, but it wasn't. We slipped their sights, but they landed anyway, Gwendolyn, it's the Reaper. Dirk is here."

Gwen closed her eyes for a moment then looked at Braxus, "Most of the crew stayed aboard the ship, but a number of us came out to find you so that you wouldn't be taken by surprise if he found you. We encountered these snake men that seem to be all over the island. They pull your fears out of your thoughts and bring them to life or trick you into falling to your death. Those not trapped in the nightmare see the monster for what it is. Four members of the crew are dead, and I lost two. We have to get off this island. What ever they have found here, those snake men want to keep it and they are more than happy to kill for it."

"Braxus take care of him." she left Stiele's side and ran for the edge of the clearing. "What are you doing? You can't confront Dirk; you don't have to. We'll wait for the others and get to the other side of the island where the ship is waiting."

"Two members of my crew are lost, if there is even a chance that Dirk has Konrad, I need to know." She ducked under the tree line and ran back the way they came. She stopped often to listen to the silence that surrounded her. Without the other sounds of the island, it was easy to listen for someone on her heels. The sun had started it's decent and the red of Lelandra's Tear made the sky, the trees and the ocean beyond the canopy catch fire in the most brilliant display of colour. The sound of movement behind her got her attention. Gwen turned and crouched low to the ground. When Dirk cleared the grove, he looked right at her.

"I knew it was you." He walked toward her with arrogance as she froze for a moment, "Shame about your men, or at least I can only assume they are yours."

Gwen's stomach was knotted but the mention of her men suddenly released her, she drew her sword and got to her feet. "I am not letting you leave this island Dirk."

To Gwen's shock, the pirate that had been the source of all her nightmares since she was just sixteen widened his eyes and stepped back and disappeared into the trees.

"Get back here!" Gwen gave chase but quickly remembered what Stiele had said about the serpents luring crew members to their death. She moved quickly but not so fast that the next step was unseen. She raced after Dirk until he got to the beach where he ran along the water's edge. Gwen sped up with plain ground before her and clamoured over the few rocks that had seemed to slow Dirk down. Behind her she could hear

Savane screaming something at her and could see them coming out of the trees, but he was so close. Dirk tripped and Gwen could hear the sound of bone cracking as he fell between the rocks, his leg twisted at an odd angle as the rocks crumble under his footing. "Gwen stop, you're not thinking clearly." Dirk raised his hands up and held them out for her to see. "No weapon, I'm not going to hurt you."

"Going to hurt me?" she balked, "I have spent the last ten years of my life healing from how you hurt me!"

"I didn't hurt you Gwen."

"Liar!"

Savane was racing down the beach screaming at her, with Balae on her heels.

"Don't do it Gwen it's not what you think."

Gwen looked down at Dirk as memories of her father pinned and dying against the wall as his wife and daughter were fed to Dirks men. She raised her sword and without a moment's hesitation she drove it through Dirk's chest.

In the moment the blade slid through the bone and into the softness of his chest the air rushed out of Gwen, the comet in the sky exploded and the light shattered into a thousand flaming stones that burned up and rained down into the ocean. It was so intensely bright for a moment that everything was cast into darkness. When Gwen's eyes opened, the blood on the ground was pooled and seeping into her.

A rush of memories washed over her and she could feel the life force she had taken, the memories washed over her mind like the blood over her feet showing a life of joy and a daughter and a first true love in the Angry Maiden, Konrad's life washed over her. Her eyes opened and where Dirk had been trapped in the rocks lay Konrad, lifeless and still, the tear no longer in the sky and Savane and the others had stopped running toward her.

Savane fell to her knees, sobbing, Theries and Balae were wide eyed behind her.

"No, No..." Gwen pulled Konrad into her arms and choked in air as screams tried to come out. "What happened, how did this happen?"

"The serpent, it was the snake men." Savane sobbed.

"Why, why show me this? How did he even get here?" she screamed. Braxus cleared the trees helping Stiele walk. Both froze until a horrid sound escaped Braxus. Such a pained cry that it brought fresh tears to Savane's face. He lowered Stiele to the ground before running to his sister, pulling her crumpling form into his arms, as if his strength could somehow hold her together as she wept. "Oh Gwen, what have you done?"

Balae looked out on the water. The Reaper was a short distance off the coast, and she could tell they saw everything. Gwen looked up to the ship on the coast, the Reaper, with its gun ports open and brought to bare on the beach. Gwen choked out a breath. If he were to open fire, the pain would be no more, she could leave it all behind. Braxus followed her gaze to the guns. "UP, everyone up!" he had just uttered the command when Dirk opened fire and cannon fire blasted the beach creating waves of hard driven sand into the air to wash over them. Everyone raced about, seeking the safety of the treeline. Braxus had to rip Gwen away from Konrad's body to save her from the onslaught. Danica and Dayin had only just made the clearing and were driven back into the trees a small way down the beach, "Get to the Angry Maiden, we need to get out of here." Braxus shouted.

"I can't leave him here!" Gwen resisted as Braxus tried to pull her into motion.

"Captain." he used her title in hopes of separating the woman from her role. "You have nearly a hundred men that look to you to keep them alive. If the reaper clears that coastline and finds the maiden on the north eastern inlet, not a single one of those men will ever make it home again. I know you are hurt, I loved him too, but right now, right now, you need to be the captain of the Angry Maiden and get us out of here."

Gwendolyn's face was covered in sand, tears left clean streaks down her cheeks. The hopeless gaze gave way to her obligations and though there was no fire erupting behind her eyes, there was movement and purpose, which in that moment was all Braxus could hope for. He took one more glance back at the beach and broke into a run after Gwen with the remaining members of the crew in pursuit.

The Angry Maiden sat in the inlet as Stiele had said. The crew, oblivious to what had just transpired, except perhaps the shattering of Lelandra's tear, were busy on the deck when Gwen and the others rowed up in the long boat. "Mr. Stiele can you get us out of here?"

"Aye Captain, I can."

"Braxus, stay with Stiele, just in case he is not as

fit as he believes himself to be."

"Captain?" Braxus was fully aware that the order was given in front of all her men with the intent of keeping him on deck so that she could be alone. To her credit in front of her crew, her mask was concealing her emotions. Savane was still trembling when Gwen went below deck, without a backward glance she called out. "I am not to be disturbed."

Dayin looked to Savane, "Let's get you below deck as well."

Savane looked up into the darkening sky, it was the first time in a while that the sky was not illuminated with the beauty of Lelandra's Tear.

"What does this mean Dayin?" she rolled her head side to side with the weight of it.

"Was it them? Was it Gwen and Konrad all along? Is that why it was above us the whole time we were on the island? Cause they were with us?"

"Don't think on it now Savane, we will rest and take care of wounds and talk about it over dinner in the galley."

Dayin put a protective arm around her shoulder and guided her to the stairs. Her eyes caught

Danica; she was about to go below deck but instead she ran to embrace her. Danica froze as Savane's small form caught her in her embrace. Her hesitation seemed to matter very little to Savane. Danica guarded her hands as she returned the gesture. She wanted to give her something positive and uplifting, but her emotions were raw from the serpent's deceit. Nothing would come forward, but the closeness seemed enough. As Savane pulled away she looked to Danica's hands with a look of empathy before turning to Dayin to be guided below deck.

Balae looked to Theries who seemed to take in the horizon with passivity that Balae was unaccustomed to. "Are you okay?"

"Not much takes me by surprise Balae. I like to think that I am a good judge of people and so I see things coming." he looked back to the island and then to the doorway to the lower decks, "That, I didn't see coming." he looked past Balae to where Gaelan sat on the barrels. He, like most of them, seemed dumbfounded and aloof. "I'll speak to him." Balae offered, then smiled at the relief that washed across her brother's face.

"Gaelan, are you alright?"

"Why did she do it? Why would she set us on this path? To go through the trouble of awakening Savane and driving her into all she has done, show her an image that we had no possibility of stopping. Those tears that Savane touched on Lelandra's face, that was what it showed her. The two that were to bring about the child, and now he's gone. Why?"

Balae's eyes widened, she looked at Boeden then back down at Gaelan. "You know, I'm not much for supplicating to the Gods, I believe they are there, that all the legends of their battles and successes are true, but here is what I think. When I fight a battle, most of the time I believe I'm coming out of it alive. I have trained all my life, and that lends me a certain confidence when I fight. My allies, however, I don't know how hard they trained, or even if they have the same will to live that I have, so I don't own what happens to them in a fight. It's up to them to win or lose, I can help them along. I can do what I can to make it easier but, in the end, it is on them to survive. That's what I believe it is for the Gods. They can point us in the right direction, they can show us what they will, but in the end, what happens to us, falls to us. Lelandra showed us her vision of how to save us. If that has failed than we need to create a new way."

Gaelan looked at Balae and took a deep breath. "That is an incredible light in an otherwise very dark day."

"Come on now, let's get you fed so you can keep everyone else entertained with some music. I think we're going to need to keep spirits lifted, cause this crew is going to feel Konrad's death as much as the Angry Maiden herself."

The crew fell into their routine of preparing to sail in ignorance. The sun had set and for the most part they were concealed by the darkness as they left the inlet. With the sails raised and the island and the day slipping behind them, some slept, some ate, Gwen sat on the floor of her quarters, lulling side to side with the ship on the tide. Her tears were dry on her face and she wrung her hands repeatedly leaving them feeling raw. Everything felt raw as the scene kept replaying in her memory.

They had been sailing for a few hours when there was a banging below deck. It vibrated through the floor of Gwen's cabin. She could hear Seraphic whinnying in his stall, and his occasional foot stomp. But the banging was something else. Then foot falls overhead that sounded muted compared to her men. Her door opened moments after to Danica standing with her weapon in hand and bloodied. "What is going on?"

"The serpents are on the boat."

Gwen's stomach instantly knotted. How many of her men would she face and not know who they were? She pulled herself to her feet and grabbed her sword, still blood stained. "Lock your door Gwendolyn, I will make certain we don't harm anyone. The illusions they cast are powerful but if I listen and use my sense of smell, I should be able to discern the serpents from the crew. They fooled me once, they won't a second time."

Danica's hands still shook as she held her weapon. The pain she felt was secondary to the need to put an end to the serpents that had awakened the pain of Urrie's death and brought about Konrad's.

Gwen closed the door and slid the lock home, grateful that Danica had a viable reason for her to hide from the world just a little while longer. She slid down the wall and closed her eyes to the sounds that were already starting on deck.

Danica moved through the lower deck and stopped at Savane and Dayin's room. "Dayin?" he opened the door with his sword drawn. "The serpents are on the ship. I'm not certain if they were meant to keep whatever was in the tomb locked away or if they are just malevolent."

Dayin looked back at Savane, "lock it, don't open it for anyone." Dayin pulled the sword of Lynstrom off his back and left his own on his hip as he closed the door behind him. "Do not allow us to become separated."

Danica took a deep breath. Her mind replaying her betrayal against her friends and allies, this southern warrior with as much courage and strength as any of her tribesmen. If that truth of what she did when they were fighting for their lives in Ilvaran were to come out, she was certain he would not be so willing to trust her with his life.

They turned the corridor and up the stairs to where the crew's quarters were. Hammocks lined the room, some were occupied. Danica looked at the first of the men sleeping until the stink of blood flooded her senses. "Be cautious Dayin, I smell blood."

Dayin looked in on a member of the crew, his neck soaked and clothes dark in the poorly lit room. "They mean to kill them all. We need to wake them." Dayin was about to sound the alarm when Danica clamped her hand around his mouth. "if you do that, they are at risk of seeing what the serpents want them to see, that included you as a threat. Just clear the room and lock the door, we'll find them one at a time. We are their best hope at getting them through this alive." They moved to the back of the room and locked the door then moved forward checking each sleeping member. Danica hovering over them to see if the scent was human or not, the heartbeats awake or slumbering, or racing. She hovered over one of the crewmen. His heart racing as he feigned sleep. She hadn't thought of that. The serpents were capable of attacking the minds of men and were able to let them do the killing. The crewman slashed out at Danica with a knife in his hand, Dayin looked up just as Danica narrowly pulled her neck out of his range.

In that moment the man shifted into a serpent and Dayin lunged with his sword toward Danica's assailant.

Danica shifted her blade and the man, pulling him in with the knife hand, held under control to protect him from Dayin's attack. "Dayin he's one of us. See it as it is!" As though she had illuminated the darkness, the illusion disintegrated before him and the crew member was held at arms length, in Danica's hand. His weapon still in his grasp with Danica fighting to free it from him. He fought against her as the serpents controlled what he saw, she imagined in his mind she was a serpent. Dayin used the butt of his sword to knock him unconscious.

"So not only do we have to worry about what we see but we have to worry what they see as well?" A look of desperation fell over Dayin. "If I don't try and kill it, you shouldn't either, agreed, knock them out. Wound them if you must, but don't try to kill anything unless I tell you too."

"Why did it have no affect on me in the cavern?" Danica paused as the memory of Urrie returned, "because you weren't his target."

They moved through the room. Some crew members slept while others were already dead. One crew member got out of his hammock panicked, as though he were alone, he went to the lantern and held it against the darkness beyond it. Danica froze so as to avoid him seeing them. Then looking to Dayin, she motioned for him to go around behind him. Just as she was about to move toward him, her sense of smell found him. He had shrouded himself in illusion to avoid being seen by her, but once she smelled him it all fell away. He was heavily muscled in the torso with skin that was so pale that the blue of his veins beneath lent a hue to his hairless skin. His coiled tail gave him added height, as he postured up, it lifted him to the full elevation of the room. His face was human aside from the slight curve to his ears and a protracted jaw that made room for the serpent fangs, that he barred in the realization of his detection.

Danica called to Dayin, "knock him out Dayin, don't let him..." she was about to warn him of the fire in the crew members hand when the serpent turned his head to one side. The crewman upended the oil on himself, instantly released from the serpent's control, he panicked and raced through the room to get topside to where he knew he could find water and salvation, leaving a flaming prison to all those on board.

"Dayin get the others!" Not positive that he would not be tricked a second time, Danica faced off against the serpent. It loosened it's coils to reveal a barbed tail that he let fall to one side. "Ah child of Vetis, you are still so lost."

Danica tightened her burned hands against her weapon. "I am right where I need to be." She lunged forward as Dayin woke and helped the crew escape the room. They raced to the back corridor and unbolted it. Opening the door to Boeden who looked annoyed, "Saving all the battle for yourself hey Pretty boy?"

"Boeden he can manipulate your thoughts; you could end up fighting Danica."

"That girl can take care of herself, get them out of here." Boeden raced into the room. Danica's hands were covered in blood and her attacks were sloppy as she fought with the burns on her hands. The serpent had already made multiple cuts in her shoulders with his barbed tail. He had pulled his torso back to coil around a support pillar behind Danica. He yanked with incredible force, splintering the wood and sending tremors and protests from the beams above. Boeden lunged at him, his coiled tail still wrapped around the beam thrust it up, landing squarely into Boeden sending him sprawling across the deck. The serpent released his oversized club and spun back on Danica. He raised to his full height and lashed his tail toward her, she felt the barb sting her shoulder as she gripped the tail, twisting it around her wrist and forearm. He instantly started squeezing pressure which made her horribly burned hands feel as though the were going to pop of her wrists. Her weapon clamored to the floor as her body started to numb. She dropped to one knee and smiled. The serpent read her intentions just a moment too late at Boeden's axe drove through the torso, shattering his shoulder. His tail let go as an agonized scream rang out. Boeden swept past Danica grabbing, both she and her weapon. Despite her height, he carried her like a child. They cleared the first room and closed the door behind them, barricading it from anything behind them as they made it up the stairs. Deck hands were shouting about the fire and trying to put it out from above, while Braxus had already freed Seraphic from his holding. A blindfold aided in keeping him from terrorizing the deck, but it was only time before the smoke and flames would drive them all off the boat.

Gwendolyn's crew were trying to contain the flames as best they could as Boeden and Danica came from below. Danica's only movements on the deck before she stumbled like a new fawn, throwing her body over the gunwale to violently empty her stomach.

Dayin looked at Boeden in shock. "The snake caught her with the barb on his tail." he shrugged.

He crouched down beside her and checked her wounds while Savane moved in to be closer to her.

"Danica?" he sat beside her on the barrels. She lifted her gaze to the water, her hands vibrating as blood pooled in her palms. Savane ripped the sleeve from her blouse and bunched it up for Danica to hold. She clutched it loosely at first, then her hands tightened around it.

Gwendolyn's crew were scarce as they tried desperately to get the ship closer to land and control the fires below deck. The group of them stayed together as the ship limped its way back to the familiar coastline of Abarris.

Braxus had been taking care of the ship, he stopped and looked at the small group. He looked to Danica's hands and muttered to his goddess, "By Shoanne girl, you are a mess." Danica looked up at him before turning and heaving her stomach over the rail. Savane grimaced. "Dayin, let's leave her a moment."

Braxus sat next to Danica and patiently waited for her to regain control of her stomach. She sat back down on the barrel and looked pitifully at Braxeus. He took her hands in his and began to whisper prayers to Shoanne. His eyes stayed closed and in such a state he was so peaceful, his brow relaxed, his jagged teeth almost concealed behind his slack jaw. He used his amulet from around his neck in much the same way she had seen Dayin say his prayers, but at the end he produced a flask that he uncorked and poured over her wounded hands and shoulder. Saltwater rushed over the wounds and turned pale red as it mingled with the blood of her burns. He emptied the contents of the skin until the water ran clear. She looked at her hands to reveal raw pink new skin.

"How can faith in a God bring about healing?"

"Ah Danica, perhaps it is not my faith in Shoanne that healed you, but her faith in you. I am just an instrument of her power, perhaps you still have much to learn." Danica opened and closed her hands, the skin looked soft and free of the burns that touching the sword had caused. "I feel like I betrayed them."

Her eyes locked on Savane and Dayin as they tried to keep Seraphic calm. Braxus looked at them then back to Danica, "Guilt is a blight to a child of your blood. Carry it and it will get heavy, let it go and there is nothing to weigh you down and corrupt every good deed you do."

"Thank you Braxus." He placed a hand on her good shoulder. "It was my pleasure."

Chapter Twenty

The Angry Maiden was almost to the port of Abarris when the storm hit. Waves beat against the hull tossing her off course and trying to pull her back out to sea. Gwen, despite the weight of losing Konrad to her own blade was still composed, keeping her men focused on saving the ship if possible, but getting as close to land in the event that the damage the Maiden had taken was too much.

On a clear night the port would have been easily identified by moon light or braziers would line the coast, but the darkness gave them a false sense of distance when the ship ran aground and lurched heavily. It threw a few men overboard including Dayin and Gaelan who had been standing closest to the barrels that Savane and Danica were seated at.

While crew members floundered in the water, Savane was horrified when Dayin didn't even surface once. "His armor!" She cried; her voice elevated in panic. Danica cast off her cloak that she had been wrapped in since Braxeus had healed her hands, grabbed a rope free of the rigging and dove into the water where Dayin had disappeared. The water beneath was black but Danica's sight could pick up Dayin's sinking form, struggling to free himself of the armor that weighed him down. She swam toward him, pulling him into her as she reached hand over hand along the rope. His back against her body, the sword that had already burned her so badly pressed against her as she carried him to safety. This time, layers of clothing she wore, and the swords scabbard protected her but the fear of it touching her drove her to get her and Dayin to the surface.   When they surfaced, they both drew in deep breaths. She transferred Dayin's weight to the rope she held and swam to where Gaelan clung to a barrel that had gone over with them. He had a miserable look of someone reluctant to confess his inability to swim. Danica pushed him toward the rope and looked toward the shoreline. Above, boats were being lowered into the water and Braxeus had already strapped Seraphic into the sling and was lowering the horse to the water.

Danica released him from the sling and the beast, true to its overprotective nature swam to Dayin and brought him easily to shore. Dayin lay on the beach for only a moment before he pulled himself free of his armor and started helping other people to shore as they pulled themselves out of the long boats. When Savane reached the shore, she ran to Dayin. He caught her and pulled her in, holding her against him for a moment, his face buried in her hair. "I can't do this without you Dayin, don't do that again." he lifted her face with his hands and stared down into her beautiful purple eyes. "I'll try." he whispered, before kissing her forehead and placing his chin on top of her forehead for fear that he would break his promise to himself and give her the false hope of a kiss. He could feel her shoulders fall in disappointment as the anticipation went unanswered. "We have people to help." he whispered in her ear then pulled himself away from the safest place he knew.

The ship had drifted off course from the docks of Abarris some distance. It was decided to light a fire on the beach and try and get some rest. Take stock of the lost crew and do their best from where they were to get the Angry Maiden repaired. Gwendolyn had found a quiet place away from anyone while Braxeus was resolved to take on her responsibilities, allowing her the time she needed. From a distance Savane watched her silent torment, feeling helpless as the memory of what happened replayed in her thoughts.

Theries sat a short distance from Savane by the fire and Balae and Boeden were helping to bring items from the ship to shore with Dayin and Danica.

Gaelan walked over and sat next to Savane producing a small fish on a stick he had roasted. There were dozens such sticks surrounding the fire for any of the crew to take. The fire burned so hot that it cooked them quickly. Savane looked up at Gaelan, his eyes were tired, his expression drawn. Savane looked up at him then watched as his gaze fell on Gwendolyn. "I would try but I know better. You on the other hand need to eat." She gratefully took the fish and peeled it apart on the stick. "I don't know what to do now Gaelan,"

He looked at her then up to Balae who was still smiling. After all that they had been through, she could find humor in something that Boeden had shared. He looked back to Savane, "We find another way. We pick up all the broken pieces Lelandra's Tear cost us and find another way. The tear was just an omen of those who were meant to birth the child to hold the darkness at bay. What about the events in Abarris, the bloodlines, surely a child would not have been able to save us from the likes of that for at least fifteen to twenty years. Would you sit idly by and wait for a child to lead us?"

Savane shook her head. "There is still much to do, and it seems to me that this group is the only one who knows it. We have to stop the Gatherers, find out what they are doing, preparing for, and put an end to it."

Savane took a deep breath and looked at her mother's book sitting by her feet in the satchel. "Even my mother was unsure of her role in all of this. I have limited spells in this book and no idea of where to start."

Gaelan looked at the book before looking back at Savane, "Then that is where we go next. Find you more spells. Learn more about who they are and what they are trying to do. To do that, we have to bring you home."

Savane choked, going home was the last thing she wanted to do. Even being on the coastal port was enough to make her stomach twist and knot. "We'll let them know and get some rest, I'll go talk to Gwendolyn."

Savane stood and walked solemnly over to where Gwen sat on rocks. "Gwen?"

When Savane was close enough to her she could see the suffering had taken its toll. Gwen looked exhausted, tears along her cheeks, her body hunched in a desperate attempt to disappear. Savane sat next to her for a moment and didn't speak. Gwen watched her through her hair before she pulled it all back and lifted her chin to look at Savane.

"How did you know it wasn't him?" emotion made her voice crack almost brought forth a new wave of tears. "When we were in the God's house there was a statue of Lelandra, she was crying. When I touched her tears, I saw you chasing Dirk down the beach, but it wasn't Dirk. When he turned around it was Konrad, I saw it just as it happened. Only with an awareness of what I was seeing versus what the serpent wanted you to see. We tried to reach you in time."

"You did, I just didn't listen to you. I was so driven by hatred, so poisoned in that moment, I felt like a wild animal chasing its prey. Why would he run from me?"

"The serpent's may have corrupted his thoughts as well."

Gwen choked, "I left him on that beach, and I can't go back."

"Do you want to?"

"My ship is in no state to sail, and even if we made these repairs within the fortnight his body would never be there. It would be in no condition to move, the tide would wash it away or the crabs on the beach..." it brought a new wave of emotion. "I've lost him, and what is worse, I feel him inside me, like his feelings, the essence of what he was transferred into me as he died."

"It is the bloodlines, the Divine blood passes from line to line with the death of one who has it. In a way, he is still with you. We are going to my father's manor, to put an end to all of this. When we return, we will help you finish the repairs and sail back to that cursed island to put Konrad to rest. You are not alone Gwen."

Gwen shook her head, "we aren't going back, not there, I've lost too much on that island. Konrad, my men, I can't go back for a dead man."

Savane nodded her head and stood. She brushed the sand off her clothes and crouched down in front of Gwen.

"Whatever you want to do, that's what we'll do."

"Go to your father, end this if it can be ended, then we'll see what the Gods have planned for us this time." She placed a hand on Gwen's shoulder and stood, turning back to the fire and leaving the Angry Maiden's namesake to stare out to sea.

The crew had their fill of food and had tended to the wounded. Settling in along the beach, wrapping themselves in cloaks and torn sails. Dayin kept watch as they slept. They were a desperate, weary looking lot, exhausted in more than just body. The serpents had devastated their trust in their own eyes, leaving them to question the comfort that ignorance of such creatures had previously afforded them. A sound drew Dayin's attention. Danica slept away from everyone as she often did, but it was a restless sleep.

Danica lay on the beach under what should have been the Tear of Lelandra. It had become such a comforting sight in the sky that its absence was now as odd as it's arrival had been for her. So much had changed since that tear first lit up the northern sky above the hut she occupied with Kazmir. She pulled her fur around her shoulders and let the silence pull her under. Until there wasn't silence, a heartbeat. Faint, and fast, faster than any she had become familiar with. A child's heartbeat. A baby. She rolled onto her back and listened to the child growing inside her. Her betrayal to her friends, she closed her eyes and placed her hand on her stomach. Not a betrayal, she thought, a child, that would be everything that she was, and bear no loyalty to the man who sired him.

Dreams were waiting for Danica just inside her sleep, as though Svetovid waited for her. He stood above the beach and beckoned for her.

She looked back at everyone sleeping around her and moved along the ground soundlessly. She joined Svetovid on the hill and looked past him to the darkness of the estate. The sky swirling as though the land had gone mad. "When we arrive there, you will have to make a choice, the choice you make will determine what happens next, so be certain that you make the right one."

He turned her back to take in the sight of the beach. As far as she could see the dead covered the sands. Some were floating in the water sloshing ashore. Dayin, Savane everyone that held meaning to her lay lifeless and the ocean was red crimson. "You have already lost your people once Danica."

Danica woke as Dayin shook her. His eyes exhausted and drawn. "I'm sorry Dayin."

Dayin looked at her confused, "for what Danica?"

"The night in Ilvaran, when you were fighting the gathers, the Northern Gatherer came for me. I'm carrying his child." The anger that washed over his face evaporated his fatigue and was quickly replaced by sympathy, "Oh Danica," she realized in that moment that he didn't suspect her complicity in the conception and was about to clarify when he pulled her in to console her. She was so afraid of that kindness being turned into hatred that she took the embrace in silence. Feeling in that moment, that there was nothing she could do to feel less of who she thought she was.

"I'll keep watch Dayin, you need to sleep." He pulled her away confused by her lack of emotion over her revelation. He reluctantly moved away from her and pulled the sword off his back. He held it in his hands for a moment and looked into the polished pommel, age had not touched the blade.

Danica watched as Dayin held the blade in his hands, as though he were no longer in control or acting on his own accord. He slid his hand along the edge, fresh blood painted the blade as Dayin sat seemingly unaware. "Dayin?" Danica crouched down beside him. She shook him to no response, only the silence of the beach. She clenched her fists, feeling a helplessness sink into her stomach. She sat across from him and stared into his opened vacant gaze and waited for dawn.

Dayin had waited a lifetime to hear the voice of his God, he had prayed, served, fought and devoted himself to his God and on the beach, with everyone else asleep, his God answered.

Chapter Twenty One

The estate was wrapped in shadows. The sky had taken on a ghastly yellowish hue as sunlight failed to breach the fog that had begun to take over Savane's home. The silence on the road that once bustled with life and activity only bore greater witness to the changes the land had suffered. The people were long gone, dead or otherwise, birds no longer filled the air with song, having sensed the darkness, they were all gone. The fog in the air left everyone feeling as though they had been standing in the rain. The chill felt deep inside.

Dayin was still on Seraphic riding next to Savane as she walked, drawing closer to the foreground of the estate. There had been no change in him. His eyes had become dark and tired looking as they stared blindly before him.

He didn't react to anything Savane had attempted, no words or tears had moved him to return to himself. Even this place which held such a horrible combination of good and bad memories for him had no apparent effect on his condition. She pulled her gaze from him and let her eyes scan over the land that had once been her home. Every building and shelter bore the scars of having been neglected following the days of the Dukes fall. Balae had slowed her pace and Theries was silent with his lips parted in the closest expression of shock that Savane had ever detected. Danica had been distracted ever since they had started that morning. She was still present, acknowledging everyone, unlike Dayin, but there was a definite chill to her demeanor that Savane knew she was not imagining.

The sword of Lynstrom, in its scabbard now, seemed so plain and harmless. But the knight who had searched for it and the Northern warrior that seemed invincible, both bore the wrath of its power. They continued to walk in silence drawing nearer to the estate. The gates were battered and fallen. Though it was impossible for such rot to have taken hold in so little time, there was definitely rust on the hinges and the softness to the wood was undeniable.

Savane tied Seraphic's reins to the stables before turning to the others. She paused a moment at Dayin, weighing whether he would be better on his horse or inside the estate. With the silence outside and the swirling sky above the tower, she clenched her jaw and left him mounted on his horse while she turned her focus toward the fallen front doors.

"You gonna leave him here?" Boeden's voice was like a dull knife in her ears. His tactless arrogance and indifference to rank had been his identifying characteristics since he joined with them in Ilvaran. Despite successfully having found the sword, she still questioned his need to be in their company. Balae, on the other hand, had found a training partner and someone who she could confidently entrust with the lives of her friends. His skill with a weapon was unmatched in their group. He was a furious fighter with an undeniable blood lust that Balae felt better used to her favour, rather than have their enemies redirect him against them. Savane shot Balae a withering look, Balae allowed a guilty grin and walked toward the estate grounds taking the barbarian with her.

She could hear him talking with Balae in a way that made her blush; she looked away trying to ignore his vulgarity. looking to Danica who watched the two as they walked toward the entrance of the manor. "Are you sure he isn't from the North?"

Danica looked at his sun bronzed skin and lighter hair and shook her head. "I'm certain. A man with a mouth like that would not last in the North lands unless he was a Chief and even then," she shook her head again, "Our women would not let him speak as he does."

"Are you well Danica? You seem to be far away and struggling, ever since you touched that sword..." Danica's gaze fell on her hands and then back to Dayin. "None of my kind should touch that blade, it is not meant for us."

Savane stared at her, her lips parted in shock at the division Danica had placed between them. It had been so long since she had brought attention to her origins, but it was the blood in her veins that Danica was referencing, not the place of her birth.

Savane looked to Theries, his eyes trained on the swirling sky overhead. Its unnatural colour and eerie cyclonic movement made him feel as though they had reached the end of the world and everything was going to be sucked into the deadlands from this very point. "Seems about right that the place I was to meet my bride to be would be the beginning of the end of the world."

Savane and Danica both looked sharply up at him, a pause lingered in the air before the two both let amused grins creep in at the morbid humor. "Come now, bride groom, let us meet your father-in-law."

The Manor was as decrepit and devoid of life

as the rest of Savane's home. There was blood, long dried on the walls leaving dark shadows in places that were once filled with light. Tapestries tattered and crooked on the walls, paintings slashed and stained, debris in doorways that had been an obvious attempt to hold something at bay. Whatever the something was, it no longer roamed the halls. Everything was dead.

Savane entered the grand hall where Balae and Boeden had gone. They stood silent, staring at the eye of a vortex. A figure hovered in deathlike stillness; robes as tattered as the manor clung to the bones of a man far thinner than Savane had ever seen her father. His visage, a mask of death with wisps of white hair sparsely covering his thin-skinned pate. Age spots speckled his blue hued skin. The sight of him stole Savane's breath and made her nauseated and dizzy.

"Is he even alive?" Behind him the vortex seemed to be expanding and breathing for him. Boeden looked to Savane and aloofly pulled his axe from his back.

"This is it, and this is why we're here? We end him and it all ends?" Savane nodded and shook her head in confusion and wide-eyed disbelief. Balae looked to Savane with a sympathetic gaze before pulling her sword from her back and advancing with the barbarian. Behind Savane, Theries was whispering, then louder.

"Nothing has been that simple" the words fell too late as the first fall of the axe awoke Savane's father. Soulless eyes and an ear-splitting scream threw the warriors into the air and against the stone alter that sat in the aft part of the room. Balae pulled herself to her hands and knees while Boeden seemed completely unaffected. He stood up and raced back to the center of the room. He ran forward like a bull and was met with the same repellent scream that drove him back.

It seemed to make little difference who advanced; Theries drew his attention with only a step to the doorway, as though the revenant knew his thoughts and diverted him before the idea had ever bore fruit. He judged Savane with horrid concentration, his eyes devoid of colour or emotion watched her indecision. Danica was still beside Savane, her eyes focused on the monster before her. Svetovid's words echoing in her thoughts.

"Only you can save them Blood Bringer, but to do so, you must let go. You don't belong here."

"It has to be me." she said finally, her expression was one of total resolution but in that there was suffering.

"Theries, Boeden, get them out of here!" Savane looked toward Danica as she advanced on her father. She felt Theries grip her shoulders and pull her back toward the door. There was a moment of realization for Savane that Danica was employing the people who were notorious for doing whatever it took, rather than finding another way.

Danica drew her weapon from her back and moved toward Savane's father. Despite the colourless eyes, Savane could see the recognition in his face. He snarled like a caged animal as Danica advanced. The first blow he evaded with otherworldly agility, clawed hands lashed out and shredded through leathers and flesh leaving black rivers of blood along Danica's arm and shoulder. Boeden drew into attack again while Danica had him distracted, but again was met with the same cold gaze as he in turn was a distraction for Danica. Her movements were deadly and fast, as though she had been granted a moment of sight to predict every action he would take. In one flurry of attacks, her weapon finally slid home under his ribs. Blood, black like ink splattered to the floor and burned a trail along the ground toward Danica's feet. She choked in a ragged breath as the others watched in horror, the blood of Savane's father burned darker than any before along the ground and seeped into her veins blackening and racing through her skin. Her eyes losing their colour to pools of obsidian. Then there was stillness. The vortex seemed to dissipate.

The man at her feet looked less like the bone cage he had become and more like the father Savane had lost. Danica stood motionless, the essence had ebbed back below the surface of her skin and aside from the cold eyes and drying tears, she looked like Danica. Danica who never wept, and Danica whose doe like brown eyes were always filled with fire.

Now they were black.

Footsteps echoed through the hall. Mist flowed from the alter at the front of the hall through what seemed to be a gateway. A voice broke the silence. His accent was unmistakable. The Northern Gatherer stepped from the shadows. Savane had forgotten his beauty, he hadn't been there the last time they faced them.

"You thought it was an ending little duchess, this time, it wasn't about you." His one arm wrapped protectively around Danica's waist, his other hand reaching up and caressing her throat with an armored hand. His touch was the tender touch of a lover. He whispered to Danica, as much to the friends that watched, frozen in awe.

"Now she's mine."

Savane felt a wave of nausea wash over her, and she pulled against the grip that Theries had already tightened around her. Boeden and Balae, however both moved to advance, but the gatherer took one step back and was enveloped in shadows that moulded around him and pulled him into nothing. The scream that came from Savane was a wretched sound, that despite their past, made Theries pull her in to an embrace, both to hide her from what had happened as much as steal a moment for himself.

They stood in silence for a few moments before Savane pulled herself from Theries and looked up through the window in the great hall. They had expected the darkness to dissipate. For there to be some evidence that her father's death had meaning and closure. The sky however was still an eerie green. Fog descended and rolled across their feet. She closed her hands into fists, her stomach still rolling, and weakness plagued every limb. She stepped backward to the door then turned just in time to run heavily into Dayin. His eyes were wild and panicked as he scanned the room.

"Where is she?" he looked to Savane, then to Balae and then scanned the room again. "Where is Danica?"

The panic in his voice brought a new wave of emotion over Savane. "He took her." she whispered. "The northern Gatherer, he was here, and he took her, after she saved us."

Dayin slumped against the wall. His face reflecting Savane's anguish back at her. "We've lost her. She's carrying his child."

Savane stared open mouthed at Dayin. "How could you possibly know that?"

Balae, Theries and Boeden had joined them at the entrance of the great hall. His eyes fell to the blade strapped across his back. The legendary sword that had driven him into the trance and left him there. The sword that had made Danica feel like she was different from them, which had opened her back up to the blood that rushed through her veins. "Where were you?" Savane spat, "What happened to you, where did you go."

"I'm here now." he whispered, holding her hands as she tried to beat his chest plate. "I can't lose her Dayin, not now, not like this."

Dayin met Theries gaze, "It isn't the end of Danica Savane, she'll be back."

Savane lifted her head in time to catch the ominous glance between them. "What? What aren't you saying?"

"The child she was carrying was not forced upon her Savane. Lynstrom showed me things. Powerful images, of both the past and what is to come. Of who you are and destined to be. Dry your tears Duchess, you have a long road."

Epilogue

The empress looked at me as though her story were finished. A look of such finality that made my head shift backward as though I were avoiding a slap to my face.

"It doesn't stop there?" I asked incredulous.

"Of course not." She teased. She looked at the statues in her garden, specifically Dayin, where she had begun.

"It was the very last time he ever had to control the way he behaved in my company. He was never again lured into those powerful embraces, meaningful gazes or kisses on my forehead that meant the world to me.

Dayin never revealed to me what Lynstrom

shared with him in that trance, he never told me what he saw, or who he saw. My mother's book ceased being the path that we followed, and instead we followed Dayin for a time.

He knew places, things, history that we had never been taught. He had gone from being a soldier, to being my knight, to not being mine at all. Instead he found true faith in his God.

We were forever tied together, at first by our love then by our friendship and then by our battles and eventually by our children and their relationships." She stood up and took my hand, a smile lingering on her lips as she recognized the confusion on my face.

"It's time to go."

She whispered something into her closed hand and opened it releasing a tiny bird that flew toward the tower of the castle. She smiled as I marveled at its flight.

"Through every part of this story I have forgotten your magic."

"Well." She whispered, "That is not something you will ever forget again."

She produced a staff that seemed to extend from

461

a bracelet that she wore upon her wrist. With a flick, it unraveled and extended the full height of her. She caught it in her hand and tapped it in the ground. She uttered words the likes of which I would do no justice in trying to repeat and the strangest sensation washed over me. As though I were falling while standing still. In terror, I closed my eyes until the sounds around me changed into a flurry of noises.

"Open your eyes Sir Edrick."

Obeying, I was in a busy square that at first, I didn't recognize. As I took it all in, the four towers that surrounded the city, the great wall that ran the length of the castle grounds, the temple east of the city. Savane, the empress of the imperial city had brought me to the home of Ivany Olavnia, she was in no way ending her telling of the tale, she was instead introducing me to the narrator of the next chapter.

Take a sneak peek at Tina's second book.

Blood and War

Book 2

Tina Kourtras

Prologue

The walls that surrounded Danica were cold stone, etched from a cave. Centuries old pillars supported tired archways that gave the air of some sort of temple or castle. Massive braziers at even intervals forming a path to the alter that lit the room with a warm glow. She had woken here, after leaving the others in Abarris. She couldn't hear them any longer, there were no sounds, only the silence of the cave. She was in the North again. She placed a hand along the cave wall, feeling the weight of the last few nights mounting until she heard it. Soft leather boots gliding along the floor, with a familiar gait that made her heart race instantly. Her chest heaved as he approached. He came around the corner of the wall she stood against, his eyes looking to her weapon hand before grazing over her whole body. He wore only his dark leather pants and boots, no weapon or amour.

The way he watched her was enough to turn anyone. Danica had always admired the Northern gatherer. His dark hawkish features, to most were wild and fearsome, to her it was an aphrodisiac. He was scarred like most men in the North. His long brown hair was wild, and unkept, thin braids kept it off his face and hung down over his bare chest. Their eyes met and she knew there was no going back. His gaze held her to the wall that she leaned against, her head lulled back in defiance of her feelings to move toward him.

He moved closer to her, his breath smelling of salt meats and ale. It was a familiar scent that lulled her into her memories of home.

"This is that moment Danica, child of the North, Blood Bringer, Daughter of Vetis, this is that dream that you have endured in silence while others watched you thrash in your sleep. This is your destiny. This is Storm Peak. Your home." He motioned his hand to the temple surrounding them.

She stared into his eyes, the glow of firelight and her own wonder filled expression reflected back at her. She lifted her hand and felt the warmth of his chest against the cold of her fingertips. A vibration passed through them, somehow, she knew she would be forever defined by this moment. She let her hand fall slack and pressed her back harder against the wall. She looked toward her weapon on the ground.

A knowing smile intensified his expression. "Not tonight succubus, not now."

"I am not yours, or Vetis'." She spat.

"Oh, but you are. And you will see it in your dreams and feel it in your bones until you're lying in the snow, bleeding, your last breath racing away. You will call for me and. I will come for you. I will always come for you. Sweet Danica, you are my prize. Resist me if you will, it will change nothing. You still see our night in Ilvaran, I can see it in your eyes, the way your spine shifts when I come in the room."

He drew closer, taller than Danica, he shielded her, his lips at her ears. "Is there a baby in your belly?" his hands cupped her stomach and drew out the last bit of resistance against him. She softened with his touch, her muscles relaxed, her shoulders rounded and Svetovid smiled. From the day their eyes had met he had been in her head, in her dreams, poisoning her heart and now his hands poised around her stomach, she was his.

About the Author

Tina Koutras is a former aircraft technician but has always lived in the realms of magic and fantasy. For years the events of this fantasy series have been playing out in her mind, scene by scene, to bring us to a telling of their adventures as if they have lived out their lives as history instead of fantasy.

This first book introduces an epic multi-volume series with the second already in the works.

Throughout most of her adult life she has lived in Nova Scotia, Canada with her husband Paul, three sons, and their dogs. Her writings of this imaginative epic fantasy flow in amazing sequence of events from her mind to paper.

If you want to know when Tina's next book will come out, please visit her website at www.stonegardenseries.com or you can sign up to receive an email when she has her next release.